MW01222660

SIX HARVESTS IN LEA, TEXAS

By Sam Starbuck

The text of this book is set in Garamond.
Cover design by Hellen Highwater.

Cover photograph taken in Stratford, Texas, April 1935, by George E. Marsh Jr.
The original image is available at the NOAA public domain photo library here:
https://photolib.noaa.gov/Collections/National-Weather-Service/Meteorological-
Monsters/Dust/emodule/647/eitem/3001

This novel is the eighth volume published by
Extribulum Independent Press
extribulum.wordpress.com
Printer's Row, Chicago, IL

Nameless – 2009
Other People Can Smell You – 2009, Revised 2010
Charitable Getting – 2010
Dr. King's Lucky Book – 2011
Trace – 2011
By The Days – 2011
The Dead Isle – 2012
Six Harvests in Lea, Texas – 2020

ISBN 978-1-716-47588-7

This book deals with several difficult themes, including pandemic, economic depression, ecological disaster, abortion, and murder. For a full list of content warnings, please turn to page 222 at the end of the book.

Six Harvests in Lea, Texas was written in 2019, and first shared with readers at the beginning of quarantine in March of 2020. It was edited, typeset, and published during a pandemic, in a time of great social and political upheaval.

I hope that its message can be at least one light burning in a dark time.

PROLOGUE

IT MUST'VE BEEN some sort of hypnotism, because the church had always been there when it arrived one day. Everyone agreed that the church had been there as long as living memory, but some of them seemed to know deep down that it also hadn't been there the day before.

There wasn't a need for more than two churches in Lea. If it weren't for the cussedness of humanity, there wouldn't be a need for two. People have got to have something to be "at each other" about, as Mama said, which was why they had two, the Baptist church put up by the early settlers and the Lutheran church by the Germans who came after. A great many Germans had come to Texas a few generations before, and the three or four dozen adventurous souls who settled in Lea, in the Panhandle, were Lutherans.

The Baptist church was a small white affair with a gabled roof and big windows, and buckets of paper fans on shelves at the back to battle the summer heat. It was on the east end of town, the first thing you saw entering Lea if you were coming from Oklahoma. The Lutheran church was southwest of town, near Lon Platter's place. Being newer, it put on airs, with a high roof and fine woodwork throughout. Still, all told it wasn't much bigger than the Baptists' when it came down to it, at least so the Baptists grumbled.

There never was a church of any kind, let alone a little fancy-windowed thing of smooth rounded clay with a small arched bell tower, across from the bank and next to the Dry Goods on the main street (the only street) of Lea. Not until one day there suddenly was, and always had been. Of course it always had been there.

Nobody went to it. It had no priests. The window glass was cracked and the door was shut. But all the same, it was there, a low, pale monument to some other man's god.

1

A handful of the outlying farmers who went to the Lea Baptist – Wheeler Baptist was closer for some but there had been A Falling Out over music years before – said that on a hot April day in 1930 there had been terrible lightning in the sky one night. It wasn't like normal heat lightning, but looked like the clouds were ablaze, like perdition had finally come. Maybe that was when the church came, the church that had always been there.

Or maybe it was in 1929, the day of the crash, though the crash hardly registered in Lea. They'd already been struggling for some time, trying to grow more to make more, only to find the more they grew the further prices dropped.

But nobody knew for sure when it came. They only knew it had, also, always been there.

ONE

DAN ROHLF WAS one of the Lutherans of Lea, but in other ways a rare bird; he was thirty-five, one of only a handful of men in Lea of that age who had survived the war and the influenza both. There were plenty of older men in Lea, and their sons were becoming men faster each year, but from twenty-five to forty there weren't many still alive. Just names in family bibles, and crosses in the single graveyard of Lea. Dan, even rarer, had no children of his own. Still, he was of a friendly persuasion, and everyone in Lea knew everyone else, so he didn't lack for society when he was in town.

His wife, Cora, knew it too. She hesitated to send him into town on Friday morning, because he'd take the whole day there, but they needed chicken feed and flour, and it would keep him out from underfoot. She was making her famous potato salad for the church social, and he was always in the way when she was making her potato salad.

So, as he was readying the truck to head in to town, she said, "I won't look for you before sundown."

"Oh, a little before," he protested.

"I doubt it. You ain't be back before supper but you'll be back for supper, right enough."

"I ain't fixed to miss your cooking!" he said, leaning in for a kiss, then started up the truck with a bang.

"If you're fixed to loiter in town all day, get that truck seen to," she'd told him, and sent him off with a wave of a dusting rag.

He'd whistled all the way into town, a tune of his own devising, and since Cora hadn't seemed particularly upset at his being gone all day, he didn't make any hurry over it. He didn't bother taking the truck to the back of the Dry Goods where a handy youngster sometimes did fixing on cars and tractors; it had run fine, with a few adjustments he made himself, since he'd bought it in 1920. If it didn't really run fast so much anymore, well, neither did he. And anyway, why let a fella paid to fix trucks loose on his truck? The way Dan saw it, the boy would just make himself more business.

Dan stopped in the seed store for some conversation, and the Dry Goods for the chicken feed and flour, then settled on the porch of the Dry Goods with the lunch Cora had packed, looking out over the yard of the old church. Jacob, one of the young Baptist fellows, swept the porch sullenly while he ate.

"What do you think of that, there?" Dan asked after a while. He indicated the old church with a wave of his chicken leg.

"Don't make much of it," Jacob said with a shrug.

"Pretty little thing," Dan said encouragingly. "Must've taken some work to build."

"Well, your people would know, I guess."

"How do you mean that?" Dan asked.

"Ain't it the Lutherans built it? Back before you put up the new church?"

Dan shook his head. "I doubt it."

"It sure wasn't the Baptists," Jacob replied, leaning on his broom, resigned to the conversation now. Dan laughed.

"No, it sure wasn't. Maybe whoever was here before the Baptists. What do you suppose it's built out of? Looks like clay."

"Oh, they got a book about that from back east, down in the school," Jacob replied.

"Huh. Nothing good comes of books from back east."

"Plenty'a good! I like those dime novels Miss Adelaide gets sometimes," Jacob protested. "Lots of people getting killed. Detective mysteries and such."

"Trash. You stick to the Bible. Those books'll rot your mind," Dan declared.

"Will not. Miss Adelaide says books widen the horizons."

Dan gave him a dry look. "We got no lack of horizons in Lea."

"Well, at the school they got a book called South Western Architecture and it's got somethin' like that on the cover," Jacob said, as if winning an argument. "They call it adobe."

"Fancy word," Dan said.

"It ain't my church, don't tell me," Jacob sniffed.

"Hmph," Dan muttered. But he stared at the church, at its pressed-smooth walls and curving angles, its narrow windows and the white stone around the door. Someone had put on airs to make a church like that. It bothered him that he didn't know who.

"Yard around it's no good," he observed, indicating the rubble-strewn, scrubby yard full of weeds and rotten tumblebrush. "Someone ought to put up a fence."

"Someone ought to," Jacob agreed.

"Who owns it?"

"Hell if I know. Lentz Platter owns most of the city land, I guess."

Lentz Platter owned the bank, as well, and thus the mortgage on Dan's farm, which would be paid off soon; Dan tried never to draw his attention. Jacob, whose father paid rent to Lentz Platter, caught Dan's expression.

"Why'n't you ask Wild Mayer?" he said. "He'd find out for you."

"He's in Lubbock, ain't he?"

"Nah. I heard what with Lon passing, his mama called him back."

"Just as well, if you ask me. What's a man need four years of agricultural school for? He had eighteen years on the farm before they packed him off last year."

Jacob shrugged. As with most of the young men in Lea, he was a little envious of Wilder Mayer going off to school in Lubbock, but mostly overawed and apprehensive about his return.

"Besides, Lon just passed," Dan continued. "No good asking the man about his family when he's in mourning."

"Well, you're the one who wants to know if Lentz Platter owns the church."

"I don't honestly care one way or another," Dan declared, and as he'd finished his lunch, he decided he'd head west and see if John Fischer had finished putting up his new stillroom and maybe done a batch or two of corn whiskey.

It sat on his mind that afternoon and into the evening, but by the time Wilder Mayer showed his face at the Saturday social, he'd forgotten about it, mostly.

Two

THERE WASN'T A train from Lubbock to Lea, mainly because there were no trains at all to or from Lea, which was barely a wide spot in the road in the east Panhandle. Lubbock had a line that took Wilder to Carson, the Friday after school ended, the same Friday Dan Rohlf went to Lea for chicken feed. There were closer stops to Lea on the train line, but they were little podunk local stops, and it would be harder to thumb a ride from them. So Wild stepped off at the Carson stop with his father's old canvas Army bag and a sharp eye for anyone going east.

He was lucky – there was a man from Wheeler in Carson to pick up machine parts, and for a couple of tunes on the ukulele (Wild had won it in a poker game in Lubbock, not that he'd tell Mama about the gambling) he was willing to drive almost all the way to Lea. He left Wild on the doorstep of the Lentz farm between Lea and Wheeler, which suited Wild fine. The Lentzes and Platters were heavily intertwined; Wild was no real part of it by blood, being only Lon Platter's stepson, but the Lentzes still welcomed him in, asked after his health, and loaned him one of the farm's draft horses to ride the rest of the way home.

"Sure you don't want to call down there, let 'em know you made it to town?" Benjamin Lentz asked, as Wild fixed a blanket to the old dray. "Billy could come get you in the truck."

"Nah. I'll be there soon enough, and they're probably sittin' dinner right about now," Wild said, though it probably wasn't true and certainly wasn't his real reason. All the telephones in Lea were on a single line, and he didn't care for everyone for thirty miles around to know his business. "Say, you spoken to Mama lately?" he continued.

"Sure. We was down there, oh, Tuesday?" Ben said, patting the dray's pale nose, making little wickering noises to her. "My ma had some spare black cotton to send down."

"Kind of her. How'd she look?"

"Holding up," Ben said. "You need a leg up?"

"Thanks," Wild agreed, planting a boot on Ben's knee and hoisting himself onto the dray. She snorted, but her walk was easy when he pulled her head around and took her out of the barn. "I'll get this one back to you soon as I can," he added, patting the dray's neck.

"Reckon you could bring her to the Social tomorrow, and I'll ride her home from there."

"Social tomorrow?" Wild asked.

"Sure."

"So close to the funeral?"

"Funeral was a week and a half ago. What were they meant to do, wait forever?" Ben asked.

"Suppose that's true." Wild replied, tapping his heels to the dray's sides. "See you tomorrow then, Ben."

Dark was well on its way by the time he left the Lentz farm, and Wild was glad of the stars and the near-full moon as he cut through a couple of fields (careful of the new-plowed dirt) on the most direct route south, into Lea.

He hadn't really imagined Mama would make a fuss about her husband's death. Lon Platter had been a good man, not a drinker and not one to raise a hand to his wife or children. But Wild didn't expect Mama to take to her bed in grief over his dying, and he would bet Lon hadn't expected it either. Mary Platter hadn't fallen to pieces over Wild's own blood father when she was Mary Mayer, and she'd actually loved him.

Wild's daddy Gerry was barely a whiff of memory; he went to the front in the Great War when Wild was three. The war itself took plenty of men, of course, but in 1918, Gerry and at least a handful of other fellas from Lea came home, and for Gerry it was to a waiting wife and son and a good farm. Most of Lea was poor, but they'd done pretty well out of feeding the Army, so they weren't quite *dirt* poor. And the soldiers had pay, too.

Gerry poured all of his pay into the farm, and those were the memories Wild had of him, brief as they were: a few months where Daddy fixed up the farm and dreamed of buying more land. If he tried, he could recall the military erectness of his posture, and the smell of polish on his boots.

And three months after he came home, Death came from Kansas in the form of the influenza, and it took Gerry Mayer.

Same all over; what the war hadn't took the flu generally got, healthy soldiers fresh from combat and often their wives, so that there was a generation that nearly didn't exist. Wild had watched most of the survivors marry off, combining farms in order to ensure that there was someone to see to the planting and to the children. Not a year after the influenza, his own mother had caught the eye of Lon Platter, who wasn't from the rich town Platters but had good land next to hers. He was a sight older than Mary, but had two daughters – Bet was only Wild's age and Sarah even younger, hard for a widower to care for on his own. He didn't mind raising another man's son if Mary would raise his daughters, and she'd given him three sons of his own as well.

Mary and Lon's marriage had been a business arrangement, intimate and friendly but not over-loving. Lately they'd needed the large combined farmland of the Mayers and the Platters just to keep afloat. Which was maybe what had given Lon a heart attack, Wild thought.

And so Wild was home, with little prospect of returning to the Agricultural School in Lubbock anytime soon. Still, it hadn't been time wasted. He'd learned a lot in a year. For now, with his half-brothers all under thirteen and his stepsisters probably marrying soon, someone needed to run the farm, and Mama couldn't do it alone and mind the little ones too.

Lea was dark as he passed through it, just a lamp here and there lighting a second-floor window. He saw curtains twitch as curious faces peered out, but in the dark, they might not even recognize him. He concentrated on noticing what had changed, which wasn't much – a new-painted sign on the seed store, and some freshly built benches outside the bank. And on the other side –

At first he couldn't quite fathom what it was; it was so alien, so strange, and yet so familiar at the same time. Like seeing a shadow in the dark that wouldn't quite resolve into what you knew it had to be.

It took him more than a few seconds to realize it was the old church. He had the dim sense that it had always been there, another familiar landmark on the unpaved main street of Lea, but he felt like he was seeing it for the first time. In the dark, with moonlight sheening the narrow, mostly broken windows, it was like a strange animal crouched on the landscape, a well-fed coyote or a wild horse. Not threatening, not exactly, but dangerous if provoked. *Might as well let it be*, he thought.

But he couldn't help noticing there was a dirty, unswept look to the land the church stood on, which made him unhappy. Lea was a good, clean town, and shouldn't look so unkempt. Someone ought to put a fence up around the old place.

The dray kicked up dust from the road as he turned right at the church and headed west, and he thought about the stone paving in Lubbock, even the tarmacadam some of the big boulevards had. They ought to pave some streets in Lea, too, if only to keep the dust down.

Best not to speak up about it just yet, though. They'd think he was a college boy with big ideas. Which he supposed he was, but he'd play it quiet. For all the year in Lubbock and being now the man of the Platter house, he was still only nineteen and didn't have the Platter name backing him. Best to settle the farm, maybe get Sarah and Bet married off, and then see about local politics.

And first, of course, homecoming, and the church social tomorrow. He turned the dray down the rutted road to his stepfather's farmhouse. When he was close enough to be heard, he pressed his tongue behind his teeth and whistled sharply.

They poured out of the house, his mama and siblings, and when he saw his mother's face lit by the hurricane lamp she carried, he took off his hat and waved it, calling, "Evenin', Mama!"

"Wild!" she shrieked, all but dropping the lamp on the porch, and took off running down the road. He could see Sarah and Bet waiting by the house, but his brothers were at Mama's heels and then passing her. It must be Billy who was as tall as her now and outpacing her on long legs; Moses kept up, holding his mother's hand, and little Lon Junior, barely walking when he'd left, trotted behind them.

Wild threw his leg over the dray's back and dropped to the dirt to catch Billy in both arms, pounding him on the back.

"Look at you, beanpole, you got tall!" he said, pushing him back to arm's length so he could see him clearly. He only had a second to see the relief in Billy's eyes before Mama was bowling into him, arms around his chest because she hadn't been able to reach his neck since he was Billy's age. A second later, Moses wrapped his arms around Wild's waist, and Lonny was jumping up and down nearby, yelling excitedly.

Mama smelled like soap and frying oil, familiar scents he'd missed, and he buried his face in her hair briefly before letting her go, wriggling out of Moze's grip.

"Come inside, come inside," Mama urged, as if he was going to sleep on the porch if he wasn't invited. "There's cold roast left over from dinner – "

"Thanks, I'm starved," he said, handing the reins to Billy. "Put her up, would you, Bill?"

"Yessir!" Billy said, leading her off towards the barn.

"You think you can take this, little man?" Wild asked, offering his bag to Moze, who staggered under the weight before getting it over one shoulder. Mama kept one arm around his waist as they made their way down to the porch. Sarah, quiet by nature, and Bet, who hated a fuss, waved him inside.

"You should have written when you were coming," Mama said, as he wiped his boots on the porch and followed them in. "We could have sent Billy and Bet with the truck."

"Wasn't worth the gas for a trip to Carson, and I didn't know if I'd get into Lea tonight or tomorrow," Wild said. "I was lucky. Fella from Wheeler was passing through Carson, took me as far as the Lentz place."

Mama was already taking a plate out of the cupboard for him. Moses clattered into the back of the house with his bag as Bet, Sarah, and Lonny settled at the table.

"Ain't got beef this good in Lubbock," Wild said, tearing into the food hungrily.

"Well, city food," Mama said, and then burst into tears, sitting down in the chair at the head of the table. Bet and Sarah both looked pointedly at Wild.

"Mama, now," Wild said, putting his fork down.

"Oh, just let me have a minute," she said, wiping at her eyes with the flour-sack dishtowel she always had over one shoulder. Wild slid down to the end of the bench and leaned over to wrap her in a second hug. "I'm so glad you're back, Wilder."

"Well, so am I," Wild said as she sniffled. "I'm sorry I couldn't get back for Christmas – "

"I know, I know. We agreed, and you had your studies."

"Well, all of it's over now, anyway," Wild said, returning to his dinner to give her a little space.

"Ain't you going back, Wild?" Sarah asked.

"Not this fall. Someone's got to supervise the harvest, and Billy can't see above the corn now, let alone when it's full-grown," Wild said. "You all need me home, so here I am. I figure I wrung just about all I could out of those college fellas this year. From here on it's all speculation and bookkeeping."

"I could'a supervised the harvest," Bet said.

"Good, I'll probably need your help," Wild said.

"Bet took the prize for mathematics this year," Mama said, giving him a weak smile.

"Well, now! Nobody told me," Wild said. "That's great, Bet. I – hiya," he interrupted himself as Moze clumped back into the room, hopping up onto the bench next to him and taking a slice of beef from the plate.

"Moze!" Mama scolded.

"That's fine. He's almost eight now, ain't you? Got to feed you up," Wild said. The door opened as Billy came in, dusting himself down with his cap.

He had written to all of them while he was in Lubbock, though usually he'd just sent Mama a long letter with notes for the others. Still, there was a lot he hadn't been able to put into words, and of the rest of the family, only Mama and Billy were much on writing letters. Sarah hadn't ever got much to say, Bet cared more for numbers, and Moses was still clumsy with a pencil, let alone Lonny who was still learning his letters. Wild ate and listened to them tell him all the latest news, carefully dancing around the subject of the funeral. He'd get that later, either from Bet or, more likely, from one of the church elders at the social.

Once he'd kissed Mama goodnight he saw Moze and Lonny to bed in their room, then followed Billy to what had been his room. It wasn't fair to make Billy go back and share with the little ones now that he'd had his own room for nearly a year, and Wild didn't mind sharing. In Billy's room, now he supposed his and Billy's room, he opened the drawstring on his bag and took out his carefully folded Sunday suit, hanging it up to air out for the following day. Billy splashed through a perfunctory washing in the basin, then changed into his nightshirt while Wild washed.

"How'd planting go?" Wild asked, scrubbing behind his ears.

"Well as can be expected," Billy answered. "Corn, wheat, some oats. Imagine we'll have a good harvest if the weather cooperates."

"So another break-even year?" Wild asked mirthlessly. Billy shrugged.

"Better than not breaking even," he said. "Besides, didn't they teach you all kindsa crop magic at the aggie school?"

"Some. Too little, too late for this year," Wild said.

"Then what's the point?" Billy asked, echoing everyone Wild had talked to before he'd gone off to college, as well.

"What's the point of anything, Bill?" Wild replied tiredly. "If you think college is pointless, try farming a topsoil plot in Texas for decades and then coaxing good crops out of it."

Billy gave him a slightly impressed look. "Didn't think of it like that."

Wild rubbed his forehead. "Yeah. Me neither, before school."

"You think Mama will want to sell up?" Billy asked.

"Anyone ask you about buying?" Wild asked sharply. They'd better not have; it was cruel to ask a woman or her sons about selling up with her husband barely in the ground.

"Not yet, but they were waitin' on you, I expect," Billy replied.

"Good. Ain't something they oughta be asking you about anyway," Wild said, but then, "Do you think we oughta?"

"What's there for us if we do?" Billy asked. "Ain't no jobs in town we could do. Farming's all I know, Wild."

"You're a kid, Billy. You could learn more."

"Don't care much for schooling, not like you did."

"Well, maybe if you weren't farming every hour God gave, you would," Wild sighed. "I don't know. Maybe if we sold up we could go to Lubbock. Get a house in town for Mama, I could work at something or other. If you didn't want schooling you could drive a cab."

"Gosh," Billy said thoughtfully. He was kneeling down, and Wild knelt next to him; Billy was clearly waiting for him to say the prayer.

"We thank You for this day You have made," he said, as Billy squinted his eyes shut and bowed his head. "Thank You for my safe passage home from Lubbock and for the health of all the family. I'm pretty glad to be home, Lord, and glad to see everyone so well, and I hope Daddy Lon's had safe passage up there. Please bless Mama and the crops and the folks here in Lea, Amen. Billy, you got any words to share?"

"Bless Mama and the crops and please let it be nice for the Social tomorrow," Billy mumbled, and Wild grinned sidelong at him. "Amen."

Billy clambered into bed and Wild followed, the two of them curling up back-to-back; when winter came they'd be glad enough of the shared heat, but with high summer on its way, they'd have to learn to sleep as far apart as possible and tolerate the brutal warmth of a Texas July.

Just before he drifted off, Wild heard Billy say, "For sure Daddy's in Heaven, and I bet the yellin' about being took before the crops got in ain't stopped yet," and he laughed.

THREE

THE NEXT MORNING, the house was all a riot; the boys were too excited about the Social to behave, and Sarah and Bet too distracted with their own dressing to keep them in line. Wild saw to himself, letting Mama make sure Moze and Lonny were tidy and seen-to, and hoped that either Billy could also look after himself or Sarah would make sure he was presentable.

He was just pulling on his suspenders, smiling at the sound of Billy and Moze whooping in the kitchen, when Mama came in to see him.

"Don't you look nice," she said, smoothing down his shirt. "I swear you grew half a foot since leaving for school."

"Just looks that way, I expect," he replied.

"Well, either way, you're a credit to the family," she said. She looked troubled, though, and Wild frowned.

"You all right?" he asked, taking her wrists in his hands. "The little ones giving you any trouble, Mama?"

"No," she said. "No-one's troubled me at all. But you know…" she shrugged. "You're the man of the house now, Wild. That changes things."

"Don't I know it," he said. "I wasn't fooling about Bet having to help with the harvest this year."

"That's not exactly what I mean," she said. "Lord, you're like your blood daddy sometimes."

"I wouldn't know," he said, but he gave her a smile to show it wasn't bitter. "I hope I can live up to Lon, anyhow."

"And you do. But that's the problem, ain't it?" she asked. "Wild…folks'll see you different, now. The other men, they'll want to talk crops and town business and…"

"Aw, if I can't do that I'm pretty useless," he said. "Won't be a problem, Mama."

"I just want to be sure you know, so it don't take you by surprise."

"I know," he assured her.

"Maybe they'll ask you about selling up," she said, eyes cast sidelong.

"Billy said harvest should be all right if the weather holds; time enough then to decide, I imagine."

She nodded, still not quite meeting his eyes, and he wondered when his own mother had become afraid of him. "Mama. Man of the house I might be but boss of the farm I ain't. I wouldn't sell up without asking you. We'll weather this the same we always did, together."

She pressed her forehead to his chest. "I was blessed to have you, Wilder."

"You been blessed more times than just me," he said, laughing, and she gave him a smile as she leaned back. "I've got to bring the Lentz dray to the Social."

"Don't let your suit get dusty," she said.

"I'll do you credit," he promised, and just then Lonny sent up a wail, and Mama bustled off to see what was the matter.

The Lutheran church was close to the Platter-Mayer farm, but the soil was muddy; Wild, thinking of this, put Sarah and Bet up on the Lentz's dray and led it by the bridle, to preserve their nice dresses and shoes. When they arrived, folks were already setting up and decorating the tables, and Wild helped the girls down so they could join in, before leading the dray off to hitch it to the Lentz's truck.

A few other horses were hitched nearby, and he found he could still tell who had arrived by whose trucks were parked and whose horses were tied up to posts. There was Tex Muller's tractor and Tex Junior's horse; Tex Junior's sister Dot probably rode the tractor in with her father. The whole Schmidt family, both sides, and some of the cousins who were Schmidts a generation back. Fischers, Webers. His aunt Mildred's family the Wagners and his aunt Margaret's family the Kochs had arrived, he could tell by all the cousins' horses.

Word had no doubt got around from the Lentzes that he was home. As he left the dirt lot where the trucks were parked, he could see heads turning towards him, the flock-of-birds movement as people came forward to say hello. He was enveloped first by schoolmates, fellas pounding him on the back and asking questions he didn't have time to answer about the agricultural college; then girls pushed through to say "Hi Wild," and "Hope you're well," and "Sorry about Mr. Platter," but he didn't get much of a chance to respond to those either, because Lentz Platter was coming, half a head taller than anyone else and in a suit worth everyone else's put together, pushing through the crowd.

"Well, well," he said, and the youngsters dispersed. Platter held out a meaty hand. "Back home, eh, Meyer?"

"Yessir," Wild said, shaking his hand. "Happy to be home, though not happy the reason, Mr. Platter."

"No, we were all grieved to see Lon pass. Too soon, too soon," Lentz Platter clucked his tongue. "Good you're here for your mother and the little ones."

Wild swallowed and nodded. "I think so, sir. And I don't want you to think your money went to waste, Mr. Platter. I learned an awful lot this past year."

"You're staying on here, I take it?"

"Yessir."

"Well, come speak to me when you're settled in. I'd like to hear about it."

With a clap on the back, Platter retreated to one of the gaily decorated tables, where his wife and sons (one of them a college boy himself, though at a fancier college than the Aggie) were sitting. Wild casually wiped some sweat from his forehead with his handkerchief. That had gone better than anticipated. It was hard to tell a man paying your scholarship that you weren't going back to school.

"Wild, come have some food!" Bet called, and he was grateful for the rescue, and saw she knew it. She passed him one of the church's chipped plates, hand-me-downs of hand-me-downs, and he started moving down the food line, helping himself to scoops of potato salad and slabs of cold sliced meats, kartoffeln, cornbread and deviled eggs, wursts of all kinds, and strong brown bread to sop up the juices with.

He found himself with Dot Muller at his elbow on one side and his cousin Anna Koch on the other; somehow she'd got between him and Bet, who was chatting to Tex Junior next to the cake table, where the cakes were still under covers to keep them pretty for later.

"I heard you got back into town last night, Wild," said Anna, beaming at him. "Hope you didn't get any big ideas of being a city boy out in Lubbock."

"Barely had the chance," he said. "I was studying all the hours God gave."

"Doin' Lea proud?" Dot asked.

"Sure, I hope so. Came in near the top," Wild said.

"Well, we're happy you're back for the summer," Dot replied.

"Probably back for good," Wild replied. He saw, behind her, people growing impatient to get to the food, and started to move away from the table. Anna and Dot followed.

"You ain't going back to Lubbock?" Anna asked, a little too sweetly. There wasn't a mean bone in her body so it wasn't teasing, Wild knew, but what it might be instead, he wasn't sure.

"Not with the farm needin' me," he said. He wondered how many times he'd have this conversation with people who probably already knew.

"Dottie, whyn't you and Anna go join the Ladies' Circle?" a voice said, and Wild looked over Anna's shoulder to see Tex, Dot's father, stood there with hands on hips, watching the girls. "They're working on their stitches."

"We ain't eaten yet," Dot protested.

"Well, go eat with them and when you're done, get to your sewing."

Dot and Anna exchanged a look, but they did as Tex ordered.

"They weren't bothering me none," Wild said, though it was true he hadn't had a chance to get a bite yet.

"I'll bet," Tex said, giving him an amused look. "Come along. There's some of us in the shade at the back, you can eat in peace there."

He led Wild to the sheltered wall of the fellowship hall behind the church, where the older men, the heads of households and farm owners, usually retreated with their food. Later, after the footraces and ball games and cakes, they'd return to have a quiet smoke. Wild had never been, but Lon had usually joined them. His mother should be the one – it was her farm now, really – but women didn't go back of the fellowship hall at Socials.

In the shade, a handful of the elders of Lea were chatting in German, and most of the Lutheran farmers were standing, holding plates and eating or speaking quietly with one another. Wild looked over the faces and realized he was the youngest by a bit; the only other man near his age was still years older, and there with his father. He wished desperately, not something he had done too often, for Lon's presence. You were meant to bring your son when he was ready, not leave him to go on his own.

Then Tex rested an arm across his shoulders and dragged him towards the bench under the eaves, into the knot of sun-worn men, and Wild saw his uncles and the fathers and grandfathers of his friends, and he relaxed a little.

"Fellas, pass it over," Tex said, and Wild's uncle Wagner handed him a flask, in defiance of the dry laws, Prohibition, and good sense that said drinking at noon wasn't the best idea. Still, Wild took a nip out of politeness, and then handed it on to Tex.

"Billy tells me the planting went well," he said, and there were various nods all around.

"Weather should hold," a farmer said, and another replied, "Hope to God."

"Your mama holding up?" Uncle Wagner asked. "Happy to see you?"

"I think so, sir," Wild replied. "Said she would have sent Billy to Carson to pick me up if she'd known."

"That one. Can't barely see over the steering wheel and thinks he's a man," Tex said, shaking his head. "It's good you're back."

"Well, he's done a man's work, it sounds like to me," Wild replied, feeling he should defend his brother. "I'm glad to be back, but Billy ain't one to shirk."

"True enough," men murmured, and one of the old-timers said something in German, to which the other old-timers laughed.

"Reckon you know what you'll do with the farm, yet?" Dan Rohlf asked, at the tail-end of the laughter, and most of the men exchanged looks – some seemed unhappy he'd asked, others just unhappy he'd asked first. Wild wondered if Rohlf was looking to buy, though their lands didn't border and he'd have a time managing a farm the size of the Platter-Mayer acreage plus his own.

"Got to get the crop in," Wild said. "Enough time to decide once that's settled. Besides, it's not my call to make; my mama's been running it with Lon for years and she brought half of it with her when they married. Reckon she gets to decide."

"Don't be too much tied to her apron strings, now," one old-timer cautioned.

"Just making sure my family's settled for in the way that's best," Wild replied. There must have been an edge to his voice, because Uncle Wagner changed the subject to repairs the church was starting to need, and everyone had opinions about how best to roof it before next winter, and whose job it ought to be.

"Talkin'a repairs," Wild said, as the discussion died down, "Anyone else notice how the old church in town's been failing?"

There were nods all around, and Tex said, "Someone ought to put up a fence round it."

"That's just what I told that young Baptist boy at the Dry Goods," Dan Rohlf said.

"I thought so too," Wild agreed. "But I ain't know who ought to. Most townies are Baptists. You'd think what with all their talk of respectability one of them'd do it."

"Fencing ain't cheap," Tex pointed out.

"Baptists are!" someone exclaimed, and there was laughter.

"Pull down a couple of trees, don't have to buy real fencing," Rohlf said, when it died down. "Just enough to keep folks out. And maybe pull up the trash and tumbleweeds around it."

"Who owns the land?" Tex asked.

"Baptists say maybe Lentz Platter," Rohlf volunteered. "Thought you might know, Wild."

Wild shook his head. "I could maybe ask, but I ain't know."

"Maybe nobody," George Lentz said. "They only did land grants back when for the farms. Town was town."

"Somebody owned it, though. Whoever owned the plot the town built on."

Everyone exchanged glances, but it was clear nobody knew.

"Well, maybe best to ask forgiveness rather than permission," Wild said thoughtfully. "Who needs some trees felled?"

"I got some spare lumber drying at my place would suit," Rohlf said. "Too crooked for building anything but it'd be fine for a free fence. Bring up your truck and help load and you can have it."

"That's neighborly of you," Wild told him. "Let me make sure the farm's tickin' over and I'll come down in maybe a month or so."

"Well, we got one thing settled, anyway," Tex said with a laugh. There were a couple of hearty backslaps and some finishing of food, but it wasn't long before the men were making their way back up to where the rest of the Social was, finding their wives, watching the boys gather for sports and the girls weave crowns from weed-flowers growing in the field. Wild took a chair next to his mother, who had Lonnie on her lap and was trying to convince him to eat some potato salad, and watched Billy line up with the other boys for the footrace.

"Told you," his mother said, but she looked on him a little proudly, he thought.

"Wasn't nothing I couldn't handle," he replied. A couple of the younger women in the sewing circle were looking at him, but whenever he looked their way they dropped their heads and laughed to each other.

FOUR

ON A WET Tuesday, not long after the Social, Wild put on his churchgoing clothes and took the truck into town. He'd wanted Mama and at least one of the girls to come with him, and maybe Billy too, but Mama said she trusted him and he didn't know how to ask the others, so off he went alone.

Lea didn't have a lawyer, but the lawyer in Wheeler came down once a month to take care of paperwork for the bank. Lon had apparently used him to write a will, which seemed ridiculous to Wild until he thought about it. After all, Lon had two daughters from one marriage, three sons from another, and then there was Wild, the eldest, but not his own boy. Plus half Lon's farmland was technically by marriage, and while Lon had owned the deed, Wild supposed by rights the Mayer plot, long since incorporated into the Platter holdings, should be his. Disposing of the farm could be a tricky business.

And anyway, Wild had been the one the lawyer had called, the previous week, to ask if they could meet and go over the will. So here he was, looking like he was going to a prayer meeting, heading for the bank. The lawyer's office was a dim cubby inside the bank, and the lawyer was a Baptist by the name of Briggs. Wild wasn't sure he trusted him.

"Mr. Briggs," Wild said, taking off his hat as he shook the other man's hand. "Sorta surprised to hear from you. I didn't figure Lon had much of a will."

"Well, the farm," Mr. Briggs said, and Wild nodded. "Did he ever discuss its disposition with you?"

"Not with me. Figured he had another ten years in him at least, I imagine," Wild said.

"I am sorry for his passing."

"Thank you, sir. It's been a blow to the family."

"Yes, I would guess so. Well, I can't say the will is complicated, but he did have me draw up something official, just in case, and he left a letter for you," Briggs said. "I'm…not sure he anticipated a longer life than what he had, Mr. Mayer."

"How so?" Wild asked. "He tell you he was feeling sickly?"

Briggs gestured to the letter in front of Wild. "You may want to read that, then we'll go over the particulars."

Wild unfolded the letter and read it, perplexed, but soon he was distracted; Briggs had clearly gone through and added all the right grammar, but the letter itself was pure Lon.

To Wilder Mayer,

It seems by rights I should be leaving the farm to William, being the son of both your mother and myself, but I have a great fear he'll be too young when I go to my reward and I know you are a trustworthy man. You will look after your mother and make sure the farm prospers, God willing.

I hope you will think of your sisters and brothers as well. When you think of my children I hope you will remember I tried to do as well by you as I could and not hold any errors I made against them. You should not split up the farm but if any of your brothers has a head for farming I hope you will settle him with some land somehow.

There should be a little set out for the girls' marriages &etc. which Lentz Platter will know about and make sure you are given title to. In particular please do not abandon Elizabeth no matter how she may try you as she is headstrong but not wicked.

Trust your mother and do not listen to any other advice. Be guided only by good sense. I had never wished for a better son than yourself even from my own blood and I hope you will care for your brothers and sisters in the same spirit.

Yrs

Lon Platter

Wild felt a pain in his heart he hadn't expected; he'd liked Lon, considered him a decent father, but he hadn't thought Lon was all that fond of him. To find out in a letter was…hard.

Briggs cleared his throat softly as Wild folded up the letter.

"He left me control of the accounts?" Wild asked.

"Mr. Mayer, it isn't just the accounts," Briggs replied. "Mr. Platter left you the entire farm. The deeds to the Platter and Mayer plots, both houses and the single remaining barn, all the equipment and any livestock."

Wild stared at him. "But my mama – "

"Mr. Platter felt it would be more secure in your hands. A woman owning that much land has…potential threats, and he seemed very sure in his belief that you would be a good steward of the land and, well, listen to your mother," Briggs said.

"Yes, but…" Wild scratched his head, bowled over by this. "It ain't like a woman can't inherit. Didn't leave nothing to Bet, even? She's got a better head for numbers than I do and he knew it."

"Bet?"

"My stepsister by his first wife."

"Ah, yes. I believe she comes up in the letter." Briggs steepled his fingers. "Mr. Mayer, I need to warn you that if you try to reject the contents of the will, the entire property may become the domain of the state, and be put up for auction. I'm certain you don't want that."

"No, I just don't want…" Wild trailed off, unsure how to put it into words. "I never wanted to become rich off my stepfather's back," he said.

"Hardly rich," Briggs said drily. "Farmland's not worth what it was, you know."

Wild nodded. "That's true. But it's still ours and he was proud of it."

"He had every right to be. And he left it in his will as he saw fit."

Wild nodded. "I take your meaning, sir. I'll take the farm on myself. Once I have it, can I give it away? Can I give the accounts to my mama?"

"I suppose you could add a name to the accounts. You'd need to speak with the bank about that. Mr. Platter has made it clear in the will that the farm can't be divided up until after it's sold on to someone outside the family. There are ways around that – if you wanted to sell off some of the land or gift some of it to a family member, you could, but you'd need a survey and a redivision of the land, plus some legal appeals. Costly. I don't recommend it."

"The Platters won't be pleased," Wild said, mouth twisting up in a half smile. "I expect they thought it'd stay in the blood family."

"Mr. Mayer, in my dealings with the people of Lea, I find nobody is every truly pleased after a will is read," Briggs said with a low chuckle. "But it's my understanding Lentz Platter likes you, and his family steers by his star."

"Let's hope that don't change," Wild agreed. "All right. Might as well show me what I need to sign. I don't read as fast as a lawyer, and I'll need to look it all over."

He spent most of the morning reading through all the documents Briggs gave him, even the duplicates. Bank access letters, deed transfers, all kinds of things he barely understood but made sure weren't some kind of swindle. He sat at the table outside the lawyer's office and read them all, overhearing farmers from as far off as sixty miles coming in to take money out, some to plead for their mortgages. There was a drought on, some of them said, though Wild hadn't heard of any such thing among farmers in Lea.

Eventually he got all the paperwork completed, signed for the deeds to the farm and for access to the various bank accounts. Lon hadn't lied; there was some money set aside for the girls, and the farm was in good condition, with all the taxes done up proper. When he signed the last paper, Briggs gave him a toothy smile.

"A pleasure doing business with you, Mr. Mayer," he said. "And if you ever need a will for disposal of the property, please feel free to tell the bank, and they'll get in touch."

"No insult intended, Mr. Briggs, but I hope to God I won't soon," Wild said.

"None taken. I know many a farmer in your shoes," Briggs replied.

As he drove past the little ruined church on his way home, Wild reminded himself to talk to Rohlf in another few weeks about getting that timber for the fence. It'd be something nice and simple, putting up a fence. He wondered if the bell tower still had a bell, and if someone ought to salvage it, maybe put it up in the graveyard as a monument of some kind.

When he got home he shed his boots, washed up, and found Mama at the kitchen table, mending shirts. He kissed her hello and sat down across from her, and she set her sewing aside.

"Might as well say it," she said, no doubt seeing the look on his face.

"Lon left me everything," he told her. "And he begged me not to screw it all up."

"That's Lon for you," his mother answered, unperturbed, and picked up her sewing again. "All that high drama just to know the farm's safe. I know you won't break it, Wild."

"Won't I?" Wild asked. "It's not an easy life, Mama."

"Well, no," she said. "But if it were easy, would it be worth it?"

"Dunno," he replied. "Say, you hear anything from the church women about a drought coming on?"

"A drought? No. Why?"

"Well, there was talk at the bank. Not anyone I knew, so they must be far-out from Lea, but…" he shrugged.

"If we lose the crops…" she began.

"Lon has some set aside. If we lose this year's crops we might have to take a new mortgage on the farm for seed, but we'd eat." He didn't mention that what they'd be eating was his sisters' weddings.

"Well, I don't imagine God found me your stepfather and then took him from me only to take the farm too," she said. "Rain follows the plow, as they say; we'll work hard and leave the rest to Him."

Wild resolved to talk to Bet about going over the accounts at the bank. She'd know down to the penny what they could afford, and how much they'd lose if the crops did fail.

FIVE

IT WAS PAST high summer by the time Wild drew the old truck up alongside Dan Rohlf's barn. He'd already packed a lunch and a dinner, a post-holer and a shovel, saw and a mallet, and some good rope. There was a bucket full of rawhide sinews soaking in water, and a jug of ginger-water for Wild himself.

"Surprised when you called up. Figured you'd be bringin' in the oats Lon and Billy put up in the north field about now," Rohlf said as they loaded the wood for the fence. That was like him – he always knew what other folks were planting, even when it wasn't none of his business.

"Nother few days, I think," Wild replied.

"Oats were lookin' ripe when I drove past."

"Sure they are, but not dry enough yet," Wild said, annoyed. Billy had made the same argument, but it was too humid yet to harvest; they'd need a dry spell for the best yield. Trying to convince Billy it was more scientific to risk the crop and wait another week or two for a dry patch was tough going; he didn't need to have it out with Rohlf as well.

Besides, he hated oats, and Billy had planted them regardless, so Billy could mind him.

"Well, you're the doctor," Rohlf said, without resentment. "You need help putting up that fence?"

"Only if you've a mind to spend all day post-holing. You're already givin' the wood," Wild said. "Don't feel obliged."

"Well, I'll take a pass then, as I got chores around here. Say, if your brother's old enough this year, think he'd like some cash helping with the corn harvest?"

"When you thinking to harvest?"

"Don't rightly know, yet. Planted about a week before you did."

"Well, if we can spare him, he's free to help if he wants," Wild said.

"But with Lon gone, we'll already be hiring on hands."

"Fair enough. If I know of any good ones I don't need, I'll send 'em your way."

"Much obliged," Wild said, still feeling oddly uncertain at how easily the men of Lea were treating him as one of them. Rohlf helped him tie down the lumber and waved him off, and Wild turned towards Lea and what Mama fondly called his Fool Volunteering.

When he pulled up to the church in Lea there were old-timers, Lutheran and Baptist alike, sitting out front of the Dry Goods; they sat on separate benches according to their faith, but didn't seem especially bothered by one another as he parked the truck and began unloading his tools. It was apparent that he was the most entertaining thing they'd seen in some time. He left the lumber in the truck for now; he'd pace out the post holes first, then drive posts two at a time and lash the crossbeams with rawhide. When it dried in the sun, it'd hold tighter than wooden pegs or nails, and be less work for him, too.

He surveyed the yard and the church inside it thoughtfully. There was a rusted chain with an old padlock on it running through the big heavy door handles. He decided he'd save cleaning away the trash and tumbleweed for some other day, or maybe he'd make Moze and Billy come up and do it.

"You planning on a sermon?" one of the old-timers called.

"Yeah!" Wild called back. "On the message of high fences make good neighbors!"

They cackled at that as he began pacing out the fence, dropping handy stones every so often to mark where the posts ought to go. By the time he'd paced all four sides of the yard, other fellas had passed by to inspect what he was doing, and two were sitting on the edge of the truck bed – Micah, a Baptist who'd been two years above him in school, and Tex Junior, Dot's brother, who'd come up with him in school as far as the tenth grade, when he'd left to work the farm full-time.

"Ain't you got chores?" Wild asked, a little surly at being watched doing work.

"We got chores, Tex Junior?" Micah asked.

"I haven't got any," Tex Junior replied.

"Thought we'd lend a hand," Micah added.

"Looks like all you're lending right now is your asses," Wild pointed out. Micah grinned. "You want to help, sure. Tex Junior, you want to drive posts? Micah, you follow behind him, lash the crossbeams up to the posts with rawhide."

"Suits me fine," Tex Junior agreed. Wild took the postholer out of the truck as the others began unloading lumber. "Why'd the Baptists build this old thing, anyway?"

"We didn't," Micah replied. "We all thought you Lutherans did."

"Hell no," Tex Junior said.

"Watch your swearin' there," Micah scolded.

"Mind yourself," Wild warned, driving the postholer deep into the ground. "You two gonna fight over theology I can do this just fine on my own."

"Nah," Tex Junior assured him, as Wild pulled up the first plug of dirt. Under the top layer it looked to be good soil, actually, dark and rich, better than he'd have expected from town. He dropped the postholer twice more, widening the hole, until Tex lifted a post and fitted it in snugly, twisting it to seat it fully before tapping it in with a mallet. "Yep, that'll do."

The work went pretty smooth. Wild would posthole one side of the yard, then go back while Tex Junior drove the posts and help Micah with the rawhide. They had a couple of problems with the lumber being too long or not straight enough for Micah's liking, but by the time they stopped to eat and pass around the jug of ginger-water, they were near half done. They sat in the shade, backs to the church wall, and ate their food and speculated.

"You reckon there's anything left inside?" Tex Junior asked, jerking his thumb behind them. "Old pews, moldy Bibles?"

"Bibles don't grow mold," Micah said. "Well-known fact."

"What, on account of that paper they print 'em on?" Tex Junior inquired curiously.

"On account of the Holy Word," Micah replied.

"Theology," Wild muttered.

"Our pastor says the Holy Word lives in the hearts of men," Tex Junior proclaimed.

"Lordy, hallelujah," Micah replied drily.

"Moldering bibles and rotten pews," Tex Junior said.

"I reckon not," Wild replied. "By now someone coulda got in and stole everything."

"So why not tear it down?" Micah asked.

"Who knows? If it ain't belong to the Baptists or the Lutherans, better just to leave it," Wild said, and he felt like the smooth adobe warmed under his back, but maybe that was just his imagination. It was hot enough out to start with. "That's the point."

"Point 'a what?" Tex Junior asked.

"Point 'a putting up the fence. Keeps it safe. Keeps people safe from it," Wild said vaguely. "Best to leave it be unless you can't. That's what Lon always said about things. If you can't fix it, best leave it be."

They sat around after eating for a while, chatting about nothing consequential, until finally they felt like they'd digested; then Wild went back to post-holing, and the other two carried a pile of lumber out from the truck. There was no way to answer the question of what was inside the church, anyway; the windows were too high up and narrow for them to see through.

The sun was getting lower in the sky and they'd nearly finished the fence when *it* happened. Tex Junior and Micah were lowering a post into the ground, and Wild was digging the last post-hole, when the metal tip of the postholer hit something. There was a brief flash of blue, and a sound – later Wild said it was like the sound of a metal nail tapping against a china plate, only a thousand times louder.

All he knew at the time was that when he thrust the postholer down into the soil, turning to make some smart remark to Micah, it impacted something. The collision sent a jolt back up through the metal, through the wooden handle, past Wild's gloved hand and into his flesh. Every nerve in his body lit up in pain at once, and he had a sense of motion, of the world spinning and heaving around him, the smell of burned meat, and then...nothing.

The panhandle of Texas around about Lea was flat, and prone to storms; mostly sheet lightning in the summers, but sometimes bolt lightning would strike the tallest thing in the area. Given how bare and empty it could be, often the tallest thing in the area was a man standing up. You learned early, in Lea and the surrounding countryside, to lie flat in a ditch if a storm rolled up. There were some men who had died from lightning strikes, and a few who had survived. Those that did were never quite right – some stopped watches just from wearing them, and the unlucky ones "went strange" as they called it. Most were marked – some for only a few days, some scarred permanently by the strike.

They said afterward that Wild must have been struck by lightning, some kind of freak accident, but the skies were clear and it never did rain that day. Micah and Tex Junior knew, too, that it couldn't have been, because the blue light that threw him off his feet came up from the ground, not down from the sky. One minute, they were both putting a post into a hole Wild had dug; the next, Wild was lying halfway across the yard, motionless, and both of them were blinking afterimages of a pale blue light out of their eyes.

When Wild woke, later, he was in his own bed, which was a surprise. He'd known enough as the electricity struck him to wonder if he'd wake up at all.

The last thing he remembered was driving the postholer into the ground and the world exploding in pain. He sat up, saw that it was light out, and wondered if Billy had seen to the chores.

He realized he was naked, and when he looked down at his arms he let out a noise of surprise. There was a fine, lacelike network of raised scars, like curled willow branches, starting at his shoulder and going almost to his wrist, curving around his bicep, across the inside of his elbow, and down the inner part of his forearm. When he looked down he saw the scars continued, across his pectorals and over his abdomen. They rose up his left leg, too, starting at the heel of his foot and wrapping up towards his thigh, meeting the scars from his arm just above his privates.

He'd seen other lightning-strike scars, so he knew what they were, but these were different – not red like a fresh one, but paler than his light brown skin and barely raised at all. They looked like old scars, and he wondered how long he'd been unconscious, but he decided it couldn't have been so long – a glance out the window showed the crops about what they had been when he'd gone up to town.

It felt like he'd been marked, but when he stood, when he dressed, the scars didn't hurt or pull at all. He felt all right, if a little dry-mouthed, so he did up his clothes and walked into the kitchen, and just about scared Mama to death when he did so.

"Wild!" she cried, dropping a pan in the basin, and ran to hug him with dish-wet hands and her apron still on. "Jesus *Lord* we was worried about you," she said.

"What happened?"

"You've been out a day and a half. Tex Junior and that Baptist boy brought you back, said you got knocked flat while you worked. We were set to get a doctor if you wasn't up soon, but Bet said she'd read to leave you be, so…"

"I suppose she was right," Wild replied. He disengaged himself from the hug, holding her shoulders to steady her. "I feel fine, Mama."

"Well, you looked like electrical death," she declared.

"I imagine I did. Tex Junior and Micah say what happened?"

"Just that you were putting up the fence when something struck you. Freak lightning, Tex's father called it."

"You know if they get the fence finished?" he asked.

Mama stared at him. "That's what you want to worry about right now?" she asked, pulling him to the kitchen table to sit down.

"Well, you know what Lon always said, fella has to make sure if he starts a job it gets finished," Wild managed weakly.

"I ought to hide you," she told him. Mama had never hided him once in his life, and at this point she was about half his size, but she sounded so mad he almost believed she would. Instead, she went to the pantry and took out some bread, set it down in front of him with butter and a pot of jam.

"Eat," she commanded, pouring a cup of water from the pitcher. He took it and drank before he even tried to eat the bread. "Yes, Tex Junior finished the fence," she allowed. "He told me he was aiming to when he went into town today, anyway. I suppose he knew you'd want to know. He said there weren't much left."

"No, that's true. Billy saw to the chores?"

"He did, him and Bet."

Wild looked at her over the rim of his mug. "Imagine you saw what it done to me," he said.

She nodded. "Do they hurt?"

He shook his head. "Feel like they've been healed over much longer'n a day."

"I'll order some of that scar balm they advertise in the almanac."

"You know that's all snake oil, Mama," Wild said. "Anyway, they don't bother me."

Mama looked down at the tabletop.

"Don't you scare me like that again," she said. "You're my baby and all I got left of your daddy."

"Well, I won't if I can manage it," he said. "Promise I'll make Billy mend the fences from now on."

She laughed a little at that, but she let it go. Wild worked his way through another few slices of bread while she changed the subject to other, less weighty matters.

The next day, a dry spell set in. In four days' time they were bringing in the oats, even though Mama didn't like him doing such hard work so soon after having his sense knocked out of him. Still, nothing hurt, and it had to be done. Anyway it was fortunate, Wild thought, that they had such a well-timed dry spell. He worried what it would do to the corn, but once the oats were in, the rain came again.

They set aside some of the oats for feed and stored the rest for sale, later in the year. When the wheat harvest was in, Wild told Billy, they'd drive the wheat and oats into Carson and sell them to the fellas who came through on the train, taking the crops down to Lubbock to be shipped, who knew? All over the world.

"The wheat and corn money'll go to the farm," he told Billy, driving into Lea in the rain to pick up some supplies mama had asked for. "But the oats were your idea. If you were a tenant farmer you'd pay a third of the crop for tenanting, so I reckon two thirds of what we make from the oats'll be yours."

"I'll give it to Mama," Billy said staunchly.

"Well, that's nice, but you ain't have to. Set some aside. Time you're ready to be a man, maybe you'll have enough for a year in Lubbock too," Wild said, tousling his hair. They rolled down the muddy, rutted main street, and the church across from the bank seemed to loom up at them out of the rain, two small bell towers like long locust antenna, watching them.

Something seemed different about it, Wild thought, but maybe it was just the fence. Good strong fence, and he was proud of that work.

He parked the truck in front of the Dry Goods and he and Billy both leapt out, running inside, Billy with an oilskin bag under one arm so the goods they were buying wouldn't get wet. Through the window, while Billy bought the flour and a few other incidentals, Wild stared at the church, and it seemed like the church watched him back.

The very edges of his scars tingled slightly, but that was probably just the rain.

HARVEST 1930

THEY BROUGHT IN the wheat in July; the corn wouldn't be ready until autumn. The wheat was beautiful, thick pulpy heads of deep gold-brown, and most of the farms around Lea had produced the same. Late July was a harried process of bringing in the harvest and then running to the next farm to help them bring theirs in; Wild figured over the course of the month he'd loaned out the tractor at least half a dozen times, and he'd worked some part of a dozen other farms along with his own.

They'd likely have labor roll into town for the corn harvest, but this early, for the wheat, it was mostly the men and boys of Lea, burning in the sun, bringing in the grain so that it could be threshed and sold in Carson. There were already plans for the men of Lea to caravan into town, trucks and trailers full of bushels of wheat and oats, and hopefully the crop buyers offering futures on the corn, a certain dollar per bushel ahead of time guaranteed. Maybe not so much as you'd have got on the day, depending on scarcity, but a dollar guaranteed was worth a dollar-fifteen uncertain, most of the Lea farmers thought.

Wild, sitting at the kitchen table with Bet, watched her pencil go, impressed as always by the speed of her mind.

"What you figure we'll take on the oats and wheat?" he asked, as she consulted an almanac with last year's crop prices.

"You figure a dollar?" she replied, looking worried. "Last year was a dollar twenty but…"

"It's been dropping for years," he agreed. He'd only had the one class in farm economics, but the aggie school had made it clear – grain crops were the most lucrative, and still didn't pay much.

"Ninety cents to be safe?" Bet asked.

"Say ninety, and do the math for lower as well," he said. "We'll hope for higher."

"Well, the wheat'll take us through December either way," she said, as she wrote. "Is the corn safe?"

"Even if we don't get more rain, we'll get something from the crop," he said.

"How much, you think?"

"Maybe eighty cents if we get it in just before November, which we ought," he said. "Sixty if we got to bring it in between now and then."

"Well," she said, "if it's a good crop, that'll be seed for next year and a little over."

"Can't rely on luck," he said. "What's the worst?"

Her pencil moved again, the scratching somehow louder. "If the wheat don't fetch over ninety and the corn fails and comes in at sixty…well, at least Daddy paid off the mortgage," she sighed. "We'll keep the farm."

"That's something," he breathed, leaning back, shoulders relaxing slightly. "Enough for seed for next year? Without a loan, I mean."

"Yeah. I think so," she said. "We're lucky, I suppose."

"I know." He rubbed one eye with the heel of his hand. "Lord, I'm tired."

"I ain't surprised. Even Daddy had you to help," she said. "Which reminds me, now that you're man of the house, you been thinking about settling down?"

He laughed. "Why, have you?"

"No, but I ain't own two farms' worth of prime acreage," she said with a grin. "You pick a wife now, you got your choice. Best baker in the county could be yours."

"Yeah, who's that?"

"Dot Muller, I reckon. Or you could court Leanna Webber, her mama keeps a clean house and she's won prizes for her quilts."

"They payin' you to sell them to me?" he asked, amused.

"Not exactly, but I've had questions."

"I suppose I'd better, sooner or later," he said. "It ain't like deciding what to plant, though, you know that."

"Well, yes, but your Mama and my Daddy did all right marrying in haste."

"Mama had good taste and Lon got a bargain."

"That's what he always said too," Bet agreed. Wild thought about Lon's letter, how he'd begged Wild to make sure Bet was looked after.

"What about you?" he asked. "You're a Platter, and my sister, you must have courters come calling."

"One or two," she said loftily.

"Sarah?"

"Oh, I imagine soon enough. Might as well ask about Billy, at this point."

"Well, hell, Billy could go courting, I gave him the oat money."

"Don't change the subject. If you marry off me and Sarah before you get wed, who'll look after the little ones with Mama? No, you got to find a wife first," Bet said decisively. "You ain't want to pick, I'll find you one."

"Easy, there! I can find my own woman, thank you."

"Best get to it once the crops are in. It'll be a long, cold, boring winter," Bet advised.

Wild had to admit she was right – it'd be his winter for courting, and he could marry in the spring before the planting. Besides, he ought to start thinking on having his own children, sooner rather than later. And his mother wasn't getting any younger; a good wife would take some of the burden off her shoulders, especially after his sisters left.

"I'll think on it," he told her. Bet tapped her pencil against the paper. "I will, Bet, honest to God."

"You get spoiled by those city ladies in Lubbock?" she asked.

There had been women in Lubbock – the daughter of a professor, *very* briefly, until he'd realized the trouble that might cause. There had been a bordello the fellas had gone to sometimes, and he'd gone once with them, but he didn't like to spend his money on a woman that way. It didn't feel right. Even if it was winnings from poker and not the allowance Mr. Platter had sent him, it felt wasteful of the money and cruel to the women. He'd felt poorly in spirit after. Most of the other women he met were city-bred, and, well…

"I wouldn't take one of them to a farm in Lea if you paid me," he said. "They wouldn't come anyhow."

In any case, there was the oats and wheat to sell and the corn to get in, and he'd consider it all after that.

The caravan to Carson was delayed three days; there was a

downpour the day before they'd meant to go, and the road was no good until it had dried. It didn't hurt the harvested crops or even the growing ones, so the men only complained the traditional amount.

Wild brought Bet with him to check the math and Billy to learn how it was done. It was how Wild had learned, riding in with Lon, watching him talk with the buyers and load and unload the grain. Bet rode up in the cab, but the day was fine, so Wild let Billy ride in amongst the wheat – he'd hitched an old cart to the back of the truck to haul it all, and the road was full of trucks with trailers and carts and racks, farmers at the wheel, sometimes wives or sisters in the cabs, young men riding in the open air.

It wasn't good fortune, when they got to Carson. There were buyers, but they weren't offering above seventy cents. Lon had taught Wild to haggle, but there just wasn't the demand for wheat there used to be.

"Even with Oklahoma and Kansas poorly, we got mostways what we need," the buyer said. "Where'd all this come from, anyway? Didn't you know there's a drought on?"

"Not in Lea," Wild said.

"I guess not." The buyer shrugged. "Seventy's a favor."

"Give us seventy-one, and we'll drop to sixty-eight after sixty bushels, and give you eighty across the board for the oats," Bet said. The buyer looked at her but she looked back, guileless; Wild knew they didn't have much over sixty bushels of wheat, but the buyer didn't. He looked to Wild, confused.

"She's the bookkeeper," Wild said. "This is my sister, Miss Bet Platter."

"How do," the buyer tipped his hat courteously.

Wild clapped her shoulder and left Bet to her discussion with the buyer while he went to help Billy with the rest of the unloading. They poured sack after sack of oats into the big hopper on the scales, and then watched the crane pulleys whisk the hopper off, dumping it into a train car before returning to swallow their wheat, as well.

"Thank god for oats," Uncle Koch said, joining Wild and mopping sweat off his forehead with a handkerchief. "Prices ain't what they used to be but I don't think anyone'll fail this year."

"We been lucky," Wild agreed.

"Wild!" Bet called.

"Best go make the handshake," Uncle Koch said, and Wild hurried back.

"Your sister here is a very thorough young miss," the buyer told him. Bet rolled her eyes, but Wild grinned at her. "Now, she's gone over this bill of weight and the payment here, surcharge for shipping, and here's your total – that all right, miss?"

Bet gave Wild a nod, so he signed the receipt and shook the man's hand, helped Bet up into the truck, and whistled for Billy, who came running. They pulled out so another farmer could pull in, then headed for the main street of Carson.

"Well done," Wild told her, when they were out of earshot of the buyers. "I don't think anyone else got seventy-one for wheat."

"It'll see us through January at least," Bet said. "Did you hear what he said about Kansas and Oklahoma? I hear there's two whole states gone dry from lack of rain."

"And parts of the panhandle too," Wild said grimly. "We'd best hope it doesn't come as far as us."

"Well, at least we won't fail this year," she said.

"Uncle Koch says probably no one in Lea will," Wild agreed. "Hell, we could probably pull down the corn now and bring it in and be all right. Not what I hoped for, but all right."

They treated themselves to a meal at a lunch counter in Carson, and over hot sandwiches and coffee Bet worked out what they'd need to set aside for next year's seed, and what Billy's percentage from the oats was.

"Now, what's five percent of total before the shipping charge?" Wild asked, and Bet frowned but did the math. "All right. We'll put that in the bank for you, Bet, as our sales agent."

"Wild, no, we need that for the farm."

"Not if the corn goes well, and anyway, you live on the farm," Wild pointed out. "If we need it, I know you're good for it. You did the work, ought to be paid."

"No more than you ought to."

"Hell, I didn't even plant the stuff." He tapped the number she'd written out. "Take it, Bet. Lon'd say the same, you know he would."

She gave him a smile and drew a little circle around it. "All right."

"Once it goes to the bank in Lea, I'll make the transfers," Wild said, satisfied.

Most of the other farmers in Lea seemed pleased, too, even with the low payment for the wheat. The mood as they drove away from Carson, later that evening, was joyous; boys whooped from empty truck beds, and women with packages of goods on their laps and maybe a few treats for the folks back home smiled out at the golden fields of corn still growing around Lea. By the time Wild pulled off for the Platter farm, there were lanterns lit on the porch.

"Your uncle Wagner got in ten minutes ago, and Mildred called over to tell me," Mama said, coming down the steps. Wild tossed the keys to Billy, who got into the cab to put the truck in the barn. "You did well!"

"Sure did," Wild agreed, spinning her around. "Come on inside, Bet'll give you the numbers."

Two weeks later, the price of wheat dropped to 27 cents a bushel. Wild saw it in the paper and sent up a quiet prayer of thanks.

Six

CORN IS A picky crop, and a risky one. It has to rain at the right times, and sometimes it can't rain; a corn field is a mysterious place. Getting in the harvest is difficult and time-consuming, and it's a son of a bitch to get to market.

The migrant laborers arrived in early September, rough men and women who pitched tents when they weren't permitted into barns, or slept in makeshift homes in the back of their own trucks. There were more than usual, that year, and some with kids; plenty said they'd been tenant farmers or even owners until now, until the one bad year had done for them. They'd overextended on mortgages or farm equipment payments from previous years, or just slowly been worn down until finally this was the end. He heard it half a dozen times.

The sheer number of them drove labor prices down, at least on some farms, but Wild couldn't look at the gaunt faces and not pay them a fair wage; he hired the kids to de-tassel the corn, too. The least he could do was pay well enough they'd eat something other than pan bread. And if some corn went missing, well, who was to say it wasn't raccoons or wild hogs?

But once the harvest was underway, everyone was already looking ahead, looking past the worrying news and the dim hope for a good price for corn, to the social.

The Lutherans and the Baptists had agreed that it would be better this year to have one harvest social, where everyone could celebrate, and the Johnsons offered their farm; true, they were Baptists, but Gert was the midwife for all of Lea and her mother had been a Lutheran, and everyone agreed that was close enough.

So Wild and Bet and Billy drove into Carson with the caravan again, followed by trucks and carts driven by two of the men who'd helped them bring in the corn. Anyone who didn't go to Carson went to the Johnson farm to help prepare for the social: putting down boards for dancing and stringing lanterns from poles, setting up tables for the food, hanging the ragged bunting that came out for the Fourth of July and New Year's and school passing-out.

Before the harvest took up every waking hour, Wild had spent a little time with the other musically-inclined Lutherans, and it was agreed the Lutheran string band would take up the first half of the social, and the Baptist organist would play the piano for the second.

Wild wasn't sure that a banjo, two guitars, a harmonium, and a ukulele were really the height of culture the Lutherans had to offer, but they'd do their best.

And so the night after they came back from selling the corn, feeling like the richest man in town despite low pay for the corn too, Wild put on his Sunday best. He crammed Mama and Sarah into the cab with food on their laps, loaded Bet and the boys into the back, and drove them carefully up to the Johnsons' farm.

A harvest social even in a bad year was a good time, but Wild didn't remember much about it later. There was food, singing and dancing, and he played until his fingers hurt – even played a solo, since the ukulele was a mystery to most of them and they wanted to hear what it sounded like without a banjo overwhelming it. He played *Second Hand Rose*, which amused them, and then at the very end, to give the other fellas time to put their instruments away and someone to find the Baptist organist, he played *Shine On Harvest Moon*.

Shine on,
Shine on Harvest Moon
Up in the sky
I ain't had no lovin' since
January, February, June or July…

He remembered handing the ukulele to Billy, so he could run off and show it to his friends, who were mostly clustered around the bonfire at the edge of the party. And he remembered the Baptist organist striking up a dance hall number on the piano, and he must have joined in the dancing because he remembered stopping, suddenly, as he caught movement under the lanterns ringing the makeshift dance floor.

Sam Starbuck

There was a woman on the edge of the floor, surrounded by farmers' sons and children, and Wild didn't know her; couldn't have named her, and that was so unusual in Lea that he was stunned by that alone. But she was also just about the most beautiful woman he'd ever seen, even in Lubbock, with a sweet oval face and skin a shade darker even than his own, deep brown eyes and thick black hair done in neat plaits, wrapped up on her head like a crown. She was looking at him like she knew him, too; when their eyes met the scars from his shock throbbed, once, sharply –

"Wild," Sarah called, grabbing his arm to pull him forward, and the feeling fled. "Wild, come meet Miss Adelaide."

He managed to touch the brim of his hat respectfully when presented to her. Miss Adelaide nodded, lips curving gently.

"Miss Adelaide's the schoolteacher, you ain't met yet," Sarah continued blithely. "She came after you left for Lubbock last year. She went all the way down to Dallas for the summer, to give music lessons to rich folks' kids, and now she's back to teach once school starts."

"Well, now," Wild said, bewildered by all this information.

"I think you played beautifully," Miss Adelaide said.

"Thank you, Miss. Ma'am," he managed. He felt like he'd been plunged into deep water. The sound all around was muffled, and he wasn't sure which way the surface might be. "Would you like to dance, Miss Adelaide?"

That probably wouldn't help his confusion, this feeling of drowning but enjoying it; still, hard to make things worse. Some of the fellas standing around her looked at him angrily, like he'd stolen their march, but it wasn't his fault they hadn't asked. She took his hand, and that let him break the surface; he breathed in wood smoke, night air, and kerosene from the lamps, as the Baptist organist struck up a two-step.

Miss Adelaide more or less kept up, though he could tell she didn't have much experience with two-steps on the whole. Maybe she knew new dances from Dallas, and thought theirs were old or boring. But just leading her around the floor left him breathless, and when the music stopped, she laughed.

"I haven't done a two-step quite like that before," she told him, turning but keeping hold of his hands, so his wrists were crossed. "That

42

was nice, Mr. Mayer."

"I thought so too," he said. "You'll save me another dance for later, won't you?"

"Why not now?" she asked, and Wild glanced over her shoulder, where Abe Weber was making a determined path towards them.

"You got other fellas wanting a dance, I imagine," he said.

"Well, what if I don't want to dance with other fellas?"

He laughed. "Then you ought to sit out — ain't fair of me to monopolize a pretty dancer like you."

"Thank you, that's kind of you," she said. "Why don't you walk me back to your sisters?"

Wild shot Abe Weber an apologetic look as he led her away from him, back to the edge of the floor.

"That's a fifty-cent word I didn't expect to hear in Lea, you know," she said.

"What's that?"

"Monopolize. I hear you did a year of college in Lubbock, that's why you weren't in Lea last year."

"Yeah. I had a scholarship, but they need me at the farm now."

"I was sorry to hear about Lon Platter passing. I met him a couple of times last year. Seemed like a good man."

"He was, thank you."

"And now you're here," she said, sitting down, and only then letting go of his hand.

"Yes, Miss Adelaide, I am."

"Well, you should come to the schoolhouse sometime, tell the little ones about the college life."

"Wild, will you get us some punch?" Sarah asked, giving him a significant stare he couldn't interpret.

"Oh! Sure. You want some, Miss Adelaide?"

"Yes, please, Mr. Mayer."

He fetched punch, but he felt strange hovering on the edges of the women's' conversations, and Miss Adelaide had a lot of admirers to speak to, not just the young men but the children who had missed her over the summer. At one point he took Dot Muller out for a spin on the floor and caught a view of Miss Adelaide speaking amiably with Moze, obviously reassuring him about the start of school.

"You ain't all here tonight, Wild, I swear you ain't," Dot said.

"Maybe not," he replied. "Just thinking about the winter, I suppose."

"What about it?"

"Nothing much in particular. Do you suppose yours'll need help weatherproofing this year? Wet summer means a cold winter."

"Sure, I'll tell Dad you'll come help," she said, pleased, looking up at him through lowered eyelashes like he didn't know that trick. He grinned down at her, and when the dance was done he walked her back to her father with a nod. Tex Senior looked...perplexed, like he was just noticing Dot was of courting age.

By the time he made his way back to his sisters, Mama was holding Lonny, who was sleeping, and Moze was looking cantankerous.

"Glad to see you," she said to him. "The boys are tired and I could do with going home – I thought we'd hitch a ride with the next folks leaving, and you could drive the girls home when you're done."

"Nah, you take the truck," Wild said, looking for Billy near the bonfire. "Billy can drive you."

"I'll go too," Sarah volunteered. "My feet ache in these shoes."

"Bet and I'll catch a ride, or it's not a bad walk," Wild said, seeing Mama waver. "Go on. I'll fetch Billy."

He found Billy with a group of boys, learning to strum the ukulele, and passed him the truck key, cautioning him to look after Mama and the ukulele both. When he got back to Bet, one of the Lentz boys was just taking her out for a fast polka.

"I believe you asked for another dance, Mr. Mayer," Miss Adelaide said. "I've never done a polka, though."

"Well, step out a little and I'll teach you," he told her, and led her off into the hard-packed dirt beyond the dancers, pulling her back against him, maybe a little closer than he had to. "Starts out like the two step only you step in place a little more, like so."

It took them nearly the whole song for her to learn the steps, but that wasn't really any matter. By the time the song was over, the Baptist organist was stretching her fingers and looking tired; Wild fetched Miss Adelaide another cup of punch, but people were already starting to wander towards trucks and horses and tractors, now that the music was over.

"Where're you staying at? In town?" Wild asked, watching the steady but slow drift away from the dance floor.

"Yes, I'm boarding with Lentz Platter's family," Miss Adelaide said. "I understand you're relations?"

"Not by blood – Lon was my stepfather, he's a relation to them on the poor side," he said with a smile. "My brothers and sisters are, though. Who's taking you back to town, the Platters?"

"Yes. Do you and Bet need a ride as far as town?"

"Well, we might presume," Wild said, looking around for Bet. He caught her arm as she ran past with Anna Wagner. "Bet! Where you think you're going?"

"Uncle Wagner's got a spot for me in the truck," she said. "They can take me back to the farm on their way."

Wild looked at her and then at Miss Adelaide, torn, but Bet saw it and laughed.

"There's no room for you, I'm afraid," she said, nose in the air. "Cousin Neil's jealous you played the ukulele so well."

"That's all right, I think I can go most of the way with the Platters," Wild said, grateful to her.

"What's this I hear?" Lentz Platter's voice boomed. "Wild, you need a ride to the farm?"

"Just into town, I'll walk from there," Wild said, and followed Miss Adelaide and the Platters to the big open touring-style car Lentz Platter favored.

When they stopped in town, Miss Adelaide reached for his hand and let him help her out of the car, and then in a whirl of activity, keys and doors and wiping boots, they were all gone inside. Wild saw the lights going on, but he didn't linger; it would be a long walk back, and Mama would worry if he didn't show.

Walking through town, it felt like the first night he'd come home – only he was settled back in now, secure in his place and with a good crop behind him. Not to mention plans for the future.

The moon and stars threw enough light to see by as he headed towards the main street, passing the bank and coming up on the seed store. The church was up ahead too, and he was struck as always by the incongruity of it, the strangeness of an abandoned house of worship, the unusual sinuous shape of it among the squat, square buildings around it. It seemed wrong that it just stood there empty, even though he had reason to know that it might be abandoned because it was...dangerous. Or at least, incomprehensible.

He stopped at the junction of the roads to regard it, its little narrow windows in the front, the padlock on the door –

He didn't move when it did. He didn't even, thinking about it after, feel fear. He just looked up at it, awestruck, as the adobe façade shifted, expanded and contracted, moving like something inside was breathing. A hole opened up above the door, blossoming like the world's largest flower, and colors unfurled from it, jagged, bright, unbelievably beautiful.

He watched, frozen, scars beating in time with his heart, as a huge wheel of glass burst out of the darkness, locking into place as the church began to settle. Before, there had only been a handful of little windows high up on either side of the door. Now, above the door sat an ornate rose window, glorious and intricate, all blues and greys in the dim light. It was split into six equal wedges, with a circle in the center, and each wedge had some irregular shape he couldn't quite make out.

But he could see where part of the roof had fallen in when the church twisted and grew and put forth the window, and he was pretty sure when it was light out, the sun would shine right down through it.

He didn't dare go near it – didn't dare cross the fence that had nearly killed him once already – but he gave it a nod and a tip of his hat as he passed on.

SEVEN

AFTER THE HARVEST there was still plenty to keep busy with, at least in the first few weeks. Winter would be on them soon enough, and the house needed repairs. He had some special treatments for the farm soil he'd been wanting to try since learning about them in Lubbock, and he wanted to diversify the crops for the following year, which meant a lot of time bent over a map of the farm, dividing and re-dividing the land, trying to figure how to earn a good dollar from some of it and feed the rest of it so the soil wouldn't die. With school begun, the older boys were out of the house all day, but that meant Mama had to send them off with lunch pails daily, and Lonny had to be looked after the rest of the day. Wild and Bet had to help them with their lessons when they got home, while Sarah helped Mama with dinner.

Even so, after a while he began to run out of chores to take care of, and to remember how Lon had always spent a restless month before settling into the stillness of wintering over. Lon had favored whittling and reading, though books were hard to come by and he wasn't a fast reader.

It was wasteful to drive into town just to fetch the boys from school, since the walk wasn't bad and gasoline was dear, but once in a while Wild schedule a trip into town to coincide with picking them up, and maybe he'd stop and speak to Miss Adelaide for a minute or two. He was still a little in awe of her, and he could feel his heartbeat in his scars when she looked at him. It wasn't unpleasant; sort of warm and nice, and he enjoyed talking to her, too.

The third time he picked up the boys in as many weeks, she said, "You should come again tomorrow before school lets out. You could talk to the children about college in Lubbock."

"Suppose I could," he said, rubbing the back of his head. "Some of 'em ought to go, probably, if we can afford to send 'em."

"I guess that's the problem, isn't it? But we might as well try," she persisted.

"Well, I'll come a little early then," he said. "And maybe you'd like to come to dinner – I could drive you back home again after, if you wanted to come down to the farm."

She beamed. "I'd like that a lot. Oh, Billy, don't forget," she called, as Billy ran to the truck. He trooped back, apparently anticipating homework, but instead she handed him a cheap-looking book, like a Sears catalogue in miniature. "Billy won the book prize this week," she told Wild. "You should be proud. I'll see you tomorrow?"

"Yes ma'am," Wild said, blushing to the tips of his ears as he climbed into the truck, Billy and Moze wrestling for space on the seat.

"She's a Baptist, you know," Billy said to him, on the drive home.

"Half the folks in this town are Baptists," Wild replied, not sure how exactly this was a defense. "What's this book prize she mentioned, now?"

"Miss Adelaide gets these little books in the mail, every week," Billy said, waving it. "They're published up north, they're full of stories. And the best reader in the class gets to take one to keep."

"What's it about?"

"It's a bunch of stories all in one," Billy said, thumbing through it. "But Miss Adelaide saved this one specific for me if I was top this week."

"Oh?"

"It's called *science fiction*," Billy told him. "She said it's about all kinds of future things, like flying cars and machines that can talk, and people from the moon coming to visit."

"Sounds…" Wild searched for a word. "Imaginative," he finally decided.

Wild possibly could have timed his invitation to dinner better; when they arrived home and he told Mama that Miss Adelaide was coming to dinner the following night, she swatted him and called him a couple of names, and he realized that maybe he should have extended the invitation for the following week to give Mama time to prepare.

Still, she kept a clean house, so all there was to do was scrub down the table with salt and bring out the tablecloth, kill a chicken for roasting, and sweep out the sitting room. While the rest of them worked, Billy read to them aloud from his book, with the result that they all gained an education in what some fool from a publishing house in Chicago thought men living on the moon might look like.

The next day, Wild drove in to town early, wearing perhaps not his Sunday best, which would be a little much, but clean trousers without any patches and a good shirt. The kids had mostly heard stories about the aggie school in Lubbock second-hand from Billy, and those were heavy on what Lubbock was like, what it was like to live in a boarding house with electricity and a "flush" toilet. So he told them about the school, about the crop science he'd learned and how they'd made him learn extra math to help calculate the operations on the farm. Some of the children had questions, and he could see one or two starting to scheme about how they might get the mystical blessing of a scholarship, too.

Then Billy and Moze clambered up into the back of the truck, settling among the empty sacks and farm tools, and Wild helped Miss Adelaide into the cab before climbing into the driver's seat.

"You're lucky to be so close in to town," she said, as they headed for the farm. "I think it must be hard for the farms furthest from Lea."

"Well, I suppose without much more effort they could get to Carson or Wheeler, which are bigger," Wild said. "But our folks prefer Lea. You know a fellow in Lea, where you wouldn't in Carson."

"I prefer Lea," she said, smiling out at the flat Texas scrubland on the edge of town. "You've been to Lubbock – which did you like better?"

"Well, ma'am, Lea's my home," he said. "Been here since my father's grandfather came over from Germany. My mother's people were Texicans – they go back here even further. Lubbock's all right, I suppose, but I was happy to be home. Can I ask where you come from, Miss Adelaide?"

"Oh, outside of Texas," she said. "Nowhere you'd know."

"How'd you come to Lea?" he asked, not wanting to pry further if she didn't want to say. Maybe Missouri. He wouldn't say if he were from Missouri.

Maybe, a little voice suggested, *much further than Missouri*.

"Not really sure, in the end," she said. "I suppose you needed a schoolteacher and I needed somewhere new."

"You must like it, if you came back from Dallas to teach again," he said with a sidelong grin.

"I do like Lea. Dallas was all right, I suppose, but it's like you say. You know everyone in Lea. In Dallas you don't know anyone, ever."

"That's how Lubbock was. Still, the school was small enough."

"And it helped, it sounds like! All this talk of crop rotation and soil restoration. It's very new and scientific."

"Yep. I'd like more of the farmers hereabouts to do it. We were lucky with a good rain this year, want to make sure next year we take measures in case we don't get so lucky again."

"It seems so precarious," she said. "Trying to pull enough to survive on out of the earth."

"They say at the aggie school we've been farming for thousands of years. Since Jesus and before. And you know the Bible says God made Adam a farmer."

"After he threw him out of the garden," she said softly.

"That was his own fault, I imagine," he replied. "Anyway. I suppose it is precarious but we're like corn, you know."

"Like corn!" she laughed. "How so?"

"Well, you cut down the corn stalk and take the corn, but you put aside seed for next year. A farm might fail, a whole lot of farms might fail, but the farming goes on," he said, wondering if he was putting it into words properly. "Farmers die. Farming don't. So every year…new corn."

She nodded. "Not like a tree with deep roots. More like…an unbroken cycle."

"Well, that's what we hope. If I can plant crops for forty years and give the farm to my children at the end of it I'll have done my part."

"It doesn't bore you? The idea of forty years of harvests and plantings?"

"You teach the same lessons each year, don't you? Different children, but the same learning."

"Yes, but I've only been teaching a year. I don't plan to teach forever."

"Well, my mama would tell you forty years of laundry and cooking and raising a pile of kids ain't much better, but I think secretly she likes the cooking," he said.

"Not the children?" she asked, eyes bright.

"We're tolerable enough in small doses," he said, turning down the road to the farm house. "See how you feel after dinner with six of us."

For all the flurry of excitement before dinner, the meal itself went fine – Miss Adelaide complimented Mama's embroidered tablecloth and the food, and Billy kept them entertained with a summary of another story from his prize book. Moze seemed awestruck to have his teacher at his own dinner table, and Sarah and Bet caught her up on some of the gossip among the girls who had just left school. She even promised to lend Bet a book on higher mathematics she'd had from the publisher who sent her Billy's book.

Wild knew how courting was done, more or less, when it was the daughters of farmers or even most girls from town – a man should show he could provide, and for a farmer that meant showing the farm. With a woman like Adelaide, earning her own way, possibly destined for more than a farmer's wife, he wasn't so positive. But other than play the ukulele, which she'd already seen him do, all he really had to show was the farm. So when dinner was done, the boys were set to their lessons and Sarah and Bet had discreetly disappeared to their room to sew, he said, "Would you like go walking, Miss Adelaide?"

They couldn't walk the whole farm, but he took her down the path past the big, well-kept barn, the tractor and the horse cart, to one of the harvested fields. From there, you could look out and see pretty much to the edge of the land. Off in the distance his own father's house, not lived in since Mama remarried, was a shadow on the horizon. The light turned everything gold and then blue, and she glowed through both.

"You must have one of the larger farms in the area," she said, as they strolled down rows of earth strewn with dried out corn silk and leaves.

"Some have bigger. When the Germans came to Lea, mostly only small plots were left. Lon's family bought from a Baptist who was selling up, and my father's grandfather bought the plot behind it, but they were both small. Lon's plot is only half of what the farm used to be when it was deeded. The rest got split longways between the Mullers and the Fischers when he bought his piece."

"Glad I never had you and Tex Junior for students," she said. "I've heard enough stories to think you must have been hellions at school."

"We got in our fair share of trouble, but I liked learning. Still do. It's why Lentz Platter picked me to go down to Lubbock."

"I thought it might be family – you being Lon's stepson."

"Sure that didn't hurt, but if they wanted to send one of the family, they could have sent someone with the name. Or a Lentz. Mayer's hardly a dynasty," he added drily.

"You never know. It might be yet," she said, curling one hand around his elbow, and his breath caught. "Do you like reading?"

"Sure. Planning to borrow that book off Billy when he's done with it, though I don't know if I put much stock in that kind of thing."

"You like westerns?" she guessed. He laughed.

"Nah! They don't get nothing right about Texas. Don't let them give you ideas. I mostly read adventure stories, I suppose, when I can get them. Why, what do you like?"

"I like novels," she said, as they reached the end of the furrowed earth, where a lane cut through for access. She turned down the lane, and he followed at her side. "I like books about America. I like it when someone tries to tell a story about the country. Even if they don't manage it. Sometimes it's only a little bit of the country, sometimes they try to talk about all of it, but…"

"All the whole country," he said. "That'd be a thing. You've read a book about the whole country?"

"I've read some that tried. None did it justice. It's difficult to do. America is slippery. It's so big, and there's so much that was done…"

"The way the papers talk, you'd think we were still wild country."

"That will change, in time," she said. "I don't know if it'll be pleasant. Sometimes things are sacrificed, sometimes things that shouldn't be. But I suppose it's like childbirth – there's pain in bearing, but at the end of it, new life."

"Like the corn," he said, and she laughed.

"You and corn. Fine, yes. Also like the corn," she agreed. The moon was emerging, now, and the sky was dark, so he steered her gently back towards the house, before they were out of view of it, which would technically be an impropriety.

"I should get you home, before I catch hell for keeping you out all hours," he said.

"It was a very nice walk and a delicious dinner, thank you," she said.

"Well, you should come again," he said, before he'd thought about it. "If you have a mind to, I mean."

"I'll hold you to that. It's nice to get outside of town with good company," she said. "And I'll see if I can find you a book or two."

When he helped her out of the truck, back in town, she squeezed his hand and thanked him for a nice evening, and Wild smiled all the way home.

"She's a Baptist, you know," Mama told him, when he came in from putting the truck away.

"Everyone tellin' me stuff I know," he complained.

"But she's a very nice girl, nonetheless," Mama continued, patting his cheek. "Don't know if she can cook a lick, but Bet says she can sew, and she keeps the schoolhouse tidy."

"Not sure she'd give the time of day to a man like me, marriage-wise," Wild pointed out.

"Well, she hasn't given the real time of day to any other boy in Lea, the girls say."

"Then I ain't fixed to hurry," Wild said. "She'd like to come to dinner again, but I didn't want to put you in an attack."

Mama laughed. "Just warn me next time, Wild. Now, run help your brothers with their lessons. Can't shame the family in front of the schoolteacher."

The first time Dan Rohlf drove into town, after the harvest social, he didn't come home for dinner. Cora had expected he'd be in town all day, but when he missed dinner and then night fell, she called up to the seed store to see if he'd been there.

"Why, yes," the seed store clerk told her, voice crackling down the phone. "Picked up the new spring planting catalogue, had a jaw. He ain't come home yet?"

"You don't think he crashed the truck, do you?" she asked, worried.

"That thing he keeps fixin' himself? Wouldn't be surprised," he said. "But it don't go very fast at the best of times, ma'am. If he did, he's probably just walkin' home."

But he wasn't walking home; she called the Lentz farm next, and George Lentz drove out to hers in his truck, and they drove slowly into town, looking for Dan, looking for any sign of a crash. When they finally reached Lea, they rolled down the main street slowly, straining to see anything in the falling dark, and then –

"Dan!" she bellowed, jumping out of the truck as George Lentz pulled it to a stop. Dan Rohlf, her idiot husband, was sitting on the wrap-around porch of the Dry Goods. His eyes were fixed on the old ruined church, big and unfocused, and he barely looked away for a second when she lit into him. The Baptists would no doubt talk later about what a scold she was, and how they hadn't seen anything like it in years, but she was so glad to see him safe and so mad he was just loiterin' at the Dry Goods.

She was about to slap him, just to shake him out of whatever stupor he was in – was he drunk? – when the last rays of the sun dipped behind the buildings of town, and he startled out of himself and looked up at her.

"What've you got to say for yourself?" she asked him, and he blinked. "Well, Daniel Rohlf?"

His mouth worked its way open, slow, and she waited.

"I've had a revelation," he said, looking to the church and back to her. "I've had a revelation and I've seen God."

"Lord, you been drinking," she said.

"No," he said. "God's here in Lea, honey, and I seen him in the church. We got to go home," he added, suddenly, wildly.

"You're right we do, it's past dark and your dinner's cold, all this ravin' about God, I don't know – "

But he was already moving back down the street towards his truck, and she waved her thanks to George and followed. He drove home fast as the old truck would take them, and when he got there he just...went straight on through the kitchen, and into the bedroom, and shut the door.

She tried to open it, but he'd propped it closed somehow. And when he finally let her in, after another forty minutes of banging and pleading and then silent sulking while she threw out his dinner, she almost cried with relief.

"What's happened to you, Dan?" she asked.

"Nothin," he said to her. "Nothin, honey, I'm so sorry. I can't think…it just gripped me of a sudden. I'll explain everything. Only I got to sleep first."

And she cried a little while, but they both slept, and in the morning he didn't say a word about it to her.

He went back into town again two days later, and he came back with paper and a new pencil, and after that he commenced to writing, and he didn't stop for some time. But at least he came home by dinner, even if he went into town a lot more often, after that.

Eight

"YOU KNOW, IT occurs to me," Wild said over breakfast one morning, when the frost hadn't yet hit but would, and soon, "we got a whole other house on this farm."

"Your daddy's old place?" Mama asked.

"Yup. I showed Miss Adelaide the other night where it was, but it was too far to walk."

"Just as well. It's not in very good repair. You ain't thinking of moving back of beyond in that old thing, are you?" she asked.

"No, but I took a look at it during the harvest, and it's built pretty solid," Wild said. "So I had an idea."

"Oh lord," Bet muttered to Sarah.

"I was thinkin', we take some axes and some rope out there, me and some of the fellas, and pull it up off the ground," Wild said. "Put it on a couple of logs. Once the ground freezes it'll be plenty firm and mostly flat, and we could hitch the truck up, roll it straight across."

Mama cackled at him. "To where?"

"Why, to here. We settle it on the back of this house and that'll add plenty of space to the kitchen, and a room for me so Billy ain't have to share, and if Bet or Sarah wants the other room they could have it so they ain't have to share either."

"Sounds tomfool to me," Billy said, from behind his book. Miss Adelaide had found him another book of science fiction stories, and he barely took his nose out of them, these days. Billy said she had a way of knowing what a person would like to learn about and teaching it, and Wild believed it.

"Tomfool?" Lonny asked.

"Means especially foolish," Wild told him. "I seen it done in Lubbock," he added stubbornly. "They rolled a post office down the street on logs."

"Oh, well, if they done it in Lubbock," Mama said, rising to help herself to some more pancakes. "If it'll keep you busy, Wild, you have my permission, but if you pull the house down around your ears, don't say I didn't warn you."

He brought it up after church the next Sunday, and the farmers all thought it was a fine idea. Some of them had seen it done to a farmhouse decades ago, and they reckoned the old Mayer place had a similar construction, so it wouldn't be hard to pull it up in one piece. You couldn't raise a barn this late in the year, and there weren't many other excuses to gather together and sweat and drink, so they settled on it – the first hard frost on the ground, barring an ice storm, they'd come down to the Mayer farm the next day and help him roll the old farmhouse along. Wild extracted promises they'd bring food – a couple of jars of preserves and pickles, a sack of potatoes, some sausages or a side of beef or salt pork, so that Mama wouldn't be overburdened by the cooking.

The first hard frost was the second week in November that year, and men started showing up early the following morning. Some loosed the house from the foundation while others rolled felled trees into place, and some of the women gathered at the Platter house and cooked and had a quilting bee. The old house came up easy, right off the foundation once they'd loosened a few reinforcements, and after lunch they hitched draft horses and Wild's truck up to the house and began to pull.

They'd had a debate about using trucks; horses knew how to pull in unison, Uncle Wagner had argued, and trucks all pulled at separate speeds. Uncle Koch had wanted to try it, but Wild didn't want the house torn up accidentally, so they'd compromised with all the horses and just one truck. For luck, Tex had joked.

"Pull!" Tex would roar, and the men would walk the horses forward a few yards, while Wild gently drove the truck alongside them, and then the backmost log would be rolled around to the front. "Pull!"

By the time they reached their goal it was coming towards dinner time, and dark was falling. From here, Wild could secure the house down into the ground himself, maybe even soon if there was a thaw, and connect up the kitchens of the two houses. It'd practically be a mansion, the women told Mama, which was some reassurance since she didn't like the idea of knocking out any walls in winter. They made the old Mayer house as snug as they could against the Platter house without busting anything, and then unhitched the horses and put them up in Wild's barn.

Billy and the younger boys had made a huge bonfire nearby, and the men pulled the rolling logs over to it to sit on, collecting food passed out to them through the kitchen windows by wives and daughters. They settled around the fire, passing flasks and unlabeled bottles around, and Uncle Koch picked a little on the banjo for a bit while Wild strummed the ukulele.

Uncle Wagner called for a speech from the college boy, which Wild appreciated, since he did have some speaking to do. He stood up in front of the fire and thanked them all, and then took a breath.

"You all know I'm planting my first crops next year," he said, to murmured agreement. "And you all know I did a year down in Lubbock, and I thank you all for helpin' my people while I was gone. But I picked up some things at the aggie school, and with places so near suffering such bad droughts I figured I'd better not wait to tell it."

"What's that, Mayer?" George Lentz asked.

"Well, they got some new science says sometimes you got to let a field go fallow, or plant a cheap crop to feed the soil," Wild said. "Might be time we tried planting cheap crops and plowing them under, or rotating crops out of good fields. I ain't saying we have to, but I'm saying this year I'm going to plant different from how Lon did. Make sure the soil stays rich. Make sure if there is a drought, the topsoil don't blow away."

"Two years of drought in a row?" Tex asked skeptically.

"We didn't have a drought. If it hits us instead of them next year, how many of you could afford to lose crops?" Wild asked. The men looked at each other. "I'm not trying to tell you how to farm, but I couldn't know all this and just say nothing. If you want a college education for free, you come by sometime and I'll show you what I been working on."

"What if I can't afford to plant a cheap crop?" one of the Fischers asked. "My fields got to produce."

"Then you can't, I suppose. But I can't afford to lose my topsoil," Wild said. "Next year I'm leaving the oat field fallow, movin' the corn field to the wheat, and splitting the wheat with rye. Should keep the pests down too," he added. "They don't really know why it works, but they're seein' better yields since they tried it. Anyway. That's all I had to say."

"I got something to say," George Lentz said, as Wild sat down and accepted a jug from Tex, pouring some homebrewed beer into his tin cup. George took Wild's place in front of the bonfire and hooked his thumbs in his belt.

"George speaks for me too," Art Weber piped up. George gave him a nod, and Wild suddenly knew what this was about – George and Art's lands bordered the Rohlf farm.

"It's Dan, ain't it?" someone else asked, obviously thinking the same way.

"Anyone here not seen Dan Rohlf since the harvest social?" George asked. Nobody put up a hand. "Well, then you know he's…worryin' at us. And we got to figure what to do about it."

"Don't see why it's our business if Dan Rohlf's gone crazy," Tex Junior said.

"You pipe down," Tex told him. "It's everybody's business. Besides, his wife is your mother's cousin."

"He's been in town, puttin' up flyers for a revival," George continued. "Every time I see him it's God this and Blessing that. Now if it were just he was goin' Baptist that'd be one thing, sometimes you see a Lutheran lose his faith. But he ain't gone Baptist and he's goin' against the orthodoxy. He thinks God's livin' in Lea and that's why we had a good harvest. And he thinks if we ain't properly thank Him, we'll go like all of Kansas did this year."

"What the hell's he think church on Sunday is for?" Uncle Wagner asked. "He thinks I ain't thank God all year long for this year's crops?"

"He thinks the Lutherans ain't talking to the real God, and he thinks Baptists the same," George said.

This was a tricky statement for the men to wrestle with, because of course they agreed that the Baptists didn't know squat about God, but they also all knew the Baptists thought the same thing about them. And it might be a trifle uncomfortable to imagine someone who said both were wrong could be correct.

"He's got a revival going the Sunday after Thanksgiving," Art Weber said. "Plannin' on having it in the schoolhouse."

"You thinking of going, Art?" someone asked, and there was brief, awkward laughter.

"I think someone ought to, if only to see," Art said. "And some of you all are going, and some folks ain't here today. And some Baptists. I seen people taking flyers."

"It's just in fun," Neil Wagner, Anna's brother and Wild's cousin, protested. "Everyone loves a good revival, it don't mean we ain't Lutherans."

"Sure, that's how the devil gets you," Tex joked. This time almost nobody laughed.

"It seems to me," Uncle Koch said, "Seems to me he's not a harm to himself, is he? Nor to his wife? He ain't threatened you, Art, has he?"

"No," Art admitted. "Not yet. But I worry. Theology aside, Dan Rohlf's never been what you call imaginative."

"Wears on a man, though, not havin' any children," Tex said.

"Not his fault. Lost all three young," Wild pointed out.

"If he's got the religious mania, who knows what he'll do?" Art said. "What if it's a brain fever?"

"Can't force a man to see a doctor."

"So what do we do?" George asked.

"What can we do?" Neil Wagner said. "Seems like keepin' a watch is all any of us can do, unless someone wants to try to reason him out of it."

"Well, I like a good theology debate," John Fischer said. "I'll have him to dinner, if you like. See what I can do with him. But not until after the revival. I want to know what I'm dealing with."

"It'll pass," Tex Senior said confidently, as the bonfire crackled and men nodded at one another. "Dan Rohlf's down to Earth. He'll give a try at preaching, and it'll pass."

NINE

WILD DIDN'T GO to the revival, or the one after it, where more people did. It wasn't appreciably reducing the number of people who went to the Lutheran church, and the Baptists didn't seem upset, so the town just got used to the idea that every so often, Dan Rohlf would upset his wife and annoy the town and hold a revival in the schoolhouse or the VFW hall.

Wild was busy enough that winter, visiting neighbors, courting Miss Adelaide, driving Sarah and Bet to parties and quilting bees and sewing circles. Maybe he should've been paying more attention in general, and certainly more to his sisters, but he didn't think he could really be blamed when Tex Junior surprised him after the Christmas Eve service at church, asking if they could talk.

"Course," Wild said, as Tex Junior pulled him away from the family and out into the cold night air. They'd had an ice storm three days ago, and it was by grace of *something* that everyone had been able to get out to church at all. He tucked his fingers up in the sleeves of his coat. "We couldn't talk inside, Tex?"

"I wanted to talk private," Tex Junior said, though he looked cold too. "I gotta ask you something, Wild."

"Well, sure," Wild said, bewildered.

"You know Senior made me a partner in the farm this year."

"About time. You're doing most of the work."

"Well, I think so, but it's his farm, after all. And you know I brought him round to your crop-rotation idea, let you help us plan it out and everything."

"It'll do y'all more good than it does me," Wild pointed out.

"But it means, you know," Tex Junior gave him an earnest, searching look. "I'm a man now, Wild, same as you. Responsible. And ready to start a family."

"Sure, I feel the same."

"So – so you'd be all right if I was to marry your sister, right?"

Wild stared at him, floored.

"Not Bet," he blurted, horrified at the thought.

"No! Not Bet, Jesus! Sarah!" Tex Junior said quickly. "Only we been courting all winter, quiet-like, and I want to marry her before planting. And she wants to; she's eighteen now and she said she got her hope chest all done up, and I got a little money saved."

"Christ Jesus, Tex," Wild said. "If she said yes what the hell are you asking me for?"

"Because she ain't got a daddy!" Tex Junior hissed. Which made a certain amount of sense, Wild supposed. "And if your mama says no, she'll heed, but Mary Platter won't say no if you say yes. I love her, Wild."

"Of course, Tex, I got nothin' against you as a brother in law," Wild said. "And even if I did, I ain't her boss. You got my permission, if you needed it."

Tex Junior looked surprised, like he genuinely hadn't thought Wild would say yes, and then slapped him on the back so hard Wild coughed. "You won't regret it, Wild! You know I'll be good to her."

"Pete's sake," Wild said, as Tex Junior ran off, probably to tell Sarah. "For Pete's fucking sake!"

But it put him in mind of Miss Adelaide, and how he supposed he'd have to make a case direct to her, and whether or not it was one she'd likely accept. It was obvious to Lea, as it was to him, that she favored him, but that might just be because he had some looks; she might not want to marry a farmer, and keep a farmhouse, when she was used to teaching and making her own way.

He thought maybe she favored him, too, because the church did. He knew it in his bones that there was some kind of tie there – between him and the church, between her and the church – but he wasn't sure exactly what it was. And if it was something outside of the normal world, he didn't want anyone or anything *making* her marry him.

He didn't know what to do about the church. Hadn't ever, but now it was more important.

He was still mulling it over, two days later, when Christmas had passed happily and a couple of inches of snow had fallen, covering the muck that the ice storm had left behind. He thought for New Year's he might go in to Lea; there was meant to be a dance at the VFW, and maybe he'd see about buying some small trinket as an engagement gift.

Wild was watching the fire in the hearth, while Sarah and Bet sewed on Sarah's wedding dress and the boys played with their bright wooden trucks they'd got for Christmas, when there was a hasty knock on the door. Mama came in from the kitchen as Wild opened it to Tex Senior on the doorstep, panting.

"Tex, what's happened?" Wild asked, because he looked like death, and his eyes were wild.

"It's the Fischers," Tex gasped, and then he realized Wild's brothers and sisters were there. "You got to come quick, Wild," he said, voice low and urgent. "There's been a murder at the Fischers."

"Jesus, a murder?" Wild asked, stepping out into the cold and closing the door. "Who?"

John Fischer, as far as he knew, wasn't a violent man, and his wife was downright timid; they had two girls, near to Billy's age, and their son was only seven.

Tex looked him in the eye, leaned in, and said, "All of them, I think. Sorry to pull you out on such a night but you're the nearest by."

"I'll get my gun," Wild said.

"Bring lanterns, too," Tex called after him, as he went back inside.

The Fischer house lay under the fresh-fallen snow, stark in the moonlight. There was one set of tire tracks going up to it, which Tex Senior said was his from before. When Wild got out the only set of footprints were Tex's, but that didn't signify; snow had been falling all day.

"Me and the missus came up to see about borrowing his ladder – mine busted, and Dorothy wanted to bring Georgia Fischer some preserves anyhow. They weren't answering on the telephone, so we drove up, figured the ice got the phone line," Tex said. "House was dark. Windows were cold. I didn't like it, told Dorothy to wait in the truck. Jimmied the front door open and…"

"Where's Mrs. Muller?"

"I drove her up to town. They weren't gettin' any deader and someone had to call for help."

"Who's she fetchin' in town? Nearest sheriff's in Wheeler."

"She's gone to get the Platters up, they got a phone line out to Wheeler in the bank."

"Smart thinking," Wild said.

"Came to get you on account I ain't want to be out here alone," Tex admitted, as Wild hung lanterns off the eaves of the house and lit them. "And you…you got an education, I thought, you'd know what to do."

Tex was twenty years his senior and had seen his share of rough life, out in this country. But Wild could understand – no man wanted to be responsible for this alone.

"You think whatever did it might still be here?" he asked.

"Ain't a whatever. John Fischer's been shot, looks like, and the boy…"

Wild took the last lantern and walked to the door, not exactly happy about it. He wasn't sure if he should look inside or leave it for the sheriff, but they probably wouldn't get anyone out here for hours at least, maybe a day. Lea didn't rate the kind of policing the bigger cities did.

"You sure you want to see in there, Wild?" Tex called.

"Think I'd better," Wild called back.

By the flickering lantern light, Wild could see as he entered through the pried-open door that most of the lamps were smashed. He supposed it was lucky none of them had lit the place on fire. Or maybe unlucky, he thought; there was John Fischer, blank-eyed on his couch, chest blown all to pieces. His son was laid across his lap, a bloody mess of the kind Wild had only seen when a hunter didn't get a clean shot. He couldn't tell if it was a gunshot that had taken either of the girls, lying on the floor next to a burnt out fireplace, but it didn't look like it.

Then he saw the hatchet next to their bodies.

"Tex, did you see Georgia when you looked in?" he asked.

"No, but I seen blood," Tex called through the doorway, and Wild saw it too, a trail leading into the kitchen. He tried not to step in it as he followed it.

Georgia had been killed in the kitchen. This was no mystery – it was the hatchet. Wild covered his mouth with one hand.

"Wild?" Tex called anxiously. "There's someone coming!"

"All right, I'm fine," Wild said, backing away from the mess on the kitchen floor that had once been a woman, out into the cold and snow. "Georgia's dead in the kitchen. Looks like hatchet work. It's a rough one, Tex."

"Jesus preserve us."

"Nobody even disliked the Fischers," Wild, letting puzzlement at the situation overwhelm the horror he was trying to stuff down. "John Fischer could be an asshole but he never cheated anyone, never stole or started fights."

"Vagrants?" Tex suggested dubiously.

"This time of year? They'd freeze to death. Might've been a housebreaker, I suppose," Wild said. It made him uneasy. John Fischer's farm was on the same road as his own, and the only thing between them was farm fields and a low fence. "Bad business. Hey, there," he called, as another truck – no, a car, the Platter touring car – came down the road. "Hey, who's there?"

"James Platter," a voice called. Lentz Platter's son; that was all right. "Father's calling over to Wheeler for the police, sent me down to see if you needed any help. I brought Miss Adelaide," he added, sounding annoyed, just as Miss Adelaide climbed out of the car.

"I was there when Mrs. Muller came in," she said, wrapping her thin coat tightly around her. Wild shucked his and passed it to her. "Thanks. I thought James shouldn't drive down alone. Is it true, the whole family?"

"Don't go in," Wild said, as she started towards the door. "It's not something you want to see. And anyway the sheriff'll be mad if we do."

"But you've been in," she said, looking up at him. He nodded. "All of them?"

"John, Georgia, their two girls and little George," Tex confirmed.

Miss Adelaide was staring at the house's windows, as if she could peer through them in the dark.

"No one wants this," she whispered softly. The hairs on the back of Wild's neck raised. "It's not right. It's not wanted."

Wild chalked it up to shock, in the moment, and anyway she wasn't wrong; later, he thought it might've been more. That it might've been personal, somehow, for her.

"Well, we can't all four stand here and freeze," Tex said, rubbing his hands together. "But we'll need to keep watch on the place. Nosy neighbors and poker-arounders should be kept out."

"Not like us," Wild drawled.

"No, Wild, not like us," Tex replied, irritated. "Look. Miss Adelaide hasn't even got a real coat. I'll run her back up to town in the truck and get news of when the sheriff's coming. You young ones here and keep folks out, and if the monster who did this comes back, shoot 'im. I'll be back with someone from town and take second shift around midnight. Sound all right? James, you got a gun?"

James Platter showed him a Colt six-gun, and Wild rolled his eyes a little, making sure James couldn't see. A rifle was what you wanted in a setup like this.

"I'll let your Mama know what's going on," Tex told Wild. Miss Adelaide gave him back his jacket as Tex herded her into his truck, backing out of the yard before turning. She watched the two of them through the rear windscreen until they faded into the darkness.

"How bad is it in there?" James asked.

"Don't look," Wild said. "The fewer who see that the better. Poor John Fischer. Looks like he never even got to stand up. He's been shot, and his son. The women had a hatchet taken to them."

"Jesus. Who coulda done that?"

"Don't know. Must've got him first, or he woulda fought like hell, given the girls time to run. Someone…someone took their time with Georgia."

"Gives me the creeps," James said, sitting down on the runner board of his father's car. Wild hopped up onto the hood of it, setting the lantern between them.

"Makes me think of the *feldgeister*," Wild said, into the silence that followed. "All them stories of blood and guts the oldtimers tell the children."

"What, like the Bullkater?" James asked. "I always sorta liked that one."

"Bullkater, no. I was thinking of the Roggenwolf," Wild said. "Wrong time of year for it, and anyway a man done that brutality. But…it makes you think. We put a lot of stock in walls and doors."

"When really, something could just come and fetch you away at any time," James finished for him.

"I think parents just don't want their kids runnin' helter skelter into man-tall corn," Wild said. "But it's not all a lie."

"Death comes easy out here," James agreed.

"Shouldn't come easy like this. A fever or a farm accident, maybe even a wild boar gets you, fine, that's the chance a farmer takes," Wild said. "A monster shouldn't come out of the dark and take you with a hatchet."

"Well, no. Suppose not," James said, brooding on it.

They sat in silence for a long time, occasionally getting up to stamp their feet or slap warmth back into their hands, until Tex's truck, returning, told them it was midnight.

James left Wild at home on his way into town; Billy was waiting up in their bedroom, wanting all the details, but Wild just said "In the morning, I'm half-froze," and crawled into bed.

Somehow, probably James talking in town, the name Roggenwolf got stuck to the murder; not that anyone thought it was a real Roggenwolf, not that anyone but children believed the Roggenwolf was real. But the adults, as if saying "the murderer" was bad luck, took to calling whoever had killed the Fischers the Roggenwolf.

It hit the town hard. Nobody was used to it. They'd lost a whole family to a fire a few years back, and there was a farmer on the very edges of Lea, who didn't go to either church but was in town sometimes, who had killed his children, just up and went mad one day. But this wasn't like that. Someone had gone into the home of a man not ten miles outside Lea and deliberately killed five people, and there wasn't much the sheriff from Wheeler could do. He agreed with Tex, that it was likely a home-breaker who got more than he bargained for, and would be long gone by now.

"Tell me about this Roggenwolf," Miss Adelaide said to Wild, a few days later, sitting in front of a fire pit on the back porch of the "old" house, the Mayer house, which was still only partly grafted onto the Platter house. "Not the murders. The legend."

"I guess you wouldn't know. I think it comes from the old country," Wild said. "There's a German word, *feldgeist*. Field spirit. They're ghosts that live on farms. Sometimes they control the wind. When children stray into the crops, or even just get too close, they come out of the rows to hurt them. Kill them, kidnap them, torment them. The Roggenwolf's a feldgeist."

"How terrible! Why would they even make up such a thing?"

"Lord knows. Maybe it's not made up. Maybe it's how they dealt with losing children in the fields. There's lots of feldgeister; most are shaped like animals. One's a witch woman made of corn."

She laughed a little. "To be made of corn. That sounds uncomfortable."

"Maybe it is."

"So the Roggenwolf is a wolf?"

"A big one. Striped so that it blends into the corn. Its breathing sounds like the cornstalks rustling. If you go into the corn, it'll hunt you down and eat you. The older farmers always leave an offering for it after the harvest – the last few ears of corn, you set them out in the field as a sacrifice. Lon did it. Come to think, I did it last year myself without even considering it."

She draped her arms over her bent knees, considering the fire. "People love a sacrifice," she murmured. "There's so much in the world that can't be controlled, or bargained with, or bought. It must feel better to offer something and pretend it helps."

"Too deep for me," Wild said with a shrug. But the way she'd said people, it reminded him of what he'd been thinking on, lately. About Miss Adelaide, and about the time he'd seen the rose window grow.

"Maybe for me, too," she said.

"Miss Adelaide," Wild said, and she turned her head to see him. "I need to ask you something."

"Of course," she said, smiling at him, and her eyes seemed to glow gold in the firelight.

"You know those books you've been giving Billy," he began. "The...science fiction. About flying machines and traveling in time and...all that kind of thing."

She nodded.

"There was a story about men on the moon. And one about men

from Mars coming down to meet men here on Earth," he continued doggedly, though every instinct told him to stop. "And some about...supernatural things. Called 'em otherworldly."

"Yes, Mr. Mayer," she said softly.

"Well, ma'am." He paused, and then plunged ahead. "That's you, right? You and that church in town. You're connected, somehow, aren't you? The night we met, at the Social, I saw...something happened to the church, and I think it's on account of we met."

"Do you?" she asked, still impossibly gentle.

"Yes, ma'am. And you know something about the Roggenwolf, don't you?"

She looked sad. "Not enough to help. But yes. I know...a little."

"So you're....you're science fiction. Some kind of science fiction. Right?"

There was no mistaking it now; her eyes glowed, and her mouth, when she opened it, seemed to glow too.

"And if I am?" she asked. "Does that frighten you?"

He shook his head. "No, it don't frighten me. The church put its mark on me and I thought it put a mark on you but I reckon that's not quite right. I think you put a mark on me too, Miss Adelaide."

She leaned forward and kissed him, and it felt like the world was new again.

"Someday," she said, "You'll call me Adie, Wild Mayer."

"Adie," he repeated, entranced. "If you're science fiction, what does that make me?"

She smiled, and the light faded, and then she was just a woman again, with gold-brown skin and long brown hair plaited up on her head, and deep brown eyes.

"A gift to us, Wild," she murmured, and Wild let it be. It was not now, him and Adie, it wasn't to be now – but it was to be, very soon, and he was thrilled at the future she held for him.

"I'd like to marry you, Miss Adelaide," he said. "We don't know how much time any of us'll ever have. I ain't want to wait long. After I see Sarah married, after the planting."

"Why, I'd like that fine," she said, and let him kiss her again, and he felt suddenly that it was him who was glowing, not her.

TEN

SARAH WAS MARRIED before the planting, and Wild in April, after most of it was done. Sarah left for the Muller farm, less than a mile off if you went through the fields, and Adie came to the Platter-Mayer farm shortly after, a little unfamiliar, a little sweet, eager to be friends with Mama and to prove her abilities to her new family. Wild still wasn't sure how she'd fare, keeping house after being a teacher, but he supposed they'd settle in.

Wild had never asked if Adie was part Texican, or who her people had been; it didn't matter to him and it seemed rude to even wonder, especially since she so clearly didn't care to say. He'd worried the Lutherans would look sidelong at him for it, but they seemed to mutter more about marrying a Baptist. That was easy enough to set to rights; it was a Lutheran wedding, and she came to the Lutheran church that first Sunday after they wed, full of her usual charm. Most of the older folks realized quickly that it was their chance to teach her their ways – she didn't know how to make a German pickle or dance a true polka, or anything at all about sausage.

Only the young men, many of whom had been competing with Wild for Adie's attention, stayed aloof. Not all of them were happy with Wild, with his being treated as a man just because his stepfather was dead or his college-boy ways or his strange ideas about crops. Or, most of all, his pretty wife.

Wild didn't care. He'd put down his first crop, married his beloved, and with the warmer weather, was set on finishing up the combination of the old Mayer house and the new Platter one, not least because there was a bedroom for him and his new wife waiting in the Mayer house.

In June, when the corn was getting high enough that Billy disappeared if he walked into it, Wild would come in from the fields bone-tired and practically sleep his way through dinner. He knew it was just the time of year for it; Lon had been the same. He knew it would pass off in July, as the heat took hold and the crops did for themselves a little more. Still, for now, it was like sleepwalking through life.

But one fine June evening, after the coffee at dinner had perked him up a little and with no more chores to be done, Adie took his hand and asked to go walking. He would have taken her down the truck lanes that split the fields, but she walked boldly into the corn, still holding his hand, so he followed.

"What beautiful things they are," she said, fingers drifting across the leaves. "They feel like a present, just for me."

"Well," he said, still shy, unable to believe she was really his. "I imagine they are. A man's meant to provide for his wife."

"So this all belongs to me," she said, proprietary and strange, as they strayed further from the house.

"Yes," he agreed, because why else would you scratch an existence from the soil, if not for your family and those you loved? It was a hard life. Not worth it unless you had someone to give it to.

"Do you love me, Wild?" she asked, drawing him close in the rows between the corn, and he thought about science fiction, and the church, and he nodded.

"I do, Adie," he replied. "More than my own heart, I think."

"Well, that won't go without reward," she said, as he kissed the gold column of her throat.

She went down to the ground, and he went with her – the day was long so the sun touched them right until the last, when they fell in the shade of the corn stalks, the ears barely buds. They'd blossom gold and white eventually, but for now Wild didn't think of that, just of his golden Adie, with her plaited thick hair and dark eyes. It felt like a ritual, and he could almost feel a line stretching back to history, back to men and women blessing the fields this way in other times and places, further even than the old country folks talked of.

He broke, and he felt Adie break too; and the corn stalks rustled, a benediction.

Only abandon the earth, and you will be abandoned. Care for us and we will nourish you.

It wasn't elegant, and it surely wasn't clean; they were caked in soil and loose leaves, Adie's dress up around her waist, his shirttails in the dirt. But it was real, and as she looked down at him, he was reminded that the corn wasn't all that belonged to her.

"God preserve me, Adie," he said. "I could worship you like an idolator."

She smiled. "Don't bother," she said quietly. "I don't want worshipping. Just care while I'm here, and memory when I'm gone."

"Well, don't go too soon," he said, and she nodded gravely. And soon he picked himself up, helped her up and dusted her down, and by the time they came back to the house they were reasonably presentable, at least in the low light of nightfall.

ELEVEN

BET CAME TO Wild in early August of 1931, when the corn was really getting high; even Wild could disappear into it now. She came when everyone was out of the house, Billy driving the others into town for some shopping before the harvest. When Bet walked into his kitchen, Wild saw the fear in her face, and he put down his coffee.

"Do I need to kill a man?" he asked her.

She shook her head. He kicked out a chair for her and poured her a cup. She sat, and bowed her head over the coffee.

"Daddy'd be so ashamed of me," she said brokenly.

"Well, I ain't Lon. What've you done?" he asked gently.

"Figure I'm pregnant," she said softly.

Wild paused.

"You sure I ain't need to kill a man?" he asked. "Bet, if someone forced you – "

"He didn't force me."

"Well, then do I need to drag him to an altar? Does he know?"

She looked up at him, and the fear was still there.

"I don't wanna marry him, Wild," she said. "And he don't know. That ain't why I came to tell you."

"Does Mama know?"

"Not yet. Not if you don't tell her."

"Well, she'll find out," Wild said, a little confused. "This ain't a stain on a tablecloth, Bet, you can't cover it with lace."

"I didn't even enjoy it," Bet said miserably, looking down again. "Wasn't even nice like some of the girls said. Don't feel like a just punishment for it not even bein' nice."

Wild thought of Adie, and the way she smiled at him sometimes, a morning after, and wondered what boy had done this to his sister.

"What'll we do about it?" Wild ventured. "What do you want to?"

Bet's fingers twisted in her lap. "I need money, Wild."

"Bet. We ain't sendin' you away."

"No, not to go for good. I need…in Carson they say there's a lady who can help. She could make it stop. Make it end too soon."

Wild stared at her, realizing what she meant. He'd known a woman in Lubbock who talked about such things, but she'd said it was dangerous, that a doctor could rip a woman open trying.

Bet seemed to mistake his surprise, his concern, for disgust. "Wild, I got to," she blurted. "I ain't want a baby yet and I ain't want to marry yet. And not *him*," she added viciously.

He put a hand on her arm, soothing, turning a little more towards her in the chair.

"I can hitch a ride to Carson and only be gone a day. Na – " She stopped herself, sharply, before she could give a name. "One of the Baptist girls from town had it done. She said it's better when a woman does it. She just gives you somethin' to drink and it's all over."

"You're sure?" Wild asked.

"Well, she said," Bet said, and there was still so much fear and uncertainty in her eyes. "I know we got the money, Wild, it ain't much, and I can – "

She stopped when he held up a hand.

"You can't hitch to Carson. What would we tell Mama?" he said, and she nodded, because now she saw that he wasn't going to stop her. "I'll get the money and take you myself."

She leaned her head against his shoulder, her entire body going slack with relief.

"Now, pull yourself together so Mama doesn't know anything's wrong. We can go tomorrow. I'll find something to tell Mama."

She nodded and inhaled, and when she leaned back she was Bet again – headstrong, a little forbidding, but still his favorite, if he was being honest.

Wild went out to the barn early next morning. When he came back for breakfast, Adie was setting out a platter of bacon. He kissed her but didn't touch her with hands that were blackened by machine dirt.

"Moze, pour me out a basin," he called, and Moze pumped chilly water into a bowl for him to wash in.

"You been tinkering with the truck?" Adie asked.

"Tractor," he grunted, scrubbing. "Engine's gone wrong. It'll need a new part from Carson, most likely."

"So close to the harvest," Mama said worriedly. "Can you fix it, Wild?"

Bet, sitting at the kitchen table, sipped her milky coffee quietly.

"Sure, it's an easy fix, just got to get the part," he said. "Won't be so expensive. Worst comes to it, we can borrow the Wagners', but I don't think we'll need to."

"Well, better to find out sooner than later," Adie said.

"Yep. Figure I'll get the money in Lea, then drive into Carson today, they'll have what I need at the tractor supply," he continued. "Be gone until sundown most likely. I thought Bet might like to come, " he added casually.

"Bet?" Mama asked.

"Sure, she saw some ad for dressmakers wanted in Carson. Figure if she got a dressmaking job she could winter over in town once the harvest is in, if she wanted."

"You didn't say anything about it," Mama said to Bet.

"I just mentioned it to Wild in passing. Didn't think we'd get to Carson until later in the year," Bet said with a shrug. "Might not even be a good job, but I wouldn't mind seeing."

"Well, that sounds fine to me," Mama told them. "Only mind you're back as soon as you can, don't go lingering in town."

"Won't miss dinner if we can help it," Wild said, drying his hands (still grey with dirt in the seams and nails, but at least a little more presentable) and sitting down, accepting a plate of eggs from Adie with a smile just for him. "Billy, you see to the farm today?"

Billy nodded, though he was bent over a book.

And that was an end of it, at least as far as the Platters knew.

"Did you break the tractor?" Bet asked, as soon as they were away in the truck, headed into Lea to get cash from the bank.

"Nah. Took a flywheel off. I'll put it back on when we get back, say it was the new part," Wild said. "How much this lady in Carson charge, anyway?"

"Ten dollars," she said. "That's what – "

"Your Baptist friend," Wild supplied.

"That's what she said."

"And she gives you a medicine and then it's done?"

"Well, she didn't give details. Her mama took her."

"Many other girls around here need that kinda help?" Wild asked, feeling an anger inside him he didn't understand. The boys he knew were decent, church-going folk, and should know better than to get a girl in trouble. Then again, they sold rubbers in Lubbock. Not so much in the Dry Goods in Lea.

"Don't know. Don't think so," Bet said, but she didn't sound certain.

He took forty dollars from the bank, just to be safe – two months of bills on the farm, more than twice what a new flywheel would cost.

As they pulled past the church, he noticed it had grown again; he wondered if anyone had witnessed the little columns spouting from its sides. Adie would know the word for them, though he wasn't sure he'd ask her. They were beautiful things, rising gracefully into the air. Like the legs of a spider, and Wild had a farmer's respect for pest-eating spiders. But he'd heard murmurs in town and knew the same in his soul – that it was dangerous to ask too many questions about the church.

Whatever it was, best just to let it be. Dan Rohlf and his disciples, now a couple dozen strong, did enough staring at it on the way to prayer meetings on Sunday nights. The town muttered about that, too, but what could they do?

He set his resolve and focused on driving. Now was no time for flights of fancy, or even for thinking of Adie and all her delirious mysteries. Now was a time to be practical, to be the patriarch, to look after his sister.

They were quiet on the ride to Carson. Bet was clearly lost in her own thoughts, and Wild was worried and curious. He'd seen enough of pregnancy in hogs and cows and barn cats, and he'd been old enough to at least be nearby when his brothers were born. There was a baby growing in her, however small, and you couldn't just magic that away with a potion. When an animal miscarried, it wasn't easy. He couldn't believe it was easier for a woman.

"I think I got a condition of helping you," he said finally, and Bet looked over at him. "Won't hurt," he added with a reassuring smile. "But I want to go with you to see this lady and I got some questions for her. And if I think she ain't no good, we'll find another way."

"What other way is there?"

"I don't know, but we'll think of something," he said. Carson was looming ahead, a squat settlement on a flat plain. He hadn't noticed, the last time they'd come in to sell crops, but he couldn't help it now – the land around Carson, the farms through which the road cut like a scythe, they didn't look well. The cotton was stunted and sickly, and the wheat looked like it was thirsting. They'd had plenty of rain in Lea; maybe they'd caught the best of it.

They reached Carson just before lunch, and ate paper-wrapped sandwiches Adie had made. After they were done, he took Bet to the drugstore, where she had a soft-spoken conversation with the pharmacist, who gave her a slip of paper with an address on it. Wild studied the rack of rubbers behind him; a dollar a dozen.

He kept his mouth shut, but he took the paper Bet gave him and stopped a man outside to ask if he knew where Green Street was. The man pointed him south, said about eight blocks and turn right on Hecklen Street, Green would be another three blocks beyond.

It was a pretty little neighborhood of homes. Tidy, and with alleys down the backs of the houses for deliveries and collections. They took the alley behind Green Street, like the pharmacist had told Bet, and he parked the truck outside an unlatched back gate. Bet looked at him apprehensively.

"You ain't have to," Wild said to her softly. "I'll take you in there and we'll take care of it, Bet, but if you're scared we can go home. I'll make Mama understand if I have to. We can find some other way if you ain't want to."

Bet set her jaw. "Let's go in," she said.

The lady who met them at the door was short, white-haired and a little plump. She led them into a spotlessly clean sort of a room, like a small office. There was a diploma from a medical college in Oregon, with the name Emil Yorke on it, on her wall.

"The President wouldn't sign a medical diploma with a woman's name on it, not in 1890," she said with a grin, when she saw him looking at it. "One of my professors changed my name a little. I'm Dr. Yorke," she added, speaking to Bet now. "You're here about an abortion?"

"Yes, ma'am," Bet said quietly.

"And you're – "

"Her brother," Wild said.

"I see. Well, I'll need to do an examination, and if you're pregnant, I'll have some medicine for you to take. Do you have somewhere safe and private to go afterward?" she asked.

Wild glanced at Bet, who was looking at him.

"We came in from Lea," he said. "We were hopin' to be back home this evening."

"I'm afraid not. The medicine is harsh and the process may be difficult. Many women are quite sick for a day or two. If you don't want a room in town, I have a room you can stay in," she added.

"Wild?" Bet said.

"I'll tell Mama you took ill," he said, but that wasn't his major concern. "Ma'am, I ain't a babe in woods, I know this can…it can really hurt a woman. I ain't want my sister hurt."

"It's safer than most, but nothing's perfect," Dr. Yorke said. "The body has to…expel the unwanted fetus. Do you understand?"

Wild nodded. Bet looked pale.

"I have to say…for you, it's better," Dr. Yorke said to Bet. "You're a healthy young woman and it won't prevent you having future babies. I'm safer than any man you'd consult about this."

Bet chewed her lip. Dr. Yorke's face softened a little.

"The examination is two dollars," she said. "We can make sure you're pregnant. Sometimes women aren't, you know. And that will give you time to decide. Wild, is it?" she asked Wild.

"Yes, ma'am."

"This really should be a private examination. It won't take long; you can wait here, and speak with…."

"Elizabeth," Bet supplied.

"You can speak with Elizabeth after. And if you decide not to, I can give you some names of people who can help. Carson has a home for unwed mothers."

Wild stood when the women did, and watched Bet follow Dr. Yorke into the other room. What did they know about this woman, anyway, with a man's name on a medical certificate on her wall? Other than whatever Baptist girl had seen her and survived.

He didn't know much about what went on in the exam room; Bet told him later Dr. Yorke gave her the exam, but mostly she said she wanted to make sure it was Bet's choice, and that Wild wasn't strong-arming her into it. Ten minutes passed, then twenty, then thirty.

When Bet opened the door she looked shaky, but there was that set of her jaw again.

"I done it," she said to Wild.

He blinked. "You did?"

"She was very brave," Dr. Yorke agreed, patting her on the shoulder. "Now. There's a room ready for you, with indoor plumbing, which trust me, you'll want soon. Your truck's in the alley?"

Wild nodded, bewildered.

"Go park it on the main street, not in front of my house. I'll settle her in."

He watched them go, then got in the truck and drove back to Carson's big strip. Hustling with worry, he found the post office and sent a quick message by the afternoon Rural Free Delivery truck to the Platter Farm West Lea, saying Bet had taken ill and they wouldn't be home for maybe a day or two.

By the time he walked back to Green Street, he could tell whatever was going to happen had begun. Dr. Yorke took him to a bedroom, clean as the rest of the house, with a nice patchwork quilt on the bed. Bet was in the little closet off the bedroom, where an indoor toilet and a bathtub had piped water; he could hear her crying softly.

"Bet?" he called through the crack in the door. "You need me?"

"It's a cramp," she said, and then moaned again. "Just a. A bad cramp."

He looked at Dr. Yorke.

"That's normal. A few hours of cramping and bleeding, at least. Maybe even a day," she said, looking sympathetically at the door. "A hot bath will help. The red-colored tap will pour hot water into the tub. There's a pitcher of water, make sure she drinks, and don't let her eat anything until it's over."

"What if…what if it ain't going…right?" he asked. Bet moaned. "How would I even know?"

"I'll look in on you every so often. If she passes out or there's too much blood, come and get me."

Wild wouldn't have relived those hours for anything, later. Bet cramped and cried, and at one point he had to pick her up to put her in the bath, all thoughts of preserving her decency forgotten when she nearly fell to the floor. The hot water did seem to help, though he found out what the pail next to the bath was for when she began to retch. When she began to bleed, around midnight, he realized he didn't know what *too much* might be.

"Bet, I gotta get the doctor," he said. She sobbed miserably, curled up against the lip of the tub.

Dr. Yorke, when he fetched her urgently from her study, looked at Bet and nodded approvingly.

"It's all right, sweetheart," she said, stroking Bet's sweaty hair. "The worst is over now. Let's get you out of this bath so the bleeding can stop."

Dr. Yorke dried her briskly, wrapping her in cotton pads before letting Wild help dress her in a loose, clean nightgown from the closet. He carried her to the bed when they were finished. The cramping seemed to have eased, at least, and Bet's body was limp when he laid her out.

"Can I trust you to stay awake and watch her?" Dr. Yorke asked. Wild nodded. "If she stops breathing, come and get me at once."

He sat on the bed, watching Bet breathe, until after the sun came up.

They left Carson around ten that morning, after the stores had opened. Wild paid Dr. Yorke two dollars for the examination and eight for the medicine, and offered another five for the room; when she said the room was included, he offered her another five anyway.

"If you get a girl who comes in alone, that's for her," he said. Dr. Yorke nodded and accepted the money. A flywheel would have cost him fifteen dollars anyway.

Bet was pale on the seat next to him, but she said she might as well be miserable in the truck as in a stranger's home, and he agreed.

"You mind if I stop on the way?" he asked. She shook her head. She hadn't eaten breakfast, but he'd made her drink every last drop of water in the pitcher.

He stopped in front of the pharmacy and stepped inside. The pharmacist saw him alone and blanched.

"She's waitin' outside," Wild said. The man looked relieved. "Thank you for your help, sir. I got ten dollars here. How many skins can I get for ten dollars?"

The man blinked. "You opening a pharmacy or a bordello, son?"

"They ain't sell them in our town. My sister's the second girl I know of had to go to the doctor. Not fixing to see a third one out here anytime soon."

The man gave him a measured look, then reached under the counter. He took out a white carton and set it in front of Wild.

"I'll give you the bulk rate," he said, passing it across. Wild handed him the two five-dollar bills. "Come back anytime for the same."

"Thank you, sir," Wild said, and tucked the carton under his arm. When he got back to the truck, he slid it under the seat.

"What's that?" Bet asked.

"When we get home, you got a job to do," Wild said. "You tell your friends if they're going to go with a boy, they got to come to you first."

"Why?"

"Cause you got a box of rubbers in your room for them," he said, and kicked the carton with his boot heel gently.

"Wild!" she said, scandalized. He gave her an unimpressed look. "I can't be the town madam!"

"Fine, then tell 'em to come to me and I'll give 'em out, I ain't care," he said. "That doctor's all right but Carson's a long way to go and ten dollars is a lot of money," he added, because he couldn't tell Bet how terrified he'd been, how awful she'd looked. She didn't deserve that.

It was a few hours before they were home. They stopped twice to let Bet retch, though not much came up. When they reached the dirt path to the farm, Bet turned to him and said, "Thank you, Wild."

"Ain't nothing," he said gruffly. "Now let's go catch hell from Mama for worrying her."

Mama wasn't mad so much as she was happy to see them; Wild's letter had gotten through all right, but she'd been worried for Bet's health, and she bundled her to bed, which was just as well, given how pale she still looked. Wild kissed Adie hello and helped Billy set the table while Mama fussed over Bet.

"Think it was probably something in town," Wild said, when Mama finally came to sit down to eat with them. "Adie's sandwiches were fine but we stopped for a coffee and it didn't smell right."

"Can't trust town food," Mama said.

"Guess not. Anyway, got the flywheel, but had to pay for a hotel overnight, and food and some medicine for Bet," he said. "Fraid we'll have to wait for after harvest for the new boots for Billy."

"My boots're fine," Billy said. "Didn't want new ones anyway, just got these broke in."

"We'll make do," Mama said. Wild hated to lie to her, but he loved Bet more than he hated the lying.

After dinner, he went out to sit on the back porch, tired and wanting to see the sun go down, to remember there were constants in life, that everything had its season. He thought he might understand better, now, why Lon – never really much on religion – sometimes still read the Bible of an evening. *A time to every purpose under Heaven.*

Adie came out onto the porch, leaning against the rail opposite the bench he was propped on. She was smiling at him, and she looked better than the sunset.

"While you were in Carson I had a talk with your Mama," she said softly. "I needed some advice from a woman."

"Did you now?" he asked, surprised.

"Well, I had to be sure," she said.

"Sure about what?"

One of her hands touched the waist of her dress, proprietary, and she said, "I'm pregnant, Wild."

He looked up at her expression – a mixture of fear and pride – and then at her hand, and he slid off the bench to his knees, pressing his face to her stomach, and he prayed.

Thank you, Jesus and then *Please Lord, let it be easy,* he prayed, and then, *Please, Lord, I ain't want a child if it means I lose Adie.*

And, in some part of him, he prayed to the church and the corn. *Nourish me, give me this, and I will care for you all of my days.*

Her hand came to rest on the back of his head. "Are you cryin', husband?"

He shook his head, but he wiped his eyes before he leaned back. He looked up at her from his knees and saw light coming out of her like the rose window of the church.

He knew, in that moment; didn't tell anyone, not even Adie, but he knew. He knew it would be a little girl, more special than any other little girl in Lea, and he knew what she wanted to be named.

"Iscah," he whispered.

HARVEST 1931

THE HARVEST THAT year was bittersweet – not a bad harvest in itself, but also, in some ways, a terrible one.

Wild had planned for two crops of corn, an early one to come in with the wheat and a later one to come in with the harvest from the rest of the farms. As harvests went, both were fine enough. Bringing in the first crop of corn with only what labor he could scrounge before the true harvest season was tough, and with one third of his fields fallow and prices unusually low, it was a narrow margin that September. Between the money spent in Carson for Bet and the lean first crop, October was a frightening month. If the second crop didn't come in rich, it would be a hard winter.

But the last few days before the second harvest, with the corn huge and heavy in the fields, Wild began to plan for a good winter over.

The second harvest came in fine, but prices were still bare, below even what Bet had thought. There were more gaunt-faced men and women from up north, and the news from Nebraska was the same as the news from Kansas and Oklahoma a year earlier. Farms were failing. Weak crops withered in the field for want of water, and farms lost their soil to the wind.

And when they went into Carson, they saw the destitute of the midwest, refugees from the drought. When the farmers of Lea brought their corn into Carson, there were people on the street who watched the procession of cheap gold with hungry eyes.

"Best have them wire the money straight to Lea like last year," Bet said, watching them watch her. "I don't like it, Wild."

"I don't either, but it's not their fault," Wild said. And still, when they pulled up to the trains, to where the buyers were waiting, he grasped Billy and Moze (now nine years old and privileged to attend for the first time) by the arms.

"Stay close," he said seriously. "There's hungry folk about."

"Will they eat me, Wild?" Moze asked, only half-joking.

"No," Wild said. "But they might steal you away, and then I'd have to feed them before I get you back."

To his brother's credit, Moze stayed close, like Billy's shadow, and did what he could to help carry the corn to the hoppers. Bet did the math, Wild made the handshake, and they turned a little profit, at least, though not enough for luxuries, not this year.

And still there were the envious sunken eyes of their fellow farmers, some from as close as fifty miles away.

The murder that winter was even closer to Lea than the failing farms.

The family wasn't from Lea, so it wasn't the shock it had been with the Fischers, but they were still close enough to make folks wary, only thirty miles off. Lea heard about it from farmers a little closer in, and no details for months, just that a family had died on a lonely farm halfway between Lea and Lubbock, down near Antelope Flats.

Later, when Wild found someone who knew more details, he was unsettled by what he heard. It was a farmer, his wife, and two nearly-grown sons; the men had been shot, like John Fischer and his child, and the wife had been killed with a hatchet. Killed was the word they used, but Wild knew what word they meant: butchered. All the lanterns in the place had been smashed.

He didn't say it in town, or even privately, to Mama and Billy. Only Adie knew what he thought – that whatever the Roggenwolf was, it had come again, and it was whim or grace that kept it from Lea this time. And only then because she had asked him, one late night, what he was thinkin' on.

"Not sure I should even say," he said softly, in the dark, thin chill of early North Texas autumn nights.

"Why not?"

"Don't like to scare you."

He heard her laugh. "I'm not easily scared, Wild."

And anyway, maybe it was safe now – maybe the Roggenwolf had taken all he was going to take this year.

"I think whoever killed the Fischers killed that family down south," he whispered. "And I don't think anyone'd believe me."

"Why not?"

"Safer not to, I think," he said.

"Sometimes it's safer not to believe something," she agreed. "Doesn't make it untrue, though."

He tried to put it from his mind, and asked her, "How'd you get so wise?"

She smiled against the hand he rested on her cheek, then kissed the very edge of his scars, the last tendril curling down his wrist. "Practice, I guess."

And Lea, anyway, had other problems to wrestle with.

Dan Rohlf, who had seen other spiritualists from California and Missouri and New York do it, had put an ad in Texas and Oklahoma papers inviting seekers of truth and enlightenment to his farm. He'd held another revival, this one in a giant tent on his own land, that had drawn maybe half again the population of Lea to it, and maybe half the population of Lea had gone as well; not many from either camp had stayed, but enough had that you could call it a congregation, if not as big or as….well, as sane as the Baptists or the Lutherans.

Rohlf didn't have the kind of money, everyone knew, to support thirty people living on his farm, but that was what troubled people in Lea. Those that had come from Oklahoma and the southern Texas panhandle, those that stayed, they gave him everything they had. Sometimes it wasn't much, but one fellow from Amarillo had an inheritance that he gave Rohlf that some said was sizeable.

"It's the god damndest thing," Tex Junior said to Wild, as they shared a sandwich on the tailgate of Wild's truck, having run into each other in town one day. "I heard in the bank Dan Rohlf's as rich as Lentz Platter now."

"Money rich maybe, but he don't hold mortgages," Wild said. "And anyway, did you hear that from a banker, or some farmer that's annoyed about the revivals every Sunday?"

"Well, it's true the pastor don't like he took six of our congregants," Tex Junior said.

"That sermon last Sunday," Wild said, barely suppressing laughter.

"That sermon was pure vinegar," Tex Junior agreed. The pastor had preached on how easily the weak of faith were lured to the devil. It hadn't been subtle. "I talked with Neil Wagner, you know."

"I hear he upped sticks from his father's farm to join Rohlf. We should see about offering help come planting next year."

"You offer if you can. I'm thinking of putting money down on the Fischer place."

Wild looked at him, amazed. "You ain't gonna live in the house, are you?"

"Why not? Perfectly good house."

"Five people were murdered there!"

"You don't believe in haints, do you, Wild?" Tex Junior asked.

"Maybe I do."

"And you a college boy!" he hooted.

"They don't teach you not to believe in haints in college. They teach you to believe in soil erosion. I bet more farmers around here believe in haints than in soil erosion."

"Well." Tex Junior said, sobering a little. "Sarah feels like you, says if we do she'd like a new house when we got the money. Maybe get one of those Sears houses from the catalogue. I figure, it says it takes ninety days to put up. If I convince you and Art Weber to help, we could get it up in thirty, before planting started."

"I don't mind," Wild said, "if it means my sister ain't living in the old Fischer place. Hell, I'll front some of the cash myself if I can."

"Well, still gotta sweet-talk the bank into giving me a mortgage, and then I'd need extra if I buy a new house, that's a lot of debt. And I'll have to talk the Fischer cousins into selling to me. Wasn't my point though, getting back to it," Tex Junior continued. "I talked to Neil Wagner, and I asked him, what's so great about Rohlf that he went and saw and stayed? And he said a buncha nonsense about how Lea was sacred ground and needed prayer to stay that way, and that only the folks praying on Dan Rohlf's farm really prayed to the real God, which is nonsense *and* blasphemy, and then he said they're doing something new."

"New?" Wild asked, eyebrows lifting.

"They're *meditating*," Tex Junior said.

"Meditating?"

"Yep."

"On what?"

"Not on anything. Just...meditating. Neil says you sit still and quiet, and try to ignore the material world, and then all of a sudden you get real peaceful."

"Well, hell, I've been meditating for years."

"Yeah?"

"Sure. It's called fishing."

Tex Junior laughed. "Maybe. But he likes it. They're all fools if you ask me but they're harmless fools."

"Rohlf's gone strange this past year, for sure, but..." Wild shrugged. "When I ran up there to talk to him about crop rotation, he went all in. Said he thought it was a fine idea."

"You ever notice he watches you at the socials sometimes?" Tex Junior asked.

"He's got the crazy eyes, he watches everyone," Wild said dismissively.

He could see that Rohlf's congregation was causing problems – one woman had left her family over it, and both the Baptist minister and the Lutheran pastor were annoyed, and nobody liked all the newcomers they didn't know, pouring into town. Lots of folks weren't pleased with Dan Rohlf's new wealth, either. They were mostly problems of people being discontented, though, and discontent wasn't anything new to a small community. It seemed harmless enough in itself, just folks finding a new way to pray, even if their new way ruled out the old ways, which made Wild suspicious.

That night he thought he'd try it, just to see what Neil Wagner was all about; he closed his eyes and sat real still and tried not to think about much. But Adie and Bet were in the living room laughing at Billy, who was reading them the Science Fiction story he wrote, which was full of aliens who were funny rather than scary. Moze and Lon were running around, and in the kitchen Mama was humming, and the wind was blowing and a barn cat yowled in the distance – and anyway who wanted to ignore the world in front of him?

It was such a good world.

LINEAGE

GERHARDT MAYER CAME to the land of Texas and stayed in it in the time of the immigration, with many others of his country and their goods and families. And he had no wife, therefore he said, I will take a wife from the immigrants, that I may not raise my sons amongst Baptists. He took for his wife an immigrant, and she was Elise. And she bore him three sons, the oldest of which was Henrich Mayer, and he dwelt on the farm of his father, and the years of all Gerhardt Mayer's life were sixty-two.

The years of Henrich Mayer's life were twenty-four when he took for his wife the daughter of an immigrant, that he might not raise his children amongst Baptists, and she was Helene. And she bore him two sons and four daughters, and their oldest son was named for his grandfather, Gerhardt. And Gerhardt too dwelt on the farm of his father, and the years of all Henrich Mayer's life were forty-nine.

The years of Gerhardt Mayer's life were twenty when he took for his wife the daughter of an immigrant, that he might not raise his children amongst Baptists. She was Mary, daughter of Fischer the immigrant, but also of Maria Margarita Fischer y Lopes, whose family had dwelt in the land before it was the land. She was called Maria by her mother, but she was called Mary by her father, and with this name she married. And she bore her husband one son, Wilder Lopes Mayer.

And there was a great plague, and all the years of Gerhardt Mayer's life were twenty-five.

And his wife said, I must remarry, for my child is hungry and the fields of my husband are unplanted. And she was taken as wife by Lon Platter, that she might raise his daughters and give him sons. And all the years of Lon Platter's life were sixty.

And Wilder dwelt on the farm of Lon Platter, and he took for his wife a stranger, a Baptist, who had no father and no mother known. And the people of the Lutherans said, who is this woman? Who are her people, and she is a Baptist? But she said to him, I will dwell on your farm and worship as you worship. And Wilder Mayer was pleased, and her name was Adelaide, called Adie.

And the years of Wilder's life were twenty-one when Adelaide began to labor, and she cried out in the pain of women, and he heard her cries and he too cried out. For a day and a night she labored, until she bore him a daughter, as foretold. And he named her Iscah Margarita while her mother slept.

And when the sun rose he brought Iscah to her mother to nurse, and her mother laughed.

TWELVE

IT WAS STRANGE, how winter came and went as it usually did, even when Wild's whole life was different. Adie was living on the farm and Sarah was gone to her husband's farm, and those were big changes of course, but when Iscah arrived in January, it felt like the world shifted.

She was the tiniest thing Wild had ever seen, smaller than his brothers at birth, and for all of that she'd given her mother a rough time; Gert Johnson, who midwifed her, said she'd been breech, and if she'd been bigger Adie might have died. She fit in Wild's two cupped hands, but she made enough noise for at least three babies, he thought.

He almost didn't let her out of the house to be baptized; the Sunday that was meant for it was brutally cold, and she was just so tiny, he was sure she'd freeze. Adie laughed at him and bundled her up, but Wild still made Billy drive and held her close to his chest, under his coat, until they were inside the warm church. All the farmers, eager to see the newest congregant, crowded around and remarked on how she was awful small, and how she had her mother's brown eyes but her daddy's chin.

"She minds me of your grandma Maggie," one of them said to Wild. "Lord, she was a beautiful woman. No one would say a word to your grandfather about marrying a Texican once they saw her."

Wild had heard this old saw before, about how Maria Margarita charmed the whole town, and he just smiled and stroked Iscah's brow.

"I imagine you won't be headed back to Lubbock anytime soon," Lentz Platter said jovially, when he came to pay his respects to Iscah. "It's a shame, son, but I understand."

"I'd like to speak to you about that, sir, when you have the time," Wild replied.

"When *I* have the time! I remember what it was like raising a newborn. When you have the time and a full night's sleep under you,

you come and find me," Platter said. "Lon'd be proud of this one, even if you did marry a Baptist."

"I can't help what I was born, Mr. Platter, but I found a Lutheran to marry as soon as I could," Adie said, grinning at him.

"Spirited woman! Look after the little one. Don't let her get a cough," Platter advised. Wild fretted about her getting a cough for two days after.

He didn't get to speak to Lentz Platter for another month – first there was an ice storm that housebound everyone, and the truck couldn't go over the cobblestone ice for a week after that, and even when the roads were clear he had to light a fire near the truck to get the engine warm enough to turn over.

When he finally made it into town, he was distracted thinking about where all he'd need to go, so for a second he didn't notice the old church, and then when he did, he almost crashed the truck.

His scars hadn't given him any trouble in some time; they didn't ache in the cold or pull tight in the heat the way some men said theirs did. They were barely even visible now; Adie never seemed to mind them, and Wild himself didn't care. But when he looked up and saw the church, they pulsed, sharp and deep, and he swerved out of instinct, even though there was nothing to either swerve around or into.

He pulled over, heart racing, then leaned over the steering wheel to stare at it. After a disbelieving second, he climbed out of the truck entirely and stood at the edge of the street, still staring.

It had grown. The rose window was the same size, at least he thought, but the church itself had widened, adding little fancy-roofed extensions until the edges nearly touched the fence Wild had put up with Tex Junior and Micah. The fence, too, was different – less raggedy somehow, taller for sure, and with a wrought-iron gate that looked itself like a window, with an arch at the top. The lock was on the gate now, not the door, even though anyone could easily duck through the fence on either side of it.

It loomed over the street, almost the tallest building there – only the bank was taller – and he spotted two little gargoyles leering out of the bell towers. The hole in the roof had been patched, which he supposed was a shame, seeing as how the sunlight wouldn't shine through and light up the window anymore.

No one ever talked about it. Not about how it didn't used to have a rose window, or gargoyles, or more than one bell tower. It was either an unspoken agreement amongst the farmers of Lea, or somehow nobody else noticed. Or it was only Wild's hallucination.

It was beautiful, there was no doubt of that. It didn't seem to threaten the smaller buildings on either side as much as it seemed like it was...shielding them. Like an older sibling standing just half a step in front of the younger ones.

He didn't know what else to do, so he touched the brim of his hat, same as he had the night he saw the rose window blossom, and went on with his errands. He had shopping to do first, supplies for the farm, and then he'd try to talk to Lentz Platter. Mostly, he wanted to get home to Adie and Iscah.

At the bank they asked him to wait and they'd see if Mr. Platter was available. Wild sat, hat on his knee, not nervous so much as...concerned. If Mr. Platter said no, he'd be no worse off than he was now; if he said yes, that was a new set of problems to consider.

"Wild," Lentz Platter called from his office at the end of the bank's long hallway. "Come along!"

Wild rose and joined him in his office, piled high with paper. The telephone out to Wheeler, a prestigious trophy, sat next to the telephone of the bank's local line on his desk.

"Glad to finally see you. Some ice storm, hey?"

"Sure was," Wild agreed. "Froze the barn door shut and nearly took the roof off the house, it felt like."

"Your people fine?"

"Yes sir, and I assume the same of yours."

"Oh, we get along."

"It's about the family I came to talk to you," Wild said, shifting in his seat. "I know you gave me that scholarship to Lubbock partly because Lon was my stepfather, and the whole family was grateful – I've been sorry I couldn't take you up on the next year of schooling."

"It's good you're looking after your family. And you married a local girl – well, close enough to local anyway. Your mama was a little worried about you taking up with the women in Lubbock."

Wild smiled. "I remember."

"But you can't go back now, can you?"

"No. And if you wanted to give the scholarship money to someone in Lea who is askin' for it, I'd understand."

Platter fixed him with a steady look. "But you're asking for it for something else, aren't you?"

"Not for me," Wild said. "For Bet. Lon's daughter, closer blood to you than me, even."

"Bet?" Platter looked startled. "What's she need scholarship money for?"

"For a women's college," Wild said. "For a mathematics degree. You know how Bet is, sir, she's headstrong and she's got a better mind than me – not to brag, but you did send me to school on the strength of my smarts."

"What in God's name would a woman do with a mathematics degree?" Platter asked, still looking stunned by the request.

"Teach, or anyhow earn her way – be a credit to Lea and to her family, if she does well," Wild said.

"Here in Lea? You're not expecting her to take a degree in math and then come work at the bank or the seed store."

"No. I don't..." Wild shook his head. It was hard to admit even to himself. "If she left I don't think she'd come back."

"Has she done something to make you send her away, Wild?" Platter asked quietly.

"No," Wild said, thinking of Carson, and the woman doctor there. "No, she's never shamed us. I'm not trying to be rid of her. It's just...you know Bet. Can you picture her as a farm wife?"

"It's true, I can't," Platter said thoughtfully. "Bless your sister but she reminds me of the first Platters who came to Lea. I don't know if you know this, but the Platters were fugitives."

Wild laughed. "No."

"Hand to God. They were running from the law. Oh, they hadn't done anything too awful, political discontent as I understand it. Bet's got that fire in her."

"I believe you."

"I see a little of it in that Billy of yours too. Anyway. A Platter woman with a college degree, well well. Practically a bluestocking. You talk to Bet herself about this, yet?"

"Not yet. I wanted to know if I suggested it that I could – that we could – make sure it was paid for."

"You're a clever man, Mayer," Platter said. "Now, I had set aside the money for four years for you, but when you came back I invested it – year over year, there ought to be enough for a full degree, so money's not the issue. And it's my money, so the bank can't object to it being transferred between family. Where would she even go?"

"Well, I thought the Teacher's College south of Amarillo, or Oklahoma Panhandle A&M," Wild said. "But that'd be up to Bet, if she even wants it."

"A University Woman from the Platters," Platter mused again. "Very forward-thinking. Well. I'll make you a deal, Mr. Mayer, man to man. If Bet wants it and she can find a place for less than four hundred a year, the money'll be there. But I want to hear from her on the regular, so I can decide for myself if this idea of higher education for women is any good."

"Thank you, Mr. Platter," Wild said, offering his hand, almost disbelieving of their luck. "You won't regret it, you know Bet'll do the family proud."

"I hope so. Give my respects to your Mama," Platter said, as Wild hurried out, so excited to get home that the new additions to the old church went completely out of his head.

After he put the truck in the barn, he brought the parcels up to the house, letting himself in; there was a cheery glow from the kitchen, where everyone was keeping warm – Moze doing lessons with Lonny watching him, Billy pretending to do lessons when really he was writing in his "story notebook", a twine-bound ragged assortment of scrap paper, and Mama and Bet sewing while Adie nursed Iscah.

"How'd shopping go, Wild?" Mama asked, helping him set out the parcels and beginning to unwrap them as he sat down next to Adie.

"Oh, fine," he said. "Got everything you asked for and some penny candy for the boys."

Moze, Lon, and Billy all jumped up to investigate, and Wild grinned at Mama, who swatted them away gently before they could pull the groceries to pieces.

"The roads must've been awful," Adie said.

"Not too good, no, but I got there and back. Brought probably ten pounds of mud back with me on my shoes. How's my darlin?" he asked, stroking the palm of Iscah's hand. She clenched it around his finger and his heart ached.

"Hungry, like always," Adie told him. "Look at you, you're practically bursting – did you get good news in town?"

"I did, in fact. I saw Mr. Platter at the bank," he said. "I thought it was time I told him I wouldn't be taking the rest of my scholarship – past time, really, and it wasn't like he didn't know."

"Well, that's not exactly good news," Bet said.

"One year was enough for me. Here's the good news – he said the scholarship money was still good. And he offered it to you, Bet," Wild blurted, beaming. Bet set her sewing down and looked at him like he'd grown a second head.

"To me?" she asked. "For what, a dowry?"

"For schooling!" he said. "He said if you can find a school for less than four hundred a year he'd send you there. You could go to the Normal School, or the A&M..."

"Wild, are you joking?" Mama asked sharply.

"No! I'm not fooling, the money's there. If you want it. I told him I wasn't sure you would," Wild added, because Bet had no expression on her face at all.

"What would I study?" she asked. "What on earth would a woman from Lea go to college for, Wild?"

"Why, mathematics," Adie said suddenly. Bet looked at her. "You won the mathematics prize, you keep all the books."

"I don't need more math to keep a farm's accounts," Bet pointed out.

"But you wouldn't be keeping accounts," Adie said. "You could take an advanced mathematics course, Bet. You could invent new math, men are always doing that, or you could study statistics – do they have an advanced mathematics course at the Normal?" she asked Wild.

"I don't know," Wild said, because he hadn't even bothered to check. "We can send away and ask."

"Leave Lea?" Bet asked, but along with the worry in her voice there was curiosity – and hope.

"Only if you want to," Wild said. "But Bet…I think…"

"You do want to," Adie finished for him, softly.

Bet looked at Mama, who shrugged.

"Don't ask me for permission, you're a grown woman," she said. "I think it's a fine idea but I won't make up your mind for you."

It was just the right thing to say; if she'd pushed, Bet might have pushed back, but as it was, Bet lifted her chin like she'd been challenged.

"Well, I…I suppose I'll write to the Normal School," she said. "Billy, can I have some of your paper?"

Adie touched her wrist as Billy passed her a sheet.

"There's one other place you could think of," she said. "It's…far off, even further than Wild went in Lubbock, but I think it'd suit you."

HARVEST 1932

THE PLANTING THAT spring had gone well, while Bet wrote off to colleges in Texas and Oklahoma and the one Adie had suggested, which might as well be the moon, in *Chicago* of all places. Billy was sending letters too, secretively, but Wild knew what they were – he was laboriously writing out stories by hand, sending them to magazine publishers whose names he got from the backs of the books Adie gave him, and getting them back with polite rejection notices. It was true that Billy's stories weren't as good as most of the ones they read in the science fiction magazines, generally; he was only fifteen. But Wild also thought deep in his heart that Billy's stories were too funny, somehow too *modern*, and that them being handwritten in Billy's chicken-scratch might not be helping his case.

It was still too soon to tell if Wild's great crop rotation experiment with the farmers of Lea had done any good, but Wild felt like the soil looked richer, and plowed easier, in the field he'd left unplanted. The others all had opinions one way or another, but most of them, he saw, were still leaving a field empty, and switching crops in the others.

And the corn and wheat, oats, barley, sorghum and soy, it grew and grew.

Iscah was crawling, and had started to pull herself up with low tables and chairs, by harvest time that year. She followed her daddy around the room with those big brown eyes, and whenever Adie brought her outside in a sling, to bring lunch to the hands working the harvest or just to come spend five minutes distracting Wild from his work, Iscah gurgled and laughed. She liked to play with stray leaves from the cornstalks, or if she were set down on the ground, she would inevitably find a spider to tease with a stick.

He didn't even want to leave to go to Carson with the harvest, but it had to be sold. He certainly didn't want to leave for a week once it was done, but Bet was going off to college and he couldn't regret agreeing to drive her. It was probably the last time he'd see her for years.

The crop prices were pretty good that year – better than 1931, that was for sure. Once the hand-shaking was done, Wild left Bet and Billy eating at the new "soda fountain" in town while he went down to the general store. He had to pick up Bet's suitcase, anyway; that had come from her scholarship money, but they'd spent a little extra to have her initials stamped on it, EHP, and Wild had kicked in for the satin lining so her clothes wouldn't get beat up on the trip. But he'd also seen something in the window of the Carson general store that he couldn't quite believe.

"How do," the clerk said, when Wild walked in. "Spending that corn money already?" he added, seeing Wild's beat-up farmer's trousers and, probably, the look in his eye.

"Might aim to," Wild said. "Had a question for you about that contraption in your window."

"The typewriter? You care to try it out?" the man asked, moving towards the window.

"No, just wondering. It says on the price card, only twenty four dollars," Wild said. "I never seen a typewriter for twenty-four dollars, is it broken?"

"No, we don't sell broken or second-hand here!" the man said, sounding slightly offended. "It's the new Royal model, the Signet."

"Why's it so cheap, then?"

"It's built real simple. It's not meant for newspaper men or the like. They're selling it mostly for housewives, or for folks who want nice big print to read. Light, too, only weighs ten pounds. You thinking of your wife?"

"Nah, she's got real nice handwriting," Wild said absently. "Could a boy use it?"

"How old?"

"Fifteen. I got a kid brother likes to write."

"Oh, sure. Good to learn young, too. Typewriters are the future – why, in another ten or fifteen years nobody'll write anything down."

Wild laughed. "I'll believe that when I see it. Twenty-four you say."

"Yep, and for twenty-five I'll throw in an extra ink ribbon."

"That sounds fine."

"Happy to be of service," the man said, ringing twenty five dollars into his cash register.

"And I need to pick up an order we put in by mail – should be here, we got the receipt," Wild said, handing him the slip of paper. "Name of Wild Mayer, big suitcase."

"Right! Got that right here for you," the man said, pulling it out from under the counter. It was wrapped in brown paper, and Wild peeped under a fold just to make sure it wasn't damaged. "Suitcase was paid with the order so that'll be twenty five for the rest."

Wild handed over the cash and took possession of the bulky carton, carrying it awkwardly back to the soda fountain under one arm, Bet's suitcase under his other.

"Wild, what'd you spend your fool money on?" Bet asked, as he pushed his way inside. He set the box down on the counter next to Billy and handed her the suitcase.

"I got a present for the novelist," he said, nodding at Billy. "Open 'er up."

"For me?" Billy asked, and then went pale when he looked inside. "Is it real? It ain't broken?"

"I thought that too, but they had 'em cheap at the store," Wild said. "Man said they're not very complicated, is why. Figure you'll need it so you don't spend as much time scratchin' away and more time on your lessons."

"Wild," Bet said.

"It was only twenty dollars," he lied, just a little. "We made it back in the corn this year. Anyhow, you won't have to put up with it clacking, Bet," he added with a grin, tapping the suitcase. "Come on. Finish up, let's go home. No, no typing in the truck," he added, as Billy started to lift the typewriter out. "You just admire it until we're home."

Wild and Bet left two days later, Wild with his father's old Army bag and Bet with her suitcase, packed as full as a hope chest with clothes and books, new pencils, a thick coat with extra lining for the cold Chicago winter, and a few things Mama gave her to brighten up her room.

Mama hadn't birthed Bet, and she hadn't known her more than to smile at until she was six, but she had raised her from then, and she cried when they said goodbye. Bet hugged her awkwardly and then stepped back so Mama could be sad in peace, since it felt like half the town had come down to the farm to see her off. Sarah and the rest of the Mullers were there, and of course Lentz Platter and his family to give her one last blessing, and a couple of distant Platter cousins, and some other curious folks. Wild hugged Mama goodbye, promised to deliver Bet safely, and bundled her into the truck.

"Thank God that's over," Bet said as they left the farm. "I love Mama and the boys, Wild, but what a fuss."

"Well, I imagine it'll be the last fuss we see for a time, at least," Wild said. "It's pretty flat from here to Chicago, and mostly farms the whole way. You prepared to be stuck in a car with me for three days?"

"Harder for you going back alone," she said. "Imagine three days in a truck with nothing but corn to look at."

"Won't be so bad. I might pick up someone hitching, least I'll get some conversation. Now, run me through the route one more time."

"If we head north through Oklahoma and Kansas, we'll hit Nebraska," she said. "And the maps at the bank say that the Lincoln Highway picks up in Nebraska and can take us straight east to Chicago."

"You sure it's not faster just to cut across Missouri?"

"I thought so, but I guess the Lincoln Highway's still faster, and the roads north from here are better than the ones in Missouri."

"Well, you're the college girl," Wild said. "If we make it to Chicago in three days I'll be satisfied."

Wild had been looking forward to the drive; it was a long trip, but he didn't want to send Bet alone on the train, and this way he could inspect this school for himself. Even so, he was already missing Adie and Iscah fiercely by the time they reached the sign marking the Texas border, and both he and Bet were noticing something that wasn't...right.

"Look at the farms, Wild," Bet whispered, as they rolled through the panhandle of Oklahoma.

"I don't think I want to," he answered, because the world had gone grey. The farms had been steadily less impressive as they went north, but Wild had chalked that up to the harvest being in. Now they were passing fields where the harvest hadn't come in, couldn't come in, not the way the plants were stunted. Other fields obviously hadn't seen a harvest in at least two years.

"Is this what they were talking about?" Bet asked. "The drought?"

"Must be," Wild said. In the distance, a little eddy of wind swept dust up into a cone, then died out just as quickly. "I heard farms were failing but this is somethin' else."

They passed through a few small towns but there were no cars on the road, and not many people. He would have been relieved when they entered Kansas, but it was worse there. There was a haze in the air, and it felt gritty on his skin when he stopped to refuel the truck.

He'd thought he and Bet might talk or sing some songs, something to pass the time, but they were both shocked into silence, Wild watching the road, Bet staring out at the wasteland they passed through. Sometimes they saw farmers trying to work the land, but more often they saw empty houses. When they stopped in Garden City for the night, it felt like a parody of the name. Wild noticed that the windows of the rooming-house they found were sealed with gummed paper.

"Keeps the dust out," the owner said, when he asked about it. "You folks from out west?"

"Texas panhandle," Wild replied, a little proudly.

"Hear they're starting to get it too. You seen Oklahoma?"

"I have, sir," Wild said, voice dropping. "Two years of drought did all that?"

"I couldn't say, I don't farm. Barely make a living renting out rooms, these days. Normally I wouldn't take one-night guests, but, well." He shrugged. "There's a Depression on and the land's gone to dust. For all I know it's Armageddon. Everyone seems to have gone to Hell or California and I'm sure I don't know the difference."

"Well, we thank you for the hospitality," Wild said.

"Return business appreciated," the man told him with a dry smile, and left him and Bet to settle in.

It got better the next day, when they escaped into Nebraska. Here was green again, at least a little, and some signs of recent harvests. The truck had a thin film of Kansas dust on it, but even that started to blow away when they found the Lincoln Highway and really picked up speed.

"I didn't know a road could be so smooth," Bet said, as the highway stretched out before them, even and dark.

"Some of the roads in Lubbock are like this. Bet you every street in Chicago is paved," he added.

"God bless Chicago, then," she replied.

"Don't go getting fancy city-lady ideas on me, now," he said. "You got to study and get your education. I ain't saying I never had fun," he added, before she could reply tartly. "I'm just saying, it ought to be clean fun. No fast-living nonsense."

"Imagine me living fast," she laughed. "I promise, Wild."

"And if you ain't like it you can always come home. You just send a telegram or a letter and I'll send you money for the train or I'll come fetch you."

"When you were in Lubbock, did you ever worry folks would think…" Bet began, then fell silent before continuing. "Did you worry they'd call you a bumpkin? Or a hick? Chicago's a big city, bigger than Lubbock even."

"Well, now, I didn't worry exactly," Wild said. "A few did speak unkindly, at first. I suppose you can't do what I did to fix it."

"What'd you do?"

"Beat the tar out of them, generally."

"You didn't!"

"I was bigger'n most of 'em. I don't recommend it for a woman, though."

"Well, I could try," Bet said.

"Thing is, Bet, we *are* bumpkins. Lea's the back end of nowhere north of the back of beyond. No electricity, no indoor plumbing, barely anyone finishes schooling, and everything's rusted or held together with twine. But all that means is we know how to make do. I wasn't hitting 'em because of what they called me, but because they figured they were better than I was when I knew that just wasn't the case. It's easy to go to college in Chicago if you were born there. Takes strength to go to college in Chicago if you had to pull yourself out of north Texas to get there."

"And if the other girls snub me?"

"It ain't like Lea where there's only fifteen girls to be friends with. You'll find plenty of friends. They're all there to learn like you are, anyway, and once they see how smart you are they'll be friends if only to steal your lessons."

"They wouldn't!"

Wild laughed. "You want to make friends in college, my advice is, offer to help. The classes are hard, you have to study together. And you know how to cook and sew – the food in Lubbock wasn't any good. Make some fried chicken and share it around."

Bet nodded, still looking a little moody.

"People keep saying Lon'd be real proud of Iscah, and I think that's true," Wild said, finally, "but it's a strange thing to say. It ain't like I had more than a passing hand in making her and Lon none at all in making me. Your daddy would be much more proud knowing you were going to be an educated lady. And I'm sure your mama would too," he added, because it was rare anyone talked about Sarah and Bet's mama, who was lost to the flu the same as Wild's father.

"Daddy said I got my smarts from her."

Wild grinned. "Lon was a good man but he weren't a particularly bright one, that's true."

"Well, I'll try to do him proud," Bet said. "I been thinking, now that I'm in college, you think I should go by Elizabeth?"

"I don't think I could call you Elizabeth with a straight face, but you go where your heart desires, Bet," Wild said. "Look, there's Iowa City – let's find somewhere to put our heads."

The next day they arrived in Chicago, and once Wild made the harrowing exit from the Lincoln Highway, they stopped and asked a friendly-looking fellow to point them in the direction of the University of Chicago. They tried not to stare at the skyscrapers, at the buildings crammed cheek-by-jowl, at the bustle of the World's Fair of 1933 being built in the distance.

"Jesus, Wild, your Adie sure picked a place," Bet said, staring out at the campus, at the young men and women going to and fro with arms full of books. A horn blew behind them and Wild pulled over, still gawking like a rube at the spires and eaves of the buildings.

"Gosh, Bet, forget I said anything," he told her. "You put on all the fancy lady airs you like."

"Aw, Wild."

"I mean it, you'll need 'em," he laughed. "Hey, miss! Hey miss!" he called through Bet's open window, and a woman walking past looked up, irritated and startled. "Which way to the women's residence hall?"

"Why should I tell you?" she asked.

"My sister Bet here's gonna be a famous mathematician, I gotta deliver her," he said, and Bet covered her face with one hand. The woman turned and came right up to the truck, curious.

"You're a new student?" she asked Bet, who nodded, mortified. "With the mathematics program?"

"Statistics," Bet said. "With the Social Service Administration."

"Where're you coming from?"

"Lea, Texas," Wild said.

"Gosh! Sorry, I thought maybe you were going to start trouble," she said. "Just go south until you hit sixtieth, then turn left. If you hit Woodlawn you're past it."

"Obliged, miss," Wild said.

"Welcome to the University," the woman said, patting Bet's arm through the window. Bet looked out at her, letting her other hand fall from her face and beaming.

"It's the most beautiful place I ever saw," she said.

The woman laughed. "It's the most beautiful place in the world, is why! Good luck," she added, and walked on while Wild pulled away again.

The women's residence hall was, predictably, full of young women, and Wild wasn't actually allowed inside; he hovered by the truck, waiting while Bet went in with her suitcase and found her room. People came and went, some casting curious looks his way, and some of the women giggled and whispered in ways he recognized as universal, the same as they might at a social at Lea.

When Bet emerged, he wiped clammy hands on his trousers, and accepted her excited hug.

"Wild, you won't believe," she said. "There was a woman in there saying there's four thousand students here alone. That's more people than Lea and Carson combined."

"Well, I trust you'll beat 'em all," Wild said, pulling her tight. "This is your ticket out," he whispered in her ear. "Take it and run like hell, Bet."

"I love you, Wild," she whispered back, and then let him go, wiping her eyes.

"You get on now," Wild said. "Go settle in. I'll wire Mama you made it all right."

He watched Bet run back up into the women's residence hall, already chattering with other women headed likewise, and he smiled. He wasn't sure exactly what Adie had gotten Bet into, but it was clear it was the best thing for her.

"Goodbye, Bet," he said softly, and went to find a telegraph office, to wire Mama and Lentz Platter that Bet was safely arrived.

Chicago was much too bright and full of people for Wild to linger; it made him uneasy, the sheer population of the place. Once he'd telegraphed home he headed for the outskirts, parking the truck outside the city limits and sleeping in it that night.

On the road the next morning he picked up a fellow who was heading to Santa Fe and was willing to ride with him nearly the whole way to Lea. He gave his name as Odie, and when Wild said he was headed to the panhandle, Odie looked intrigued.

"You're going *back* to the waste?" he asked. "Why on Earth?"

"It ain't waste in Lea," Wild told him. "We got rain the last few years, and the earth is good there."

"I didn't know there was a place in the middle west that was still the case."

"Plenty of good farmland in Texas, if you know how to keep it," Wild said, a little annoyed.

Odie held up his hands innocently. "No aspersions on your homeland, my friend, other than I'll step off before I get there."

"Most do," Wild answered, mollified, because he recognized the harmlessness of it. Odie gave him a smile, then tipped his hat forward and went off to sleep while Wild drove. That night Wild slept while Odie drove, which was damn decent of him.

It was a tragedy to leave the Lincoln Highway, but at least he was used to the rough roads south, and when they turned off the highway, Wild knew they were that much closer to home.

They were just south of Garden City the following day when the storm hit. Wild was mostly concentrating on the road, starting to develop an ache behind his eyes from so much driving, when Odie said, "Mayer, look at this."

Wild turned his head, and at first it was difficult to tell what he was seeing. It was like seeing mountains when you knew the country was flat. There was a roiling cloud of blackness on the horizon, rising up towards them, off to the west. And it was moving.

"Jesus," Wild said. "Must be one of them dust storms."

"We're gonna die," Odie proclaimed.

"We're not gonna die," Wild retorted, but he couldn't help worrying. He sped up and kept going, keeping one eye on the storm while the other scanned the horizon. By the time he saw what he was looking for, the blackness of the dust storm filled the sky like a wall, and he skewed the truck around without any concern for the tires or the engine, turning into a narrow dirt road with a farmhouse nearby.

"We're running for the barn," he said, as they bumped down the long lane. "When I pull up you jump out and get the doors open."

Odie was breathing heavy, but his nerves were sound; as soon as Wild pulled to a stop he was out, pulling the barn door open, even though the cloud was almost on them. Wild didn't know if the farm was abandoned, but there wasn't time to ask permission; he shot the truck through the doors and slammed it to a stop, turning the engine off to keep from pulling dust into it. Odie closed the barn doors, clambered back into the truck, and pulled the door shut.

The howl that rose up around them as the storm hit would sit with Wild Mayer all his life. It was a high, whistling thing, and it brought with it a choking sensation in the throat, a harshness that bit into the skin. The air was grey, filled with fine particles, and Wild couldn't imagine what it was like outside the barn, this choking dust that stuck to the skin, clinging to any hint of dampness. Through the dirty windows of the truck he could see flashes of lightning, though he never heard any thunder – and there certainly wasn't any rain.

He thought Odie was praying, but the howling was so loud; Wild bowed his head over the wheel and thought of Adie and Iscah, and wondered what he'd do if the storms began to come south, into Wheeler County. If his good land greyed out like the farms hereabouts, if the storms blew up and Iscah started to cough, what would he do? Sell up? Abandon the farm? Pack the windows with gummed paper and try to stay on?

The howling and the flashing just kept on, it felt like forever. The dust began to cake on their skin, thin films of it turning them as grey as the farms and the air. Wild wept just to keep his eyes clear, and the tears made dots on his forearms.

What if it just never ended, he thought, terror filling him. What if for the rest of time it was just the wind and the dust, until even the barn they sat in was buried?

But it did end, eventually, and with the end of the screaming wind and the choking dust came a return to banal normality that was almost comical. He was hungry, and Odie had to take a piss, and both of them wanted a wash.

Outside, the air was still grey and the dust was in silent drifts, three feet high in some places, burying anything it couldn't scour away. They trudged silently up to the farmhouse nearby, and found it abandoned when they knocked and the door swung open. Odie drew water from a pump in the yard, emptying two or three basins of mud before it ran clear, while Wild scrounged for food. Eventually he found a single can of creamed corn, and they were so desperate they ate it cold.

"How fast can we get to Texas?" Odie asked, shoveling cold corn mush into his mouth.

"You don't want to go that far," Wild replied. "I can leave you at the Texas border and you'll pick up someone to take you to Santa Fe faster."

Odie scratched at his now-clean arms absently. "You say you got rain in Lea?"

"Have had for the last few years, anyhow."

"No dust storms?"

"No. No dust storms."

Odie considered this. "Well, I hope to God it stays that way."

"Me too," Wild said.

"There's railroad work in Santa Fe. What work you got in Lea?"

"Not much. What church're you?"

"No particular."

"Well, I suppose if I put in a good word, the Lutherans'd find you something to do," Wild said. "But if you want my advice, you'll keep on west. They say California's the land of gold."

Odie shivered. "Whatever gets me out of this kind of country."

They drove on dust for a good five miles before they left Kansas. Wild just about cried with relief as they passed into Oklahoma, and then into Texas not long after.

He left Odie at the Texas border. The man said he'd look him up if he was ever back out that way, though that seemed very unlikely to Wild.

He pulled into Lea well after dark, with the streets empty and quiet. He brought the truck up to the gate of the old church's fence, stopping curiously. Climbing out, he could see something had changed; over the church doorway, where before there had been a plain white keystone, now there was a small statue of a woman, head gently inclined, robes drawn loosely about her, slim hands clasped in prayer. Around her were delicate roses carved into the adobe. He'd seen something like it on one of the Catholic churches in Lubbock; a fellow student had told him it was the Virgin of Guadalupe. You could always tell by the roses, he'd said.

Wild went right up to the gate, resting hands on a fence he'd helped build years before, and felt his pulse in his scars. He looked up at Mary, her blank stone eyes looking at nothing in particular, her lips curved in a smile.

"I ain't saying I'm not grateful," he said to her, not expecting or getting a reaction from the stone. "I ain't saying it's not her place. What I'm saying is you let me send Bet out into that big world, you found her a place in it, and you'd better keep her safe."

Mary didn't look at him, and the rose window didn't move, but the church nevertheless gave the impression it understood.

"You look out for her now, 'cause I ain't able," he said. "And if you got a bigger purpose for Bet, I won't argue, but you better make sure it's worthy of her."

He let go of the fencepost he'd been gripping, and the pulse in his scars abruptly ceased.

"Just so as we understand each other," he added, and got back in the truck.

THIRTEEN

WINTER BECAME WILD'S favorite season, that year. There wasn't much to be done on the farm as long as the cold weather held, and where before he had been restless with inactivity, now he felt settled, dug in.

He spent hours and hours with Iscah – last winter he had too, just after she was born, but she'd been an infant then, and with the planting and growing season, and then the harvest, this was the first time he'd had much time or energy to just be with her since she was born.

After Adie nursed her in the morning, Wild would take her and wrap the two of them up in a blanket, reading to her from whatever was handy – the weekly paper usually took two or three days to get through, and then there was the almanac, the seed catalog, the Bible or some of Adie's books. Billy wouldn't let him borrow the Science Fiction, claiming he'd read that to her himself, but Iscah liked pictures best anyway. The Sears winter catalog, with its color plates, entranced her. Or he'd spread out a blanket in front of the fireplace after building the fire up and play nonsense card games with her and Lonny, or let Lonny, now five and proud of his new schooling, pretend to teach her to read. Sometimes he'd leave the two of them in Billy and Moze's care and go off to do any chores that needed doing, splitting firewood or bringing more in, going into town if Mama or Adie needed anything.

One afternoon, while Billy clacked away on the typewriter with Iscah "helping" on his lap, Wild helped Moze put together a kit he'd bought out of the back of one of Billy's magazines with money he'd made helping Tex Junior during the harvest. The magazine ad called it a MYSTERY CRYSTAL, but Wild had seen them before – it was just a crude radio receiver that didn't need electrical power to make it run, hooked up to a speaker loud enough to make the radio's weak signal audible. He warned Moze they might not pick up much; there was a radio station in Wheeler that the radios in town could get, but they had much bigger receiver rods.

Moze, when Wild mentioned this, looked determined. "Well, if we can't get it, we got to get a bigger receiver," he told Wild.

"But the power runs through the wire too, right?" Wild asked.

"Yep," Moze said.

"So we don't want it setting the house on fire, Moze."

"Oh," Moze said thoughtfully, but Wild could tell the discussion wasn't over yet. Still, Moze seemed pleased enough trying to tune in Wheeler. He mostly got slightly louder static than the normal static, but you could make out a word or a few bars of music sometimes.

In early March, Moze asked Wild if he could get up onto the roof. It was iced over and Moze was still pretty small, though he was nimbler than Billy had been when he was ten. "What d'you want to do such a fool thing for?" Wild asked, finally.

"I got some wire when you took us into Lea," Moze said. "I got an idea to tune in the radio."

Wild stared at him. "You ain't thinking of the lightning rod."

"Yeah! It'll work, Wild, I know it will!"

"You are gonna fry us all in our beds," Wild said.

"If we run the wire up to the rod and then down to the radio it'll work so long as there ain't any lightning!"

"And what happens the first time there is? I got to run out on the roof and pull it down and get struck again myself, probably," Wild said.

But then it occurred to him, there already was a wire running from the lightning rod to the ground – the grounding wire, that he'd helped Lon plaster to the back of the house years ago.

He looked at Moze, who had Mama's stubborn streak, and wondered just how long he'd be able to keep him off the roof, anyway.

That evening, having chopped open some of the plaster in the blistering cold and with numb fingers wrapped the antenna wire around the grounding wire, Wild and Moze came inside, Moze carrying the wire carefully. He attached it to the radio and turned the little dial carefully. Static, then silence…

And then music poured out.

There was a crash from the kitchen, and Mama appeared in the doorway.

"What in the name of – " she looked at Moze, beaming over his radio, and then at Wild, who felt as startled as she looked. "Is that the radio, Moze?"

"Yes, Mama!" Moze said cheerfully. Billy and Lonny crowded around, and Adie came in carrying Iscah.

"You can't have her, you're a block of ice," she said, when Wild reached for Iscah. "Go thaw out."

"Saw out," Iscah agreed. Wild squatted by the fire, warming his hands, while Billy pulled Mama into a dance to the music and Lonny danced all on his own.

"We got to take the wire out anytime we ain't using it," Wild said. "It's hitched to the lightning rod and liable to kill us all if we ain't careful."

"Well, at least we'd go out dancing," Adie told him, grinning.

The music stopped, and an advertisement came on. The hour was rung, and Wild expected another song, but instead a man's voice said, "And now we bring you a special presentation broadcast nationwide, from the office of the White House of the United States of America."

Billy, who had still been dancing Mama around the room, stopped. Moze stared down at the radio.

"Ladies and gentlemen, the President of the United States."

Adie sat abruptly. Wild stood up from his place on the hearth.

My friends, I want to talk for a few minutes with the people of the United States about banking, the voice said.

"Is that really the President?" Lonny asked.

"Hush, Lon," Mama said, pulling him into her, sitting down next to Adie.

I want to tell you what has been done in the last few days, why it was done, and what the next steps are going to be.

Adie looked up at Wild. They'd all heard that Roosevelt was closing banks; Wild had read about it to Iscah in the paper, trying to keep his voice steady, but he knew they'd all heard the worry in it. He'd put a call into Lentz Platter and been assured that Lea's little bank was just fine, but he knew Platter was concerned too.

That was nothing compared to now, though; if the President was talking about it on the radio it might be worse. Somehow, much worse.

They listened in silence through the whole of it – not a long speech, really. Quarter of an hour, if that. By the end Wild was sitting too, but in relief more than anything.

Why, when you heard the run on the banks laid out like that, sensible and plain, by the President himself, it seemed like the last thing you wanted to do was worry. Clearly they'd put the right man in the job, someone who knew what he was about.

Confidence and courage are the essentials of success in carrying out our plan, Roosevelt told them. *You people must have faith; you must not be stampeded by rumors or guesses. Let us unite in banishing fear. We have provided the machinery to restore our financial system; it is up to you to support and make it work. It is your problem no less than it is mine. Together we cannot fail.*

Another voice came on, and then music again.

"I'll go pull the wire for tonight," Wild said quietly. Nobody disagreed. When he came back inside from disengaging the antenna, they were still sitting there.

"I think he sounds like Adie when she was teaching," Billy said finally. "Or like a good preacher."

"You think he's telling the truth, Wild?" Adie asked.

"Well, if it's a lie it'll catch up to him soon enough," Wild replied. "But I think he's telling the truth."

"Imagine the day," Mama said. "I got to hear my own President speak right to me through the radio."

"Did you know, before you were born, women couldn't even vote?" Adie asked Lonny, who shook his head. "A lady in this country couldn't vote until 1920. And now your mama got to hear the President she voted for over the radio. Isn't that something?"

"Did you vote Roosevelt, Mama?" Billy asked.

"Course I did. Hoover wasn't no good for this country and anyway I like that wife he's got," Mama said, dusting her skirt off and standing. "Well. That's enough excitement for one night, I think."

Lying in bed that night, with Iscah in her crib nearby, Wild could feel how hard Adie was thinking.

"Best out with it," he said softly. She kissed his shoulder.

"I know you said the Lea bank was all right," she said. "But what happens if the bank fails? I never really had to be concerned about it before. It was just me. But now we got the farm and the baby, and your Mama and brothers – what happens to Bet if the bank fails?"

"Bank won't fail. I talked to Lentz Platter. Anyway, you heard Roosevelt."

"But if it did."

Wild shrugged. "We own the land. Don't have to pay a mortgage. I'd need to borrow to get seed for planting and pay the property tax, and we'd have a lean summer, a lean few years paying back the loan, maybe. Bet'd have to come home, likely, or find a job in Chicago, but she's smart, she'd do fine. As long as the crops came in we wouldn't be so much worse off than we are now."

"But the crops aren't coming in, not in Oklahoma and Kansas," she said. He should never have told her about the dust storm, but it had all poured out of him in a confession when he got home – he'd had to tell someone or he'd choke on it.

"No," he said. "They ain't."

"Lea needs the rain."

"We always have. That ain't a change. But the bank ain't failed, and so long as the rain falls here, well, we'll be all right."

She sighed. "I never thought I'd settle. Didn't think I'd find the right place. Never really fit anywhere. I didn't think I'd have to worry about a baby, about how to feed her and protect her. It's all so fragile, Wild."

"I know," Wild said. He thought about the time he'd asked her about being Science Fiction, and what she'd said. He thought about how Lea had the rain other places didn't. "But I'd give my dyin' breath for both of you, so until it comes to dying, I ain't fixed to worry."

She nodded into his shoulder. "That's why I picked you."

He laughed. "Well, good. Glad my martyrdom got me a bride."

"You should hook Moze's radio up again tomorrow, if it's a fine day," she said sleepily. "I wouldn't mind a dance or two."

HARVEST 1933

BILLY "SOLD A story" – that's how the publishers called it, he told Wild earnestly – in 1933. He sent it off in July, and didn't hear back until after the harvest, but with the acceptance letter came both a check for $15 and a promise of two free copies when it was published. It wasn't one of the funny stories, but a high-adventure yarn about a moon farmer who was kidnapped by space pirates. Wild detected a whiff of wish fulfillment in it, which is maybe why it sold.

"Fifteen dollars, that's not too bad," he said, when Billy showed him the check. "What're you going to do with the money?"

"Buy some carbon papers by mail-order, I expect," Billy said. "That way I can send a story two places at once. And maybe some candy for Lonny and Iscah. Reckon I'll save the rest. Might have to last me some time," he added with a grin.

It occurred to Wild that Billy was nearly sixteen, no longer a boy; as tall as him now, and broader at the shoulder. Bill had already told Mama and the others, then come running out to where Wild was splitting wood to show him, but it seemed like maybe there was something else behind it too.

"Wild, I been thinking," he said, as he sat down on one of the unsplit logs. "It was a pretty good harvest this year."

"Better than the last two, that's for sure," Wild replied, grunting as he swung the axe.

"And what with you got a year of college, and Bet in school up north, I reckon two college educated is enough for any family."

Wild stopped and wiped his forehead. "Well, if you ain't want to try for college that's fine, Bill. What're you thinkin' to do? Another good couple of years while you finish out school and I might could stake you on a plot to farm. Lon didn't want to split the land up but I figure we could go in as a partnership. If we do well, maybe make an offer on that ugly southern field Tex Junior ain't ever want to farm."

"That's the thing. I'm not sure it's worth me finishing out school," Billy said. Wild frowned. "Wild, I'm not like you and Bet. I do all right but I don't see the point of another two years of the stuff. Hear me out," he said, when Wild opened his mouth. "If I leave school now and you take me on as a hired hand – I don't want to be partner, I just want a wage and board – then I'd be able to do all the chores, and help with the planting and harvest, and instead of school I'd have time to write."

"To write!" Wild said. "What, more Science Fiction?"

"I got fifteen dollars for a story, Wild," Billy said. "And I reckon I can do it again. It don't take me hardly a week anymore to write one."

"Bill, I like your stories, but it took you two years to sell one."

"But now, see, folks will read it. And the editor says he wouldn't mind seein' more. And if some other editor sees I'm a good reliable regular, I might get on somewhere else."

Wild scratched the back of his head. "I suppose folks make a living doing it," he said slowly.

"Some do. And if I can't, well, in four years I'll be twenty, I'll get a loan and take you up on that partnership. You took over the farm when you were nineteen."

Wild considered it. He didn't like the idea of Billy leaving school, and Mama or Adie or both were likely to have some strong objections to it. But the kid had a point – he had enough math for the farm, more than enough letters, and the rest was just window dressing to keep young men out of trouble, really.

"Tell you what," Wild said. "I'll take you on as a hand at ten dollars plus bed and board a month, or cut it to five dollars and a ten percent share in the crop when it comes in."

The percentage was a better deal by far and they both knew it, but it was also perilous; if the crops failed or didn't do well, he'd take a loss. Billy considered it.

"Seven dollars and a seven percent share," he finally said.

"Done," Wild told him. "But Mama has to approve."

"But you'll back me?"

Wild spat in the dirt. "Suppose I will. Mama might hide me for it but I wasn't bringin' in fifteen dollars for a story when I was your age."

Billy nodded. "That's decent of you, Wild."

"Well, you write me that story I been wanting about Texans bein' the only folks suited to settling on the sun," Wild said.

"Can't no fool settle on the sun!"

"There ain't farmers on the moon, either," Wild pointed out.

"Well, there will be someday."

"You run on up now and don't mention this to Mama yet," Wild ordered. "Wait a few days so she don't just think you have stars in your eyes. We'll go into Lea tomorrow and you can cash the check."

The next day was a reasonably fine day for late October, and Adie was feeling housebound and Mama had some things to buy, so Wild crammed Adie, Iscah, and Mama into the cab next to him, settled Bill, Lonnie, and Moze under a thick rug in the back of the truck, and hauled the whole Platter and Mayer traveling circus into town. He left the women off at the Dry Goods, told Moze to take Lonnie to the seed store to entertain him, and took Bill into the bank to cash the check.

He saw Lentz Platter speaking with a clerk while Bill waited to cash his check, and Platter spotted him too, waving him over. Wild waited politely until they were done talking and then walked up.

"Mr. Platter," he said, giving the man a respectful nod. "How do, sir?"

"How do, Wild," Mr. Platter replied. "How's your wife and the baby?"

"Fine! They're over at the Dry Goods with our Mama."

"Glad to hear it. And how's that sister of yours? I had a letter from her last month, but women tell their family things they won't tell their sponsors."

Wild grinned. "She's well I think, sir. Working with some good philanthropic ladies, as I'm sure you know."

"Yes, she said she had a summer job teaching immigrants. I hope she's not developing any low habits."

"I don't think so. And she's doin' real good work at the school. You can't beat her for numbers. I don't understand a wink of it but I suppose that's why she's there and not me," he said.

"It must be a trial to your Mama not to see her this year."

"There was talk of a train ticket for Christmas, but we don't like to have her travel alone. I suppose we'll have her down next summer – I can go up and fetch her again, maybe take Mrs. Mayer to see Chicago."

"What a fine idea! Travel is good for the soul. Now – " Platter was about to say something, but he spotted something over Wild's shoulder; Wild turned and saw one of the Baptist farmers speaking urgently with Platter's head clerk. After a second, they hustled over to him, and Wild stepped back. Their voices were uneasy, and Wild could tell whatever had happened, it was something bad. After another moment, Platter gestured to the half-door that divided the lobby from the cashiers, and the Baptist was hurried through, picking up the phone to Wheeler. Platter watched, pensive, and Wild stepped in close again.

Anything I can help with?" he asked, tipping his head subtly towards the phone.

"Don't know. There's been a murder, I guess. He came in here like his ass was on fire," Platter murmured. "Hey, Bell," he said, as the farmer hung up the phone. "What's the news?"

"Sheriff says he can't be out before tonight," Bell, the farmer, replied in quiet tones.

"Who is it?"

"The Joseph Johnsons."

"Another whole family?" Wild asked.

Bell nodded. "Just come from the farm. It's a slaughter."

"Like the Roggenwolf?" Wild asked.

"Might be. Ain't you the one found the Fischers, few years back?"

"Me and Tex Muller, yeah."

"Anyone standing guard up there?" Platter asked.

"Not just now," Bell said. "It's Mayer, ain't it?"

"Yes sir," Wild said.

"You want to come up, see for yourself?"

Wild didn't, he didn't want to at all, but he was also curious. And after all, someone had to.

"My family's in town, I can't just run off," he said. "Let me get my brother, and then if you can take me up there I suppose I ought to go."

Bell nodded. Wild found Bill waiting for him, having just taken care of the check.

"Listen," Wild said softly, urgently. "I got business I got to see to outside of town. I didn't expect it but it's important, Bill."

"What is it?" Bill asked. Wild glanced around.

"You remember when the Roggenwolf got the Fischers?" he asked. Bill nodded. "They think there's been another. Some Baptists this time. They want me to go and have a look, but I can't run up there with the whole family still in town. I want you to round 'em up and get them in the truck, you get me?"

"Sure, Wild," Bill said.

"Take them home, tell Mama and Adie not to tell anyone what's happened. You get your rifle and give Adie mine, and if anyone who ain't me comes down the road to the farm, you keep them out of our house, you hear me?"

Bill nodded.

"Even if it's someone you know. Unless it's me, or Sarah or Tex Junior, you keep them out of our home."

"I will, Wild," Bill said.

"Someone'll run me home when I'm done. I'll call if I can. Get on, now," Wild said, and Bill ran from the bank. Wild saw him catch Adie and Mama in front of the dry goods and hustle them into the truck.

"All right, Bell," he said to the Baptist farmer. "Let's shake a leg."

Bell had a big old truck, even older than Wild's, but it ran fast enough. Platter said he'd point the sheriff towards the farm when he arrived, so there was no reason to linger, anyhow.

"You know Joe Johnson?" Bell asked, as they headed east.

"Just to speak to. Too old to be in school with me, not old enough his kids were. Baptists and Lutherans, you know how it is," Wild said.

"Suppose I do. Anyway, he ain't been a Baptist in about a year," Bell said.

"How's that?" Wild asked, surprised.

"He's one of Rohlf's flock now. Converted at a revival, he got that old-time religion," Bell said, with a hint of disgust. "They were getting ready to sell up and resettle on the Rohlf farm."

"You're sure it's the whole family?" Wild asked.

"Far as I could tell. I wouldn't go in once I saw the blood, thought

I'd better head in and call the sheriff up in Wheeler."

"He have kids?"

"Three," Bell said, gripping the wheel, white-knuckled. "Two boys. Didn't see 'em but that don't mean much."

"Jesus," Wild said.

"Daughter was in the kitchen with Mrs. Johnson. It's…"

"Yeah, I saw Mrs. Fischer," Wild said softly. "Any idea who might've done it? Neighbors get on all right?"

"Mayer, I think you oughta know, before we get there," Bell said. "It looks like Joseph Johnson did it himself."

Wild stared at him. "The hell?"

"Johnson's in the yard with a rifle next to him."

Wild rubbed his eyes. "You imagine he got some kind of mania?"

It would make sense, if Johnson was the Roggenwolf, that he'd eventually do for his own family. It had been three years since the Fischers died, and that family out by Antelope Flats two years ago. Wild hadn't heard of any murders like them since, but if it was Joe Johnson, maybe he'd been…trying to stop.

"Don't know," Bell said. "They say all kinds of things about Rohlf's people, but Johnson had a good head on his shoulders. Loved them kids. It made me send up a few prayers after I saw it, Mayer, I won't lie. Almost there now," he added, turning onto a dirt drive not unlike the one down to Wild's own farm. "I'll stay in the truck if it's all the same to you."

"Probably best," Wild agreed. He could see, even from here, a slumped figure in the farmyard. When he climbed out of the truck, his boots hit hardpan – the kind of dry, cracked soil that wouldn't take footprints. So much for the advice of the detective stories he sometimes managed to find in the back of Billy's pulp magazines.

There was Joseph Johnson, right enough, brains spread across a few square feet of soil. Wild gagged a little, taking in the rifle nearby, and the way Johnson's body looked almost tidy – no wounds on him, except the one under his head, Wild imagined.

He peered through the closest window, into the bedroom behind the kitchen. Two young boys lay in their beds, looking peaceful, almost untouched – except for the wet red stains on their pillows. The younger one looked to be ten or eleven, about Moze's age.

The kitchen door wasn't locked, and when he walked inside there was no illusion of peace here. Wild didn't linger.

"You think it was the Roggenwolf?" Bell asked, as Wild hurried back to the truck.

"Don't know. Sure does look like he did it himself," Wild said, but he couldn't deny what he saw of the women, the hatchet-marks on their bodies, one just a little girl…it looked like the Fischers.

"But the women – "

"Yeah," Wild said. "I don't know, Bell. I ain't the sheriff. Might be Johnson was the Roggenwolf to start with."

"Ain't seen the Johnsons in a month of Sundays," Bell confessed, staring at the front of the house. "They got strange after the revival. Weren't never real social folks – not unfriendly, but they kept to themselves even before."

Wild looked around again, at the hardscrabble farm and the dead man in the yard.

"I ain't know," he said quietly. "Got no answers."

"Should we cover him up, at least?"

"Sheriff wouldn't like it."

"What'd your people do with the Fischers? After, I mean."

Wild shrugged. "Buried 'em. Cousins sold the farm to my brother-in-law. Helped him put up a new Sears house so my sister wouldn't live where they was murdered. This…this is different."

"Cept how it ain't."

"Yeah. Cept how it ain't."

"Our preacher has a real good guard dog," Bell said. "Just whelped, got a bunch of funny-lookin' bull mix pups. Think I might get me one."

"Ain't a bad idea," Wild said. "He got any extra, I'll pay for 'em. Meantime, you want to run me home? Nothing we can do here."

"Sure, I'll take you back to your plot."

The sheriff agreed with Bell; it looked like Johnson had got a mania and done it himself. Maybe even done the Fischers, too, which meant he could close the book on that one, and he mentioned there was a similar one last year up by Wheeler that might fit the bill too. Wild didn't see how someone else could have done it to the Johnsons, so he kept his opinions to himself. It felt wrong, assuming Joe Johnson had the deaths of three families and his own on his head without any proof, but it wasn't his place to say. Wild wasn't the law, anyhow.

Bell came by a few days later with a sack with two squirming, fresh-weaned bull-mix pups in it. Wild had meant to give them to Moze and Lonny, to be trained up as guard dogs for the farm; Moze took to his little brindle fast as anything, dubbing him Buddy, but Lon wrinkled his nose and said he liked the barn cats better.

Wild, a squirming black pup in his hands, wasn't sure what to do until Iscah, toddling into the kitchen behind Adie, let out a squeal. She ran to him, falling over halfway, and Wild set the dog down so that he could help her up. Before he could, the dog had made a beeline for Iscah, and she had squirmed away from Wild to throw both arms around the dog's thick neck. He was a little over half her size, and he licked her face while she laughed.

"Mine," she told Wild, holding the pup close. "My doggie."

Wild raised his eyebrows at Adie. She looked pensive.

"Moze," Wild called, and Moze wandered over, carrying the brindle carefully. "You teach Iscah here how to look after a pup, would you?"

"I don't mind," Moze said. "What're you gonna name him, Iz?"

Iscah plopped onto her butt and the pup threw itself over her lap, heaving out a sigh. She patted him lovingly.

"Show lots," she said.

"Show what now," Wild managed.

"Show lots," Iscah said, hugging the pup's square head. It panted and squeaked at her.

"What is she saying?" Adie asked. "Is it just baby talk? Show lots?"

"No," Mama said, surprising them. Wild glanced back at her. "Xolotl. I think she named him Xolotl. It's a…it was the name of an old god. Your grandmother used to tell me stories about him. It's from…" she waved a hand. "Before Texas, when this was Mexican land. From your grandmother's people."

"Where'd Iscah get it from?" Wild asked.

"Search me. I forgot all about it 'till she said it," Mama said. "Couldn't tell you much about it now anyhow. It comes from your great-granny, darling," she said to Iscah.

Iscah looked up at her and said, "I know. Bisabuela said. Xolotl."

"Bisabuela," Mama said softly. "It means great-granny," she said to Wild.

Wild grinned. The most special little girl in all of Lea, for sure.

FOURTEEN

THE WINTER OF 1933 was a hard, dark one, haunted by the deaths of the Johnsons, not helped any by the bitter cold. Some of the farmers had a crackpot theory that the dust storms to the north were blocking out the sun, making for colder summers and brutal winters, but Adie said that wasn't exactly scientific. She suspected the drought was connected somehow, but who could really say?

There were church socials every once in a while, and Thanksgiving and Christmas of course, but aside from that there wasn't much entertainment to be had in Lea, and the roads were so bad it was difficult to get to Carson or Wheeler. Which was probably why the revivals got to be more and more popular, especially after New Year, when there wasn't much to look forward to for months, until the spring.

Revival probably wasn't the word for it anymore; Dan Rohlf called them Celebration Meetings. They were held in the big barn Rohlf and his congregation had put up, painted with a banner of what they'd taken to calling themselves, the Church of the Redeemed Abandoned. He'd heard from fellas who attended them that there was singing, and Dan would give a speech, and then they'd all get real quiet and do some of that meditating.

And then there'd be coffee and some food, and Dan would meet privately with folks who were poorly in spirit. That was when most people who stayed at the church made their decision, apparently.

But Wild had never gone to one, and didn't really care to, at least until round about March of 1934. Bill was stepping out with one of the Schmidt daughters, and the Schmidts from the lower farm were sort-of members of the Church of the Redeemed Abandoned – they didn't live on the farm or anything, and they still went to the Lutheran church, but Alma went to most of the Celebration Meetings and did meditation, so Bill said. And neither Mama nor Mr. Schmidt wanted Bill Platter and

Alma Schmidt going out without a chaperone, even to a revival, so Wild was elected to go along.

"I don't mind exactly," Wild said to Adie, slicking his hair down and straightening his collar that Saturday morning. "It's just the whole thing seems sorta silly to me."

"Well, I'm sure Lutherans seem silly to someone, somewhere," Adie said, but not with much conviction. "Now, don't you laugh at them either. Bill likes this girl."

"I promise I won't embarrass the family," he said, leaning over to kiss her. Iscah, sitting on the bed and playing at sewing with a bit of scrap rag and a dull needle, got up on her knees for a kiss as well. "You be good for your ma and granny," he told her, kissing her forehead.

"Daddy," Iscah said, giving him a very serious look. "Don't eat nothin'."

"What, with a good roast chicken lunch waiting for me when we get back? I wouldn't," he said.

"Don't eat nothin'," Iscah repeated, her huge dark eyes shadowed.

Wild squatted to be more on a level with her. "I promise I won't, darlin'," he said seriously. She patted his cheek with her little hand, and he leaned into it for a moment before standing. "Now, this place better not be on fire when I get back," he said, putting his hat on and heading out the door. He kissed Mama on the cheek on the way out; Bill was already in the truck, waiting anxiously for him.

"Can I drive, Wild?" he asked.

Wild, who knew what it felt like to want to impress a woman and not really know how, climbed into the passenger's seat. Bill beamed at him and backed the truck around, heading for the main road. "Hey, Iscah said somethin' funny to me just now. Well, maybe not funny, but you know," he said.

"Oh yeah?" Bill asked, clearly not very interested.

"Yeah, she said not to eat nothin' at the revival."

"Huh. Why you think she said that?"

"Don't know, but I promised her," Wild said. He felt a tingling in the very edges of his scars, the tips of the willow patterns pressed into his skin. "You might do the same, Bill."

"No skin off my nose, I ain't hungry. You think they do Communion at this thing, or she got some kind of premonition the potluck casserole's gone off?" Bill joked.

"Who knows. She's a baby, might just be nonsense."

"But," Bill said, because he knew Iscah.

"But," Wild agreed. "I promised."

"Well, then I promise too."

By the time they picked up Bill's girl Alma and made it up to the Rohlf farm, the front yard was full up with cars and trucks. Bill parked them on the road and they stepped out of the truck to the sound of singing.

I come to the garden alone
While the dew is still on the roses
And the voice I hear
Falling on my ear
The Son of God discloses…

People were packing their way into the barn, and Wild took a seat behind Bill and Alma to give them a little peace, though he still kept his eye on them. When the singing was done, with the clattering of tambourines and the distant plunk of a piano, everyone applauded, though what they were applauding, he couldn't be sure.

Dan Rohlf, in his ordinary everyday chore-clothes, was at the front of the barn, barely visible from here, but when he spoke people fell silent, and his voice rolled across them like a wave.

"Good morning, my friends," he called, and there was a murmur of voice. "I said, good morning!"

Good morning! the crowd roared.

"And beautiful it is. Truly," Rohlf said, "the glory of the spirit is available to all who are willing to make a sacrifice."

Wild felt a shiver run over his skin. The way Rohlf said *sacrifice* chilled him in a way he couldn't define.

"As farmers we don't think much about the garden, the humble garden," Rohlf was continuing. "We think of the fields to be plowed. But the kitchen garden, with its potatoes and chickens, its leafy greens and its beans! That is one more place we might find safety and protection, nourishment, and these are the works of salvation."

His eyes roamed over the congregation, and Wild was reminded of his time in Lubbock, of the professors there – one in particular who liked to lecture rather than demonstrate.

"All gardens are humble to a man used to tilling the soil for a living. Plowing a hundred acres of good land is a virtue; how does a garden compare? And yet," Rohlf said. "And yet."

There was a chorus of amens before he even got to the point. Wild squinted.

"A garden is still a great work of the spirit," Rohlf said. "Now you've heard – surely you've heard," he rumbled, "other preachers on the radio, in big tents or in rented halls, speaking about the problems of the world. Speaking about redemption and salvation. And they're quick to lay blame, ain't they?"

The crowd roared back that they were, they were.

"They blame everyone! The Jews. The Catholics. The government. For all I know they blame you and me," Rohlf recited. "They want to blame everyone from here to Kingdom come!"

It seemed like some kind of cue; without any other signal from Rohlf, the piano broke into *Thy Kingdom Come, O God*.

It seemed a little tedious to Wild. He'd never really cottoned to that particular hymn, but the folks sang it with spirit. It was six verses of more or less standard cant, so Wild waited it out, and when the last strains died away, Rohlf picked up where he'd left off.

"But we know different, don't we?" he asked, to an approving roar. "We know that even those who lay it don't really care about blame. What does the life of the spirit care about?"

The crowd roared. Wild fought the urge to cover his ears.

"That's right," Rohlf said. "Blame ain't important. Devotion is important. What is important? Sacrifice!"

"Sacrifice!" the crowd bellowed. Wild felt a strange sensation creep over him, partways confusion, partways suspicion. He didn't profess to know God's concerns, but he was pretty sure whatever they were, Dan Rohlf wasn't privy to them either. He could remember Rohlf as an awkward Lutheran alderman, as a farmer who never quite knew what to say. This…this was something different, but it felt human. Not like the church, not even like Adie when she had a glow about her. This was just…people. People who maybe didn't know what they were about, even though they were about dangerous things.

"We, here, till the fields of the farms, but we are not a farm – we are a garden, close to the kitchen, close to the spirit. And even when the fields are blown barren, the garden may survive. Because those who sacrifice will be reward...ed..."

Rohlf started strong, but Wild could see him end in confusion, in a mumble of surprise. He wasn't sure why, at first; Dan Rohlf had been eyeballing the audience the whole time, taking its measure, but suddenly he seemed to see something in it that he either didn't like or didn't understand. Wild caught his eye, saw him blink and stutter, and watched as he tried to recover.

And then it all became clear.

"There are those among us today who have sacrificed," Rohlf said. "There are those who carry the scars of their walks with the Divine. Wild Mayer, I see you there," he called, pointing. "Wilder Mayer, come out into the light."

Wild stared at him, shocked not only by the public nature of it, but by the sheer rudeness. He might not want to come forward, and even if he did, it wasn't polite to talk about a man's scars. He didn't feel one way about them or another, but that didn't mean other folks had a right to an opinion.

Go out, the crowd murmured, and hands urged him into the aisle. *Go out, Wild Mayer. Wild Mayer. Wild Mayer.*

The whisper of his name ripped backwards through the barn, from the stage to the standing-room at the rear. He was pushed gently into the aisle, where he stood with his hat held over his chest, looking around in bewilderment.

"Mr. Mayer, would you like to testify today?" Rohlf asked. Wild stared at him. "You got a story to tell, Wild, everyone here knows it."

Wild found his voice, though it took him a throat-clearing to speak. "With all due respect, Mr. Rohlf, if everyone here knows it I ain't see I gotta repeat it."

There was a small ripple of laughter, and Rohlf smiled, but his eyes looked annoyed.

"We don't testify to teach," he told Wild. "We testify to renew our faith in the spirit and commit ourselves to this garden we are building."

Wild looked around him at the expectant faces. He felt like he heard Iscah's voice again – *Don't eat nothin'* – and it occurred to him that her order might have included not swallowing down any of Dan Rohlf's patent bullshit.

"It's a nice garden you got here, Mr. Rohlf, but I don't fix myself to hoe someone else's row," he said, putting his hat on his head. "You keep on weeding your own self, and I'll tend to mine on my own."

He turned and began walking up the aisle; he wasn't sure if Bill or Alma were staying, but he figured sitting a spell in his truck wouldn't hurt.

He could see, up ahead, people beginning to move into the aisle to stop him, and he got himself ready to throw a punch or two, but they froze when Rohlf said, "Let him go. It's time for silence."

He wasn't aware of the soft background noises, the movement of clothing and clearing of throats and flipping of paper programs, until it stopped dead. Suddenly everyone was silent, frozen in place, eyes closed, faces lifted. It almost sounded like they even breathed in unison. The only noise now, which was worse than someone trying to stop him, was the noise his Sunday shoes made on the barn floor as he walked out. The only comfort was that in the silence he could hear one other set of footsteps at least, behind him.

Stepping out into the snapping cold and the sharp sunlight was a blessed relief, like being let out of the tight grasp of a giant hand. Wild bent over and breathed deep, hands on his knees.

"That weren't right," Bill said, standing next to him, resting a hand between his shoulder blades. "I ain't know it was going to be like that, Wild, it ain't noways right."

"It's fine," Wild said. "Neither of us expected it."

"Rude, was what it was."

"Well, I thought so," Wild said, straightening. Bill was alone. "You leave Alma inside?"

Bill blew air through his lips, a gentle raspberry. "I like her fine but not so much I'd stick with her over my own brother. And if she ain't leave, then that's a sign on her, ain't it?"

"I suppose. We'll wait for her, though. Bad manners abandoning her here." Wild knocked his hands together a few times to stay warm. "They still....whatever-they-are'ing in there?"

"That's the meditation," Bill said.

"Hey, what all did he mean by all that garden nonsense, anyway?"

"Dunno. Sounded to me like one of those hellfire and brimstone types turned sly," Bill said.

"How so?"

"Well, sounds like he thinks it's the end of the world."

"Aw, hell." Wild rolled his eyes.

"He ain't alone," Bill said. "You listened to Moze's radio lately? All the radio preachers talk about is the end of the world. I know you read the newspaper. Fascists in Italy, Socialists in Germany, Communists in New York. Can't nobody farm nothing, Okies going to California by the hundred, a quarter of the country ain't got no work. I know you think they're dumb stories, Wild, but the pulps are the same. Everyone's writin' about the Armageddon."

"I don't think they're dumb," Wild muttered. "Not yours, anyway."

"Well, thanks, but that's not the point," Bill said, giving him a half-smile. "Dan Rohlf is sayin' the end of the world is comin' like the dust bowl, and the only safe place is here, in his church. That's a powerful comfort."

"I seen a dust storm," Wild said, turning to walk towards the truck. "It didn't spare no garden."

"Well, we ain't, so." Bill spread his hands, following. "The dust storms are in Texas now, out west and up north. Most folks think it's only a matter of time before they hit Wheeler County too. When they do, what'll we do? What happens when our bank fails too?"

"Adie asked that," Wild said.

"Everyone's asking that."

"Well, I don't got any answers!" Wild said, climbing into the truck.

"Nobody's sayin' you have to," Bill replied. Wild started the truck and turned the little knob to switch the heat on, not that it ever worked very well, or even very consistently anymore.

"Seemed like Dan Rohlf sure was," Wild said. "What the hell was that about, anyhow, singling me out?"

Bill was silent for a while. Wild glanced at him.

"Well, you're a real Lea farmer," Bill said finally. "You keep your business mostly to yourself, and when we go to socials or whatnot, when you ain't dancing with Adie you stand with the other farmers. You don't much like Rohlf's folks so you keep your distance. Nothing wrong with that, Wild. But I ain't one of you all. So I get to talking with folks a little more."

"And?" Wild prompted.

"Rohlf's folks think Lea is blessed. They think it's got to do with that old church. Rohlf had visions about it. They know the church marked you when you put up that fence. Folks said for ages there ought to be a fence but you're the one went and did it, and it put its hand on you."

"It was an accident," Wild said.

"Tex Junior told Mama. He said it weren't no lightning strike, I heard him say it. It come up from the ground, and that's church ground. Say what you like about the old church, it's holy ground, Wild."

"Don't mean nothing."

"It does to Rohlf's folks. Then you went and married Adie and she's a stranger, nobody knows where she come from. She might've gone to the Baptist church but there's talk she didn't know half the hymns or what to do half the time, any more than she knew how to be a Lutheran when you married. So maybe you showin' up here…Rohlf thought you was…"

Bill shrugged. Wild gripped the steering wheel.

"Maybe he thought you was coming from the church, coming to finally pay him some mind," Bill said.

"Bullshit."

"I ain't say I believe it, but I ain't have to."

"It's goddamn nonsense, is what that is," Wild said, gesturing at the barn. Even from here, even with the engine running, they could hear it when the faint strains of singing began. "Can't figure out why people buy that slop he's selling."

"People are scared," Bill said.

"I can't fix the world, Bill. I can't even fix this damn truck's heating anymore," Wild added, thumping the dashboard. A little heat trickled into the cab.

"But if someone came along and said he could, people might believe him. And it ain't some slick salesman passing through. Rohlf owns his land. Folks know him, know he's not a fly-by-night." Bill shook his head. "What he says carries weight. To those people in there you're somethin' special, I guess."

Wild sighed, leaning back. "When'd you get so all-fired smart, Bill?"

"Bout when I dropped out of school, I suppose," Bill said with a grin. "Look, that meeting's going on another hour. We'll burn as much gas sitting here running the heat as we would if I took you home. I'll leave you off and come back for Alma."

"If you marry her we're gonna have some words about her churchgoing," Wild said, sliding over so Bill could hop out the passenger's side, run around, and climb in behind the wheel.

"Well, I'll try to find a nice Lutheran girl who ain't think you're the second coming," Bill told him as he pulled the truck around.

"If I'm the second coming we are in a heap of trouble," Wild told him, and Bill laughed.

FIFTEEN

WILD CAME IN from chores one day, not long before planting, to his mother saying, "I'm gonna strangle that girl, I swear to Jesus."

"He'd probably tell you to turn the other cheek," Wild called, shucking his boots in the hall.

"Even Jesus would find his patience sorely tried by Elizabeth Platter," Mama called back.

"How much trouble can she cause you? She's up in Chicago," Wild said, but his skin prickled with worry. If Bet had got herself in trouble –

"She ain't! I just got a letter from her," Mama said. "She's in St. Louis."

"Well, what's she doing in St. Louis?"

"Stoppin' on her way to Texas," Mama said.

"Bet's coming home?" Bill asked, from behind Wild. "On her own? She ain't hitching, is she?"

"No, she's in some….touring bus," Mama said, pronouncing *touring bus* the same way she might have said *bank robber*. "Says she caught a ride with some women she knows from the social work. She'll be in St. Louis for two weeks, then they're on to Oklahoma City 'fore they leave her off here. Says not to write 'cause she won't have a fixed address."

"Well, sounds like she's doing God's work," Wild said, scanning the letter Mama handed him. "What's got you so fired up?"

"There's a reason we sent her up to Chicago with a man who could look out for her," Mama said. "Driving around alone, wandering strange cities with only other ladies for company."

"Bet's good at looking out, though," Wild said. "She's been in Chicago a while now, Mama. Probably thought this'd save me a trip north during planting and she ain't wrong."

"I don't think she thought a whit about you. Or me," Mama said.

"If she wanted to come home we coulda scraped up some train fare."

"Well, no use shouting about it until she can hear you," Wild said. "Nice she gave us some warning, anyway. Moze, you'll have to bunk back in with Lonny, Bet'll want her room back."

"Aw, Wild!"

"It's all right, Moze, you can stay with me," Bill offered.

"Rather stay with Lonny, you make too much noise," Moze said sullenly.

"Lord give me strength," Mama sighed. "Your daddy was a good man but he gave me the most troublesome children. Go wash up, it'll be supper time soon. No typing until after dinner, Bill Platter!"

"Yes Mama!" Bill called.

"I don't know what she's thinkin', gallivanting across the country like this," Mama continued, as Wild washed his hands at the kitchen pump.

"Ain't you never wanted to go running around seeing the world?" Wild asked. "Chicago's mighty pretty, Mama."

"Pfft. What do I need the world for?" Mama asked, as Adie walked into the kitchen carrying a sleepy Iscah. "Especially when I got my favorite grandbaby right here?" she added, swooping down and plucking Iscah up.

"Well, you take her, I'll go see the world," Adie replied, leaning up for a kiss from Wild.

"I would, too," Mama said. "What do you think, Adie, I got a letter from Bet today."

"Oh yes? How is she?"

"Traversing the globe," Wild said. "She's got a ride on some kind of mercy-mission bus. When did she say she'd arrive, Mama?"

Which was when the door slammed, and Bet's voice called out, "Oh, just now."

"Well, it ain't my fault the mail is slow," Bet said, when they were all sat down to dinner and Mama had stopped scolding. "I put a date on it, Mama."

"How am I supposed to look at dates when for all I know you've been kidnapped?" Mama asked.

"It was a touring bus," Wild pointed out, not that either of them paid him any mind.

"I did think you still knew how to read numbers!" Bet insisted.

"I was worried about you," Mama said, stabbing her potatoes unnecessarily hard.

"Funny way of showing it," Bet sulked.

It had been going on throughout dinner. Wild wasn't one to let a family spat ruin a meal, but he could tell the others were anxious, and Adie was imploring Wild with her eyes to *do something*.

"I'm goin' out on the porch," Wild said, setting down his knife and fork. "Bet, you care to come along?"

"She don't care about – " Mama started.

"Bet," Wild repeated, cutting Mama off, feeling like a heel but doing it anyway.

Bet nodded, and Mama at least didn't object as Wild and Bet went out onto the back porch. Wild sat on the bench and Bet leaned on the railing, contemplative.

"Lord almighty, you've put Mama in a tizzy," Wild said.

"It'll pass," Bet said philosophically. "She'll be exhausted of me by end of summer."

"You only home until then?" Wild asked.

"Sure. The bus'll be back by in September, take me back to Chicago," she said, and there was a longing in her voice that he understood, even if he didn't share it.

"You look good, Bet," he said. "Sounded happy in your letters."

"It's the best thing in the world," she replied. "The math is part of it, but there's so much more. When you feel like you're doing good work, like you're making something real...I make a difference. I change lives, Wild."

"Why, I always knew you would," he said easily, and she looked so relieved. "You were born for great things."

"And you weren't?" she asked, gesturing at the land behind them.

"A farm's a farm, it ain't great or poor but the work and the soil make it so," he said. "I'm happy enough."

"I'm glad." She exhaled. "Wild, you ever think about that time we went to Carson?"

"When you were sick?"

"Sick. Yeah."

"Sometimes. Not often. Why?"

Bet shrugged. "Some of the work I do is with girls like I was. Some of 'em are in trouble. Some went and took care of it, like I did, but some ain't know how, and some ain't went to good doctors. Some don't come back."

"Damn shame," Wild said. Bet nodded.

"It gets to me, you know. How lucky we are. Me getting a college education while these girls suffer. This good farm you got while most of the country is dust and drought."

"I can't make it rain in Kansas, Bet," he said.

"I'm just saying. We're so lucky, Wild. What'd we do to deserve such luck?"

"Seems to me that's the thing about luck," Wild said. "You don't deserve or undeserve it. It just happens or it don't. Important thing is what you do with the luck. Seems you're doing a fine job with it."

Bet ducked her head and smiled. "Well, that's good. I try my hardest."

"Don't we all."

Sixteen

THE WHEAT WAS halfway to ripe in 1934 when the pavers came. They arrived in a long, slow-moving caravan of trucks and men, crawling west across the Oklahoma border, rolling out and flattening the earth, building a road Wild hadn't seen the likes of since he took Bet to Chicago.

He was out east of town when they came, so he was one of the first who saw them; he'd been returning a dish Mama had borrowed from the Kochs. He had Iscah with him so she could play with the newest Koch grandson while he had a chat with his aunt Margaret about the activities of the Church of the Redeemed Abandoned. They'd brought Xolotl because where Iscah went, Xolotl followed.

Even at three years old Iscah was still smaller than the big black dog, now that he had his full growth, and he treated her with a delicacy a human nanny might not even have shown. Moze had trained him and his brother, Buddy, as good guard dogs – any nighttime noise they didn't like or stranger coming around, they'd growl and investigate and, if necessary, bark their heads off until someone came to tell them it was all right. They damn near ran off a salesman who stopped for directions once. But with Iscah, Xolotl might as well have been a cherished kitten.

Iscah was on Wild's lap and Xolotl was riding shotgun, head blissfully cradled on the edge of the open window, when Wild pulled the truck up the road from the Koch farm and saw a dust cloud to the east. For a second he had a horrified vision of the storm he'd weathered with Odie, coming back from Chicago, but almost immediately it faded; there wasn't any wind, and the dust wasn't the even, rolling blanket it had been then. It looked like the clouds left behind when farmers went to sell the crops in Carson.

He leaned on the wheel for a minute, thinking, and then turned east. When he was nearly to the cloud he could see men out ahead of it, men and big machines, trucks full of crushed rock, the smell of diesel thick in the air.

He rolled to a stop and leaned out the window as a man with a big orange flag approached.

"Can't pass here," the man said. "You'll need to pull off and go around."

"Land's flat enough for it," Wild said with a grin. "I ain't headed east, though. Just came out to see what the bother was. You're kickin' up enough dust to be seen in town. What's the story?"

"We're the Federal Emergency Relief Administration road builders," the man said, doffing his hat.

"I'll be damned. They made it out to Texas?" Wild asked.

"Economic stimulation, my friend!" The man said. "Mr. Roosevelt wants FERA in every state. I'm from Oklahoma City myself so I just hope he gives me a ride home after the job. Meanwhile I'm makin' forty cents an hour wavin' a flag. You need a job?"

"Not last I checked. Road builders, huh?" Wild asked. "You comin' all the way to Lea?"

"We got a mandate to push through to Amarillo, so if you're due west, we'll see you sooner or later. Welcome to civilization, hayseed."

"Well, I appreciate the labor, friend," Wild told him.

"What's happening, daddy?" Iscah asked.

"Nothing to worry about, Iz. Look at those trucks!"

"Big trucks!"

The man with the flag chuckled. "Better clear out, before we pave right over you. Hey, let the one horse in your town know we're coming!"

"Yeah, I'll tell him there's a road full of assholes on the way," Wild replied, and the man laughed. He stepped back so Wild could turn the truck around and then waved the flag at Iscah, who stood on Wild's thigh to watch him out the back window of the truck.

"Looks like we're going to be city slickers, my darlin'," Wild said, steadying her with an arm around her waist.

"What're the trucks doin'?"

"Building a nice smooth road for us to drive on."

"Ain't we got roads?"

Wild laughed. "Well, we got plenty, but they're making them nicer."

He stopped in town and left Xolotl guarding Iscah while he ran into the seed store and the bank, to let them know that the road builders were coming. When he came out of the bank, Dan Rohlf was standing at the window of the truck. He and Iscah were talking; Xolotl was between them, ears laid back but not yet growling.

"Rohlf," Wild said, tipping his hat. "How's the farm?"

"Blessed, Mr. Mayer," Rohlf replied with a smile. "You should come up to another revival sometime, come witness the blessings on Lea for yourself."

"Oh, I imagine I see enough of them at the Lutheran church," Wild replied. "Hey, there's a crew outside of town paving the east road. They'll be passing through soon. Gonna be something of a spectacle, I imagine."

"Well, well, maybe we'll come and have a look," Rohlf replied. "You have a peaceful day, Mayer."

"And you do the same," Wild said, climbing into the truck. Rohlf leaned back as he started it up and pulled away, and Xolotl curled his body around Iscah.

"I don't like him, Daddy," Iscah said.

"Me neither, honey, but so long as he's polite we'll be the same."

"Xolotl don't like him."

"I saw. Good boy," Wild said, reaching out to rub the dog's ears. "Good boy, Xolotl."

Seemed like everyone in Lea and all the farmers who claimed it as theirs came out in the next few days to witness the pavers pass through. Wild waited until they were in town itself before bringing the family out to see, and felt it was worth it. The men had a truck with a big winch that rode ahead of them, to tow boulders and cars and other obstructions out of the way; the flag man told Wild, during a work break, that when they reached hillier country they'd have blasters too, who would cut right through the mountains with dynamite to make nice level roads.

Iscah enjoyed watching the winch truck pull cars away, not to mention watching people come running out of the storefronts and boarding houses to yell about it. Bill got right in amongst the pavers, peppering them with questions until the work team foreman ran him off, and Lonny and Moze ran around alongside the laborers with Buddy until they wore themselves out.

"It's a marvel," Mama said, sitting on the fence of the old church, with Wild and Adie leaning on her left, Bet on her right holding Iscah. "The way they go at it. Faster'n laying a brick or a cobble street, that's for sure. What do you suppose it's made of?"

"It's called tarmacadam," Adie said. "They take crushed rock and roll it flat, then cover it with tar."

"Looks like hell on the move if you ask me," Tex Junior said, leaning against the fence on Adie's other side. "Pitch and furnaces and rock smoke."

"Seems like that's what progress looks like these days," Wild remarked. "Smoke and a great crushing. Ain't it remind you of Chicago a little, Bet?"

"Some parts," she said thoughtfully. "I don't know that I'd call it progress, exactly. Modernization, maybe."

"What's the difference?"

"Well, progress means things're getting better. Modern just means things are getting newer. The smoke and dust I see ain't usually mean anything good for the folks who've got to live in it," she said. "Any more than it's doing those men's lungs any good."

"Most of 'em just seem happy to have honest work," Wild ventured.

Bet watched them, thoughtful, possibly a little sad. "I suppose so," she said.

Wild could hear – had been able to, for a few minutes now – the sound of the church behind him. It wasn't especially loud or terrible; just the creak of stone and wood, the soft murmur of something growing. He couldn't be sure it was Bet affecting it, but ever since she'd left for Chicago, he'd seen new little creatures or carvings pop up occasionally. After last year's harvest, wheat sheaves had appeared next to the doors. Glancing over his shoulder, he saw what he thought was a new carving on the white stone lintel, a little scale of justice balancing over the door.

He wondered what the church thought of the pavers, if it was even capable of thinking like that. A sidelong look at Adie showed nothing on her face but pleasure, and a sort of peaceful curiosity.

Bill came hustling back from the front line of the road crew, looking excited even about being ejected.

"Ain't it swell?" he asked, hopping up on the fence.

"Sure. You gonna put it in one of your stories?" Wild asked.

"For sure! Did you see the rock crusher? It just eats it up and spits it out. Must burn through gasoline. Imagine the kinda power you'd need to chew up, say, an asteroid or a comet!"

"A comet's already crushed up rock," Adie said. "Rock and ice. That's what they think, anyway."

"You know everything, Adie," Bill said. "How do you know what a comet's made of?"

"I suppose I read it somewhere," she said.

"What would you do with a crushed up asteroid, Bill?" Bet asked.

"Pave a real big road," Tex Junior suggested.

"Make some comets," Wild joked.

"Well, what if what you wanted was just in the asteroid itself?" Bill said. "What if there was a big ship that was just floatin' along, eating up asteroids for whatever's inside them. Gold or diamonds or something even better out in space. And they don't care about the rock so they just leave it out behind 'em. Building big ol' floating roads in space outta junk rock."

Wild grinned. Bill's eyes were distant, entranced by the idea. He knew when they got home the typewriter would probably get to clacking.

"Wild," Bet called, and there was something in her voice that made Wild turn to look at her. She was staring at the far side of the street a little east of them, just ahead of the lead line of the pavers.

There were a cluster of men and women there, all recently arrived, peering with interest at all the activity. They looked so strange that at first he couldn't figure out what exactly was strange about them, until he realized they were all in some kind of uniform.

They wore loose blue trousers, even the women. The trousers didn't quite fit well, as if they'd been ordered in one size large enough to fit everyone, and Wild was reminded of a chain gang he'd seen on the train from Lubbock, years ago. But over the trousers they wore bright orange tunics, with long swinging sleeves and no collars.

"What in creation," Tex Junior managed.

"Is it a chain gang?" Mama asked.

"No, ain't a chain gang," Bet said. "Ain't that Abe Weber? Boy, did he want to murder Wild over you," she added to Adie.

"Seems I made the right choice," Adie said.

"Yep, and there's Aunt Margaret's in-law cousins from south of Wheeler," Wild said. "It's Dan Rohlf's holy rollers."

"What're they dressed like that for?" Moze asked.

"Don't know," Wild said, sliding off the fence. "Stay here. Bill, keep an eye out."

"Sure, Wild," Bill said easily. Wild glanced at Tex Junior, who nodded; he and Bet fell into step with Wild as he crossed the street.

"Howdy there, Abe," Wild said, when they were close enough. He couldn't deny that their clothes looked well-made, and they were more colorful than you generally saw in the store; fine material, perhaps.

"Wild Mayer," Abe said, giving him a nod. "Ain't it something?" he added, indicating the pavers.

"Sure. Seems like everyone's coming out to picnic and watch the road get made," Wild agreed.

"Abe," Tex Junior said. "I got to ask."

One of the others, a distant Koch cousin through marriage, piped up first. "Everybody is, Tex, you ain't original."

"Now, don't be like that," Tex Junior said. "I'm not out to make trouble."

"We're just curious, is all," Bet said. "That's some fine dye work on that fabric."

"Ordered it special up from Houston," Abe said, shooting a look at the Koch cousin. "Make you one if you like, Miss Bet."

"Well, I'll consider that, and thank you," Bet said.

"But…" Wild rubbed his neck, trying to figure out how to word it. "How come *everyone's* in 'em? You all…I mean, is there a…parade?"

They looked like they weren't sure he was in earnest, but Abe spoke up first.

"No. It's just the church," he said with a shrug. "Father Rohlf says if you got your religion you oughta show it in all you do. As a sign of devotion. So he says his church wears their faith as their raiment."

"Father Rohlf," Bet murmured.

"Times is changing fast," another congregant said. "Got to have something to hold onto, Miss Bet."

"Well, now, I agree," Tex Junior said. "But I ain't fixed to write LUTHERAN on my hat."

"Maybe that says something about your church," Abe told him.

Wild rested a hand on Tex Junior's shoulder, because Tex Junior wasn't a religious man, but a church was something you defended, something you didn't leave, and he could see trouble on the horizon.

"We're all here for the good of Lea," he said. "I know you folks are farming Rohlf's patch with a good heart. No cause to fight over theology."

"Klara," Bet said, and one of the women who had been near the back of the group looked up. Wild dimly remembered Bet and Klara being friends at school. "Where's your little one? She must be going on three now, I ain't seen her since I left for Chicago."

"Back at the farm. Ain't good to bring the children into town too often," Klara said.

"But they go to the school, don't they? Inge, you got one about Lonny's age, don't you?"

"The Church has its own school up on the farm," Abe said. "Surprised Wild didn't tell you. After he married Mrs. Mayer, we didn't take too much to the new schoolma'am. Now, if you was to come back to Lea for good, maybe teach – "

"No, I'm just here visiting," Bet said gently. Wild knew from her tone this was a conversation she would have a lot, in the next few years; Lea was her birthplace, but he could already tell it wasn't her home any longer.

"Well, that's a shame, I won't deny," Abe said. "Wild. Tex. You'll excuse us – we got business in the Dry Goods."

"You all take care now," Wild said, as the group began to move away, around the cloud of dust the pavers were making, towards the store.

"What in the actual hell, pardon my language, Bet," Tex Junior said.

"Don't mind your mouth on my account, all three of us're thinking it," Bet said.

"What was that business about Adie?" Tex added. "Mrs. Adelaide Mayer, like she was some kinda celebrity."

"I don't know," Wild replied, watching them fade into the hazy air from the paving. "Dan Rohlf's got some kinda idea about me. You remember when we put up the fence and it knocked me out?"

"Sure."

"He thinks the old church touched me somehow."

"Dan Rohlf ain't even just off his rocker, he lost his rocker completely a few years ago," Tex Junior decided.

"Well, he's taking the town with him," Bet said. "Seems like there's a lot of families I used to see in church up at his farm now."

"Baptists aren't pleased neither, but what can you do? He doesn't seem to mean any harm," Wild said, leading them back towards the fence where the others were watching.

"What'd Abe have to say, Wild?" Mama asked, looking worried.

"Mostly nonsense, Mrs. Platter," Tex Junior said.

"They dress so we'll know they're part of the Church of the Redeemed Abandoned," Wild said. He took Iscah from her and clambered up onto the fence again. Adie leaned into him, watching the street with dark eyes.

"What nonsense," Mama said.

"I don't like it," Adie murmured.

"I ain't fixed to worry," Wild said. "It's like Bill told me. When it feels like the end of the world, folks need comfort. Not my business where they take it."

"Let's go home," Mama said. "I seen enough of other folks working for one day."

At home, Wild and Bill saw to the farm chores, leaving Moze and Lonny to help Mama and Adie. Wild sent Bill in early so he could get to his typewriter before dinner, and just as he was finishing up himself, Adie came out to see him in the barn.

"Don't you look nice," Wild said, lifting her onto the bed of the truck, admiring her shining hair and warm skin. "Once those pavers pass through I'll take you drivin' on that big nice flat road. Some warm night we'll just drive up and down it for the fun of it."

"They aren't wrong, you know," Adie said.

"Who ain't, the pavers?"

"No. Rohlf's people. Things are changing. Very fast."

Wild wondered how she'd heard that from across and down the street, but not for long; she was his Adie but she was, sometimes, still a mystery. And he had never forgot their conversation about the Science Fiction, where he asked what she was, and she asked if it mattered.

But that had ended with the knowing that he was a gift for her, which was all he'd wanted anyway.

She let him pick her up off the truck bed, carry her to where the timothy hay was waiting to be baled – with a blanket over top it was nearly as soft as a feather bed, and the sweetest smelling grass in the world. They had time enough before dinner, and no one would bother them here.

With Iscah, he had known her name, felt as though he'd known his daughter, only when Adie told him she was pregnant. This time, perhaps because they had been married for more than a few months, perhaps because Adie let him, he knew – he knew that his son would come from this, like Iscah from the corn. Didn't know his name yet, didn't know who he'd be, but he knew a son was heralded, and it thrilled and frightened him.

HARVEST 1934

THERE WERE FOLKS from the government in Carson that year, when the farmers brought in the harvest to be sold. Wild expected it; seemed the government was everywhere these days. A little bit of a dollar short, if you asked him, but better late than never, he supposed. After the pavers had come the social workers, to see to, or at least to speak to, the migrant crop workers who were more numerous every year. Most who'd lost their farms went to pick fruit in California, but plenty stopped on the way to help what harvest there would be at the edge of the dust bowl.

Bet didn't know the social workers, but all the same she knew them – they were people like her, earnest and smart, well-educated, and she spoke to them in their own language. Wild could see the way they took measure of his house, without plumbing or electricity, but he paid it little mind. He let Bet speak with them, and let them speak with his workers, and then he paid the workers, helped them fix their trucks if needed, and watched them move on.

Sometimes, he knew, Mama or Adie left cans of food and small sacks of flour in the trucks while he worked on them. Well, they weren't going hungry; why should anyone else, if they could help it?

That year, caravaning into Carson with Moze daydreaming in the truck bed and Bill and Bet in the cab like old times, Bill spun out his newest yarn for them, since Wild had been after him for so long to tell it. It was all about a group of folks who'd found a kind of dirt in asteroids that would let you farm the surface of the sun itself. Any old person could mine an asteroid, but the trick was that the surface of the sun was still so hot, only certain folks could stand it. So Bill's story was about a family movin' on from drought-blighted land, blastin' off in a spaceship like futuristic migrants to move to the solar town of Fearless and farm the sun, since only Texans were considered tough enough.

"Well, if you can tell it in a book, it'll be a real crackler," Wild pronounced.

"But you'll still make it funny sometimes, won't you?" Bet asked Bill. "They've got lots of Science Fiction books in the public library in Chicago but I couldn't stomach much of it. You beat half the writers in America, Bill."

"I hope to," Bill said, beaming under the praise. "I'm about thirty pages in. Hope to get it done over the winter."

While Wild and Bill unloaded the harvest with the help from a couple of field hands, and Bet negotiated and checked the numbers on the prices, Moze – now twelve and considering himself nearly a man – was allowed to wander so long as he came back to help sweep out the truck at the end. Wild, between hauling sacks of corn and wheat, saw him speaking with a nice-looking lady nearby. When he was done unloading, he caught Bet's eye. She saw where he was looking, gave him a nod and a go-on gesture, and Wild slapped Bill's shoulder.

"You do the handshake this year, as my official representative," he said. Bill hurried over to see to it while Wild found Moze.

"Hello, Miss," he said, resting a hand on Moze's shoulder. "Moze, introduce me."

"This is Miss Fein, she's a social worker," Moze said. "Look at what she give me!"

Wild took the little pamphlet, studying it. "Electricity by windmill," he read aloud.

"We're trying to educate farmers in rural Texas about electrifying their homes," Miss Fein said.

"I suppose we qualify," Wild said with a grin. "My sister's in social work, so I know an earnest face when I see one. Ain't it dangerous, electrifying a home?"

"Not if done properly! Moses here was just telling me you and he managed to build a crystal radio, and it's not much more difficult, just larger," she said. "Then you can run wires to the home for electric lights, power for a real radio, even an electric oven."

Wild raised his eyebrows at the pamphlet. "All in this bitty paper?"

"Well, no. That's just the plans for the windmill to generate it, but you can send off for instructions on laying and grounding wires, electrical safety, and all sorts of other methods of modernizing your home. Do you have plumbed water?"

"No, just a pump in the kitchen. I'm familiar with it, but the pump's always worked fine for us."

"Well, if you're interested, there's instructions for how to send off for plumbing lessons too, on the back here," she pointed. "Has your family been impacted by the dust clouds?"

"We been lucky," Wild said. "Got decent crops in the last few years. Prices weren't what we hoped in '31 but they're up now."

"And you're familiar with terraced farming?"

"Yes'm. I did a year at the aggie school in Lubbock, I been convincing the Lea farmers to try it. Seems to work. Keeps the dust down anyhow. Windmill, huh? We do get the wind," Wild said, studying the diagram.

"Can we put one up, Wild? Please?" Moze asked. "I got a cut coming from the farm this year, I'll pay for it."

"Well, we'll take Miss Fein's pamphlet and see, and if you want you can send off for the others," Wild said, stuffing it into Moze's back pocket. "We got to get back now, Miss. Thanks for your work down here."

Moze ran excited circles around him as he strolled back to where Bill was finishing the deal.

"You got to let me put up a windmill, Wild," he insisted. "We could have electric lights in the whole house!"

"Calm down, Jesus," Wild laughed. "We'll get the price on the wood and the parts and see. Mama has to approve it. I don't want us all electrocuted."

Moze stopped, suddenly, looking stricken. "Oh, Wild, I ain't mean —"

It took Wild a second to understand why Moze was upset, and then he laughed again.

"Moze, they don't bother me none," he said, shooting the cuffs on his arms so his scars showed. "I just don't want anyone being hurt, that's all. Electricity's dangerous stuff if you ain't know what you're doing. So we'll be real slow and deliberate, and do what the pamphlets tell us. Any rate, you save your money for a real radio, I'll see about the windmill."

The price on the harvest, Wild felt, was almost more than fair; so high he wasn't sure the math was right even after Bet checked it. But sure enough, pay for a bushel of corn was way up, and they'd have enough to get them through the winter and a bit besides. Maybe he could send Bet back to Chicago with a little spendin' money, and put up Moze's windmill.

And there was a baby on the way, after all, who would need to be provided for. Wild felt pretty fine with life as he paid off the last of the field hands, waved them off, and loaded the family back up in the truck.

The drive to Lea was full of chatter, Moze leaning in through the back windshield to show Bill and Bet the pamphlet and fill their ears with plans. Bet told Moze (again) about how nearly everything in Chicago was plumbed and lit with electric, and how the coal haze still hung heavy over the city from what wasn't. Wild could see Bill drinking up all the details.

They wouldn't pass through Lea before they were home, but on the road back to the farm, they passed Lentz Platter's new touring sedan going the other way, and James Platter leaned out of it, waving them down.

"You been to Carson?" he asked.

"Just got back. Why, what's the news?" Wild asked.

"Oh, nothin' much, just a curiosity. You might want to run up to town and have a look."

"Look at what?" Wild asked.

"You'll know when you see it. Sort of your area of specialty, I think," James Platter said, and drove on.

"The hell was that about?" Bet asked.

"I don't know. You want me to leave y'all at the house, or you fine with a drive up to Lea?"

"Lea, Lea!" Moze chanted.

"I don't mind," Bet said. "Bill?"

"Mama'll tar us if we're late for dinner," Bill said.

"Well, town's not far. We can be back in time," Wild said, passing the turn-off for the farm and heading into town.

He knew what James Platter meant as soon as they turned onto the paved road of the main street. He could see it up in the distance against the dim sky.

"Holy Moses," Bill said softly. "It's the Science Fiction sure enough."

Wild slowed the truck to a crawl as they passed the old church, with its bell towers and rose window, its colonies of gargoyles and sheaves of wheat sculpted into the adobe. Out front of the big old wooden door, inside a fence that had recently turned from rough lashed wood to upright metal bars, stood two lamp-posts. They flanked the path up to the door, tall wrought-iron numbers with clear glass at the top, almost like overgrown flowers.

And inside of each was an electric bulb, the coil of wire burning a vivid yellow-white.

"Well, Moze, I guess we oughta look into that windmill," Bet said.

"Yeah, I guess we oughta," Moze replied, awestruck.

Wild pulled the truck around at the turning for the bank and drove back past the church. He could see lights inside as well, burning dimly through the rose window. They pulsed almost imperceptibly, and he could feel the answering pulse in his own body.

"Nobody ever talks about it," Bet said softly.

"Nothing so much to talk about, I suppose," Bill replied. "What's to say?"

"Someday they will," Wild said, picking up speed again now that he was past it. "Come on, Mama and Adie'll have dinner on, and Iscah'll be waiting on me."

SEVENTEEN

1934 WAS A hard year for most of the country. The midwest was filled with dust, and the coasts were filled with men without work. It seemed as though nothing in the country was without despair and hunger. The newspapers and Moze's new fancy radio were full of it.

But in Lea, at least for Wild, there was bounty he was grateful for.

Adie was far enough along in the pregnancy that she was showing, and she glowed like the sun. They had money for a good Christmas, and the promise of a good planting in 1935. The dust storms and the Depression were both lurking around the edges like a hungry coyote, but neither had touched Lea as hard as they had most other towns. Bet was back in Chicago, where she sent gleeful accounts of snow and of academic drama, and darker stories of the conditions for the poor in Chicago, which only served to make them all more grateful.

Wild had got the windmill up before the real cold set in, and Moze had spent every day since studying electrical diagrams, trying to get a single light bulb in the kitchen in working order.

Two days before Christmas, Moze managed to get the bulb burning, which was very impressive and made a nice light for Mama to work by. But one of the wires burned out within an hour – too narrow a gauge, Moze said, though Wild didn't know what that meant. Either way, Moze's disappointment and his own idleness drove Wild out of the house that afternoon; he bundled up Iscah, brought the truck around, and loaded Moze, Adie, Iscah, and Xolotl into the cab with him.

"Another good year, and maybe we'll get one of those new touring trucks," Wild said, as Moze's elbow found his ribs for the fifth time.

"Be nice to have a second row of seats that isn't just the open bed of a truck," Adie agreed.

"Moze should be smaller," Iscah said, from Adie's lap.

"I can't help how big I am!" Moze protested. "Why're we even bringin' Xolotl, anyhow?"

Iscah gasped, offended, and Wild grinned.

He left Adie and Iscah with Xolotl at the Dry Goods and took Moze down the street, past the gently glowing lights of the church, to the seed store, where they also sold building supplies. While Moze examined the spools of wire and consulted with the store's owner, another "electricity" fan, about what would be ideal, Wild wandered over to the seed catalogs to see what new corns were out this year.

From the corner of his eye, through the seed store window, he caught sight of the bright orange-and-blue of the Church of the Abandoned Redeemed's uniform; a couple of them were passing in front of the church, down towards the Dry Goods.

"Moze," he called, "I'm goin' to find Adie. You all right here?"

"Sure thing, Wild!" Moze replied, and Wild hurried out into the chill, catching up to the Church members on the porch. He held the door for a few of them, and was going to follow them in when he saw one lingering at the edge of the porch, staring at the church; Cora Rohlf, Dan Rohlf's wife. He could see even from the back the tenseness in her body, the tightness of her shoulders.

"Quite a sight, ain't it?" he asked, joining her at the porch rail. Behind him he heard the door open again, and Adie call, "Wild?"

"Over here," Wild said. Standing next to Mrs. Rohlf, he could see the expression on her face— bitterness and hatred, tinged with disgust.

"Well, hello, Mrs. Rohlf," Adie said, Iscah propped on her hip. "How do?"

"I was just saying to Mrs. Rohlf how pretty I thought the church looks, all lit up like so," Wild said, when she didn't respond.

"Sure does," Adie said. "Iscah, you like it?"

"Yes, Mama," Iscah murmured, a little shy.

At the sound of Iscah's voice, Mrs. Rohlf's nostrils flared.

"I hate it," she said, her voice almost a whisper, but with the intensity of strong emotion.

"I'm sorry to hear that, ma'am," Wild said, now scrambling for a way to back out of this conversation.

"I hate it," Mrs. Rohlf repeated. "It blessed you but it drove him mad. What made you so lucky? What'd we do to deserve that?"

"Nobody did nothin'," Iscah said, her voice loud and sharp.

"Hush, darlin'," Wild said, taking her from Adie and holding her close, beginning to guide Adie back towards the porch stairs.

"But we didn't do nothin'," Iscah insisted. Mrs. Rohlf whirled, furious. "That old church done nothin' to him. He's just nasty and mean and scairt."

"Iscah!" Wild scolded. "Be told right now." She fell sullenly silent. "Mrs. Rohlf, I'm sure sorry – "

"You ain't sorry!" Mrs. Rohlf screeched. "You ain't sorry – "

She leapt towards them and Wild turned, protecting Iscah and Adie with his body; Xolotl barked furiously but, before he could lunge forward, the door opened and the other Church members poured out, surging towards Mrs. Rohlf, holding her back.

"Take your little Satan child and go!" she hissed. Wild blinked, stunned, and Adie grabbed Xolotl's collar. He was growling, hackles raised. "Your witch-whore wife and your *Satan child!*"

For a second, Wild wanted to shove Iscah into Adie's arms and lay a punch on her himself. But Adie was dragging Xolotl towards the truck, and Moze was running across the street to see what was going on, and he had other concerns, people to keep safe. Wild adjusted Iscah in his arms, holding her head against his shoulder. Mrs. Rohlf spat at him.

"Maybe you had better take her back home," he said to the others, who looked like they didn't appreciate him witnessing this, let alone remarking on it. "And I'll thank you to keep your opinion on my wife to yourself, ma'am."

She shrieked again, stifled by the other Church members, and Wild followed Adie and Xolotl, still growling, down to the truck. He tried to hand Iscah in to Adie, but she howled and clung to his neck; Moze called out, "I got it, Wild," and slid into the driver's seat. Adie moved over so Wild could clamber in, hauling Xolotl with her, and Moze pulled the truck around in the middle of the street, heading for home.

"Jesus H. Christ," Moze said. "What got into Mrs. Rohlf?"

"Mind your language," Wild told him. "I couldn't say. She just blew all a sudden."

"Nasty old lady," Iscah sobbed into his shoulder.

"Did you hear what she called Adie?" Moze asked.

"Everyone in a few miles heard what she said, I've no doubt," Adie said, looking shaken.

"No need to repeat it, Moze," Wild said.

"I wasn't gonna!"

"Did you get your wire, at least?" Adie asked.

"Sure, threw it in the back. What're we gonna do, Wild?"

"Don't know," Wild said. "Don't like to tangle with Rohlf's church, and I don't think they share her thoughts."

"If she ain't like Dan Rohlf she oughta leave him but I suppose she never would," Moze said.

"Plenty would take her in if she did," Wild said. "No love lost for the Church these days. Baptist *or* Lutheran."

"Hard for a woman to leave her man," Adie added. "And he's got a lot of folks willing to drag her back if she tries."

"She definitely ain't coming to us for help," Moze said. Wild, feeling Iscah's body relax, eased her away from his chest. She held out her arms to Adie, who settled her on her lap and stroked her hair.

"Daddy," Iscah said, big eyes watching him.

"What's that, baby?" Wild asked.

"Don't let the Roggenwolf get Xolotl."

Wild blinked. "The Roggenwolf won't hurt Xolotl. Where'd you hear that old story, anyway?"

"Bisabuela an' the ol' Church. They said to tell you."

"Well, I promise Bisabuela and the old church I won't let the Roggenwolf get Xolotl," Wild said.

Iscah yawned and her eyes drooped; she mumbled something before she drifted off, but Wild didn't hear it.

"What'd she say?" he asked Adie.

"Sounded like Spanish," she replied. "Has your Mama been teaching her?"

"You'd know better than I would, but I don't think so."

"Well," Adie kissed the crown of Iscah's head. "No figuring her sometimes."

Sarah and Tex Junior and their boys came up for Christmas eve dinner, which was nice; after they'd gone home, after Lonny and Moze and Bill were at least in their rooms if not in bed and Mama had gone to sleep, Wild sat up in the kitchen with Adie, just enjoying the quiet and the promise of the next morning.

It didn't last long.

Xolotl and Buddy heard it first; Wild saw their ears perk up, and both of them stood and went to the back door of the "old" kitchen, a side entrance now that Wild had stitched the two houses together. Wild went to the nearest window, but he didn't see anything; still, when Xolotl and Buddy wouldn't stop scrabbling quietly at the door, he looked again.

"What is it, Wild?" Adie asked.

"Don't know, but something's spooked them," Wild replied.

"Santa," Adie said with a grin.

"No...something..." Wild frowned out the window. It was too dark to see much but it almost looked like someone was moving in the fallow fields, crawling amongst the furrows. "Adie, get my rifle and then douse the lamp."

Adie went into the hallway, and he heard her take down the rifle, check it, and then her footsteps returning; after a second, she left again to fetch Bill's, carrying it back with a box of ammunition in the other hand. She leaned over and blew out the lamp.

"Get that window open," he said, and she undid the latch, opening the window a crack. He gave himself a little time to adjust his eyes to the dark, then took her place at the window, sliding the rifle barrel through the crack. "When I say, you let the dogs out. You loaded?"

She nodded.

"All right. When I'm empty you step up."

"Wild," Adie said. "Iscah. She said – "

"I know," Wild answered. "Not fixing to. Go ahead."

Adie opened the door and Buddy and Xolotl surged out, barking loud enough to wake the whole house; Wild saw someone rise from the field, unmistakably human, alarmed by the dogs, and he fired before he'd consciously decided to. The body in the field jerked, and he saw the flash of a gunshot from the field, heard it a split breath later, but the bullet must have gone astray. Xolotl and Buddy stopped at the edge of the yard, still barking. Wild fired a second time, stepping aside so Adie could take his place while he reloaded, though he could already see the figure turning to run.

Xolotl, always more eager at the chase, cleared the yard fence easily and took off after the man in the field. Adie fired once as the running figure stopped to turn, raising its weapon. Wild whistled, sharp, and the figure kept running, but Xolotl stopped. He kept barking, so Wild whistled again, and both dogs reluctantly turned back, loping towards the house.

Bill came barging out of his room, yelling about the dogs, and Mama emerged as well, her hair half-brushed. Iscah was wailing in their room.

"Bill, see to Iz. Mama, get Moze and Lonny," Wild called, and they hustled away. Adie was still at the window, one bullet in the chamber. Wild handed her his reloaded rifle so he could put another bullet in Bill's.

"What's going on?" Moze asked, as Wild let the dogs back into the house, looking them over for injuries.

"Someone in the fields," Wild said, relighting the lamp. "Think we drove him off."

Bill arrived carrying Iscah, who immediately reached out to Wild to be taken into his arms.

"Who was it?" Bill asked.

"No idea. Whoever they were, they had a gun. Just a pistol, looked like," Wild said. "Might've just been some drifter the dogs spooked – "

"It ain't," Iscah said into his chest.

"Hush now," Wild soothed. Xolotl was weaving his way around and through Wild's legs, anxious.

"You think any more prowlers're about?" Bill asked.

"Don't know. Not likely the way he took off running, but he might be back."

"What'll we do?" Moze asked. Lonny was clinging to his neck, pale and afraid in his long nightshirt.

"Moze, call across to Tex Junior and Sarah," Mama said. "Warn 'em someone's runnin' around the fields half cocked, tell 'em to call around and warn everyone. I'll start a fire in the living room and we can bed in there for tonight."

"I can stay up and keep watch," Bill said, as Moze went to the telephone. "Up on the roof I could see anyone coming even over to Tex and Sarah's place."

"You'll freeze your legs off," Wild said. "No point in that. You keep watch in the kitchen southeast, I'll watch the northwest from the sitting room. Moze can take over for you in a few hours, and Adie'll spell me. The dogs'll catch on before we do, anyway."

"Tex Junior wants to know if we want help," Moze called.

"Tell him to keep Sarah and the boys where he can see 'em, we'll handle ourselves," Wild called back. Mama hurried into the living room to start the fire. "Bill, you haul your mattress and Mama's in near the fire for sleepin' on. Lonny, help him bring in bedding. Shh, now," he added to Iscah, who was shaking in his arms. "See? Nobody's hurt, even Xolotl is fine."

"Nasty, mean ol' monsters," Iscah mumbled.

"Not monsters, just folk," Wild said. "Easy to kill with a rifle."

"Hush, don't fill her head with murder," Adie said. "I'm going to help Mama make up the beds. Pass her over and you keep watch."

Wild caught her chin with one hand and kissed her briefly as he passed Iscah over, then took up her place at the window. He could hear the others moving around, arranging temporary bedding in front of the fire, Mama making coffee, Bill calling to Buddy to come stand watch in the living room. Xolotl seemed torn between guarding Iscah and staying with Wild until Wild summoned him over.

He watched the fields for hours in uneasy silence. Iscah, Lonny, and Moze drifted off, and eventually so did Adie and Mama; Wild drank hot coffee, then warm, then cold, waking Adie sometime after midnight to replace him while Moze took over for Bill. He crawled under the blankets that Adie had vacated, wrapping his arms around Iscah. Across from him, Mama lay with Lonny asleep in her arms, but her eyes were open.

"Nothin' stirring," he said softly, trying not to wake the little ones.

"Good," Mama whispered. "Seems like a long spell to daylight."

"Be here soon. I think we're safe for tonight."

"And tomorrow night?" Mama asked. "And the night after? We can't stand guard every night."

Wild rubbed his face with his free hand. "Mama, you know what it was tonight."

"I ain't like to say," she whispered.

"The Roggenwolf. Iscah knew."

Mama nodded. "And if whoever it is ain't take us, they'll take someone."

"We told Tex and Sarah. They'll have told everyone they could by now." Wild adjusted his hold on Iscah. "Can't save the world, Mama."

"Ain't have to tell me, son," she replied. "But when the influenza took your father, that was God's will. When He took Lon, I suppose He had reasons. But this…it's man's devilment. Your father used to say that about the war, too. Man's devilment is what it is."

"What should I do?"

Mama shrugged, and Lonny mumbled a sleepy complaint.

"I raised you to do good and take care of folk," she said. "If I had more to teach you about bein' a good man, I would have."

Wild slept a little, fitfully, not least because Iscah kicked in her sleep. When he woke after sunrise, it was to Moze speaking softly with Bill. He could hear Adie in the kitchen, lighting the fire in the stove.

"Light out," Bill said, when Wild sat up, leaving Iscah bundled in the covers. "Wouldn't nobody try something in the light, would they?"

"Probably not," Wild said, rubbing a crick out of his shoulder. "Think I'll go see if there's anything in the fields."

"Want me to come?" Bill asked.

"No. Whoever it is, they're long gone, or too hurt to jump me," Wild said, whistling for the dogs as he shouldered his rifle. He stopped to kiss Adie, then let the dogs out ahead of him. They ran into the yard, sniffing around everywhere, then followed him when he hopped the fence and walked out into the field.

The hard ground didn't yield up much at first, but the dogs tracked their way across the furrows until they found a few drops of blood, baying for Wild to come investigate. He followed the droplets south, not very far, and then stopped to crouch.

Lying on the frosted ground, Xolotl and Buddy snuffling around it, was a worn wooden handle, with a wickedly sharp hatchet head attached to it.

Mindful of Billy's detective pulps, which were always on about fingerprints, he wrapped his hand in a kerchief from his pocket and

159

picked it up, feeling the heft of it, the good balance. When he stood, he looked around cautiously, as if the mere handling of it might draw its owner back here. His breath puffed in the air, and the hatchet was cold through the handkerchief.

"Back to the house," he said to the dogs, gesturing them ahead of him, and made his way through the empty field. He stopped on the way and dropped the hatchet behind the woodpile outside, before walking back into the kitchen.

"Find anything?" Adie asked, as he stomped ice and dirt off his boots.

"Little bit of blood," he said. "Reckon I'll head into town today and see if there's any news."

Tex Junior wanted to get the news too, but he didn't want to leave Sarah and the boys alone, so Wild drove Bill over to the Muller farm and left him off before picking up Tex Junior and heading for Lea. He'd left Mama and Adie bringing out presents for the children, trying to make the morning normal at least, and saw Sarah was trying to do the same. He took the hatchet with him, wrapped in a rag from the kitchen, hidden under the seat.

They were just coming up on Lea proper when a truck going the other direction slowed and waved for them to stop. It was Micah, the Baptist who'd helped them put up the church fence.

"I was sent for you," he said to Wild. "Fellas said you had experience with some murders."

Wild and Tex Junior exchanged a tired look.

"Suppose I do," Wild said. "Figured something would have happened. Who was it?"

"The Lees," Micah said grimly. "Baptist family. Don't expect you'd know them."

"Thought I knew even all the Baptists around these parts," Wild said.

"Lees were far-out farmers, kept to themselves. Follow me back?"

"Can't do nothing," Wild said, annoyed. "Ain't raising the dead just yet."

Micah gave him a desperate, pleading look. Wild supposed the town wanted someone to witness it, someone who might know what to do.

160

"Fine. I'll come. You call for the sheriff yet?" Wild asked.

"My brother's getting the Platters up now," Micah said. "Hell of a Christmas," he added.

The smell of blood was still thick in the air when they arrived.

The farmhouse was pathetically small – it looked to be one room, which the farmers of Lea were not unfamiliar with, but most of them had at least been able to separate out the kitchen, or to make a separate sleeping space. Not so with the Lees, who had a ramshackle shed insulated with newspapers, with a narrow porch and no windows.

"Lees kept to themselves," Micah repeated. "Didn't hold with telephones, either."

"How'd you find out so fast?" Wild asked.

"Word went out that someone came after your people. Our preacher went out knocking on doors. Lees didn't answer. Door wasn't locked – he saw enough."

"Explains why it was them," Tex Junior said.

"How's that?" Micah asked.

"Telephone. If everyone else knew…" Tex Junior spread his hands. Micah nodded.

"You going in, Wild?" Tex Junior asked.

"Might as well be me I suppose," Wild said.

Inside, it didn't take long to see what had been done. The men had been shot. The single woman, Mrs. Lee, butchered like the others. The single room's two lanterns were smashed. Wild closed his eyes, said a prayer for the souls of them and his own, and walked back out. Micah looked almost hopeful, as though he wished the family had just…gone away somewhere.

"It's the Roggenwolf," Wild said.

"Guess it wasn't Joseph Johnson after all," Micah said.

"Jesus God," Tex Junior added.

"Might as well swear by Satan, in there," Wild replied. "Someone's got to stop this. That could'a been my family."

Thinking of Iscah and Adie and his mama, the idea of someone taking a hatchet to them, made him sick.

"What's there to be done?" Micah asked.

"I shot him," Wild said. "I saw his blood. He ain't a monster, just a person. Swear to God I'll get him."

"Don't make promises you can't keep," Tex Junior advised.

"I don't intend to break this one," Wild said grimly.

It wasn't the best Christmas he ever spent. Wild sent Tex back with Micah, asking him to let Mama know what was going on, and then waited at the Lee place until the sheriff from Wheeler arrived.

"So you're the Mayer fella," the sheriff said, having introduced himself. "You been in on some of these before."

"Yeah," Wild said. "I was first into the Fischer house. And they asked me to look at the Johnsons after he up and did for them, least ways so we thought."

"Thought we were done with these after Joe Johnson."

"Hoped so, but it ain't look that way."

"And now you're here," the sheriff observed.

"Whoever it was, reckon he came after my family first," Wild said, not liking his tone. "Winged him with my rifle last night, out in my field. He dropped this," he added, offering the sheriff the bundle with the hatchet in it. When he unwrapped it, his eyebrows rose.

"Wicked little thing, ain't it?" he said. "Anyone else see this fella in your field?"

"My wife," Wild said. "It was a darkish night, didn't get a clear view. If it hadn't been for the dogs goin' off, we wouldn't even have known he was there. We told folks to spread the word by the telephone but this poor son of a bitch didn't even have one."

"Couldn't be a dirt farmer this far out, myself," the sheriff said comfortably, and Wild hated him a little for it, with his Wheeler ways and his condescension.

"Takes a special kind of man," he agreed. "Look, I just wanted to hand over the hatchet. Mind if I head home? Like to be with my family for Christmas."

"Sure, go ahead. Might drop by sometime if I have more questions."

"Well, mind the dogs when you do." Wild tipped his hat to the sheriff and climbed into his truck. When he turned onto the main road into Lea, he could tell the sheriff was still watching him, face turned north, away from the carnage inside the Lees' little shack.

The house was warm and cheerfully lit when he got back, with Moze's single bare lightbulb finally in full operation over the dinner table.

"Spoke to the sheriff," was all he said about it, when Mama gave him a questioning look. She nodded and checked on the nice roast she was cooking for Christmas dinner. Behind her, Wild noticed Adie slipping small scraps of prime cut to Buddy and Xolotl.

EIGHTEEN

WILD DIDN'T HEAR from the sheriff again, which might not have been a bad thing; true, they had no leads, but at least he wasn't under arrest for it.

That wasn't to say that January of 1935 was easy. It was bitter cold and the wind was cutting through the house, and Wild spent a good few hours hunting down drafts and plugging holes in the walls, re-sealing windows and doors. Bill spent the time attached to his typewriter, and Moze started wiring the kitchen for electricity so that if they could ever afford an electric stove, all would be in readiness. Lonny and Iscah mostly got in the way, and Adie had a time keeping the two of them entertained while Mama tended the housework.

It got so where one afternoon in early February, Wild threw Lonny and Iscah in the truck just to get them out from underfoot for a while, and to get himself out of the house. It didn't occur to him then that the urge to leave the house and the impetus to take Iscah and Lonny with him might not have been entirely his own.

He sent the kids to go explore the Dry Goods under Xolotl's watchful eye, then crossed the street to the seed store to see if any new catalogs had come in. There were a couple of other farmers there, looking as glad as he felt to get out of the house, and a handful of Rohlf's folks, in their distinctive orange tunics under their heavy winter coats.

"Hello there, Frank, Jenny," he said, to the two he recognized. The others he didn't know. "Who're your friends here?"

"Down from Oklahoma," Frank said. "They came back with Father Rohlf when he went on his salvation loop, searching for souls for the church."

"Nice to meet you," said one of them, offering his hand to shake. "Nice to be here in Lea, where we're protected."

The others exchanged looks as Wild shook his hand; Wild caught it but decided to ignore it.

"Well, Lea's always got a place for folks who want to be here," Wild agreed. "Guess I'll go find the kids – I left 'em making mischief in the Dry Goods."

"You should stop and say hello to Father Rohlf," Jenny said. "I know he always likes to see you, Wild."

"Well, if I see him I'll tip my hat," Wild agreed, giving a wave to the seed store clerk as he stepped back out into the cold.

He could see Lonny chasing around after Iscah in the Dry Goods, and he knew it would be stuffy in there, so he stopped out in the cold, breath frosting in the air, watching the lit windows of the church. He didn't even think about the fact that he was standing in front of it until he leaned up against one of the fence posts and felt his scars tingle gently.

The poles were a lot taller than they used to be – when he'd put in the fence with Micah and Tex Junior it'd been barely waist-high, but now the metal fence was as tall as his head, the wrought-iron gates even taller. Still, he could see the gentle glow of the big rose window, which now had several rings of stained-glass borders around the original smaller window he'd seen blossom, oh, years ago now. The night he'd met Adie. He felt as though he owed that big rose window somehow, for his wife and daughter and the son to come.

"Someday I'll make you tell me what you know about that place," a voice said behind him, and Wild turned. Dan Rohlf was standing in front of the gate, one hand on the wrought iron.

"I don't know any more than you do," Wild replied, and Rohlf snorted. "Well. A little more, maybe. But I don't understand any more than you do."

"Folks don't talk about it," Rohlf said. "Even when I'm sermonizing, I don't feel I ought to. But all I do is for the church. For whatever lives inside it and keeps us safe. You know that, don't you?"

"Rohlf, honest to God, it ain't my business what you and your people do and don't believe. But you seem to think I'm attached to your mission somehow, and I don't want to be."

"I know, I know," Rohlf said, looking genuinely sorrowful. "And it's a shame, it is, Wild."

"Maybe, but it's the way things are going to be."

"Well. Perhaps so." Rohlf gazed back at the church. "Ever wonder what's inside?"

"Sure, once or twice. Rotten pews, old Bibles." Wild snorted. "Micah thinks the bibles are fine. Says bibles can't grow mold."

"Someday I'll find out and tell you," Rohlf said. Wild narrowed his eyes. "Ain't found a key that'll open it yet, but this year…"

"A key?" Wild asked.

Rohlf rattled the gate. "Can't get past the fence less you go through the gate. I know, I tried. But that big door in there? No locks on that door, not anymore. I'll get past the gate sometime. And I'll open the church, and then, who knows? Maybe I'll see the face of God."

Wild let go of the fence, stepping closer. "You leave the old church alone, Rohlf."

"Why, Wild?" Rohlf asked, tilting his face up a little to meet his eyes. "What's inside?"

"Nothing for you. Leave the damn church closed. If it wanted to open for you it would, and it don't. You try to force it and you'll suffer."

"Doesn't matter. Gate's locked. For now," Rohlf said.

"I'm warning you," Wild said.

"I understand you are, but I got a higher purpose than your warnings," Rohlf said.

Wild tilted his head at him, thoughtful. It felt like they were having two different conversations.

"Anyone in your congregation have an accident recently?" he asked. "Maybe get winged while they was cleaning their rifle?"

Rohlf's face was impassive. "None of my congregants. Now why would you be asking a thing like that?"

"Someone's been making *sacrifices*," Wild said. "Which I hear you folks are big on."

"Strange sort of sacrifice." Rohlf shrugged. "We're a prayerful people. We only want what is good for Lea. The work we do is for the church, because the church works for Lea."

"Does it? These things – you don't understand them," Wild said. "I don't either, but I know better than to – "

"Marry them?" Rohlf asked. "Father their children?"

"Adelaide is not a *thing*," Wild hissed.

"Are you so sure of that?" Rohlf asked.

Wild felt like lashing out, even though he knew it would do no good. He could feel the church watching them both, waiting to see what would happen. So instead he inhaled and exhaled, and gathered his thoughts.

"Leave the goddamn church be, Rohlf, or you'll answer to me, and I won't come alone," Wild said.

"I hear you, Wild, but I got to follow the spirit," Rohlf replied.

"Let the spirit guide you the hell away from my family," Wild said, and headed for the Dry Goods.

"Wild, Wild!" Lonny called, as soon as he was inside. "Can we get some penny candy?"

"Not too much," Wild called back, as Iscah ran up to him to be picked up. "Hello, darlin', are you behaving yourself?" he asked, hefting her in his arms.

"Yes, Daddy," Iscah replied. She wrapped her arms around his neck, and he held her tight. She mumbled something into his shoulder, her face warm against the chill he was carrying with him.

"What's that now?" he asked, gently tipping her chin up.

"Don't let him open it, Daddy," she said, eyes big and serious. "It ain't for him."

"I won't," he said seriously. It wasn't exactly like he could see the church in her eyes, or that it spoke through her, but she spoke as part of it, he could tell.

Science Fiction, he thought.

"Long as I'm around, you'll be safe," he added, and meant it as much as he could.

NINETEEN

THE LETTER FROM the publisher arrived four days before the dust storm and Gerhardt did, though that was probably a coincidence.

It was a thin letter, and when Wild passed it to Bill while they were resting from planting, he could see the annoyance on Bill's face. It had happened once or twice before – Bill had sent off stories to the publisher, including return postage for the story, but hadn't gotten the story back, just the rejection. Usually he had copies, and Wild was pretty sure he had a carbon of the precious novel, but it was still a pain to have some careless publisher toss out his hard work.

"Maybe you can telegraph them to send it back," Wild said, laying their lunch out on the truck bed as Bill slit open the letter.

"Might try. Not worth it for the short stories, but that was a lot of paper – " Bill began, then stopped. He set the letter down on the bed of the truck and smoothed out the creases.

"They mention sending it back?" Wild asked.

"No," Bill said. His voice was oddly hollow.

"Bill? You all right? You look like a haint grabbed your heels."

"They ain't sending it back," Bill said. "They say they're gonna publish it."

"What?"

"They say they're gonna publish it. They got a contract they're sendin' but they'll send it with the...corrected proof," Bill said, eyebrows drawing together. "Guess that means they fix up the typos and such."

"You sold your novel?" Wild asked.

"Looks...looks that way. *We are pleased to accept your novel* Fearless, Sun *for publication...*" Bill trailed off. "Holy Jesus, Wild, they're payin' me two hundred dollars for it, advance."

"Two *hundred dollars?*" Wild asked.

"That's half a new truck," Bill said, staring at the letter still. "New shoes and clothes for everyone in the family. Hell, Wild, that's a stake in the farm."

Wild rubbed the back of his head. "Or an awful long time not having to work, to write another, Bill."

"Did all right working and writing the first one." Bill folded the letter up. "Don't tell Mama."

"Don't – you ain't gonna tell Mama?"

"Not yet. What if it's a con, Wild? Wait till the check comes, and the contract. Give me time to work out what to do."

"It's your funeral when she finds out," Wild said.

"Well, in that case I leave you two hundred dollars and my typewriter," Bill replied.

Bill was understandably quiet, though at that time of year they all were; plowing and planting was a series of long days, even with Tex Junior helping, and they'd have to help at his once they were done. Moze was old enough to lend a hand, but not quite old enough to carry a man's load, and Wild didn't like to drive him too hard. Lonnie, eight and with a double-dose of his father's cantankerousness and mama's stubbornness, mostly got in the way, but he tried.

Adie had wanted to come out and help the planting, as she and Bet sometimes had in the past, but she was carrying big and low, and it was as much as she could do to help Mama with the cooking. At night, she hardly slept; Wild fretted, but she said she didn't want a doctor, and Mama said it was normal, that she had carried Wild the same way. Wild remembered and renewed his prayers: *I ain't want a son if it means losing Adie.*

On that Friday in April, the day after Bill got his letter, Wild woke to find Iscah in the doorway of their room, apparently waiting for him. She was sleeping in with Mama now, to give Adie the best chance at a night's rest, and she clearly knew she must be quiet. Wild listened for Adie to stir, and when she didn't he climbed cautiously out of bed, scooped Iscah up, and took her out onto the back porch, in the humid but not completely warm spring air. He wrapped both of them up in an old blanket that smelled like horse, and said, "Well, little prophet, you got some news for me?"

Iscah seemed to be watching the fields, but she wasn't anxious, and Xolotl wasn't even awake, so Wild didn't worry.

"Daddy, mama can't stop it," she said. "Bisabuela can't either."

"What can't they stop, darlin'?"

"What's comin' on Sunday morning. Can't nobody stop it. It'll ruin all your nice corn."

Wild tightened his arms a little. "The corn is only just planted. Not even fully planted."

"I know. I'm sorry."

Wild considered this. "Something's coming to ruin the corn?"

Iscah nodded against his chest.

"Well, sweet pea, what should your daddy do about it?"

"Nothin'," Iscah said.

"Nothin'?"

"Stop plantin'."

"It's planting season, Iz, I can't," Wild said. "If we don't plant now, we won't have a crop. And uncle Tex is waiting on us to help him, too."

"Plant on Monday." Iscah shrugged, such a grown-up motion that Wild felt a little apprehension for his daughter.

"Can you tell me what's coming on Sunday, Iz?"

She pressed her face to his chest and made a small, sad noise, so he didn't push the matter.

"Should I tell the rest of the farmers?" he asked, after a while.

"They won't believe you," Iscah said, which was as much good sense as it was prophecy.

"How do you know all these things?" he asked.

"Just do," she said, and Wild nodded.

"You ready to go back to bed?"

"Yes, daddy."

He put her back in the bed with Mama, who barely stirred, and then went back to Adie, who was sitting up, rubbing her face.

"Where'd you go?" she asked softly.

"Iscah came to visit. I put her back to bed," he whispered back.

"What's she frettin' on?"

"Ain't sure. She says we're making no point in planting. Wants us to stop dead until Monday."

Adie looked uncertain. "You think it's…"

"Can't say. You ain't know nothing about it?"

Adie shook her head. "Ever since Iscah started talkin', things have been…disconnected. Silent."

"Maybe for the best," Wild said, unsure if he even meant it.

"Maybe," Adie agreed. "One witch in the family's enough."

"Hey now. My wife and daughter ain't witches."

Adie smiled. "And then what are we?"

"Science fiction," Wild said loftily. Adie's smile broadened, but then she flinched; the baby was kicking strong these days. Wild rested a hand on her stomach, felt the flutter of another kick.

"See you soon enough," Adie told the baby. "Let your mother sleep, you little beast, or I'll tell your daddy. What'll you do?" she asked Wild. "About the planting."

"Two days ain't so bad," Wild said. "We could go help Tex Junior plant. But – I think I'll tell him what Iscah said. Maybe ask if he don't want to wait too."

"You know if nothing comes up on Sunday you'll be a laughingstock," Adie said.

"Well, I won't be the worst Lea's ever seen," Wild replied. "Think you can sleep again?"

She shook her head. "You sleep. I'll get started on the bread for this morning. Might as well be moving around, maybe it'll shake this one loose faster."

"Sure you ain't want help?"

"Unless you can birth him for me, Wild, you can't help," she told him sweetly, and he let her go out into the kitchen. He fell asleep to the sound of her humming gently as she began setting out flour, as she fed the starter and warmed it to rise.

Later that morning, Tex Junior pulled into their yard same as he had for the past week. Sarah and the boys were in the cab; Sarah had promised to come help with the housework to take some of the strain off Adie, who could watch the children while sitting down, at least. Wild met them in the yard, and Sarah, at least, immediately knew something was up.

"What's wrong, Wild?" she asked. "Is it Adie?"

He shook his head. "No. Not yet. I got…something's happened. I think we ain't gonna plant anymore until Monday."

Tex rubbed the back of his head. "Why the hell not? You ain't sick?"

"It's Iscah," Wild said. Sarah and Tex exchanged a look. "She told me somethin' bad's coming. Something that'll ruin the crop, make planting pointless. She said we shouldn't even bother, that can't nothing stop it."

"Iscah's four," Sarah said.

"Iscah ain't four," Tex Junior said. Sarah looked at him. "You know she ain't, that child was born old. And weird."

Wild wouldn't have taken that from anyone else, but Tex Junior was family, and he knew about Adie, about Iscah. Not from telling, just from…being family. He didn't mean harm by it, only to put a name on it.

"I don't deny she's got a blessing on her," Sarah said, "but you can't just up and stop planting because a little girl says so, Wild."

"I aim to. You want us to help you plant your patch today, Bill and Moze and I'll come help, but I ain't recommend it, Tex," Wild said. "I'd get called a kook in Lea, but we're neighbors and you're kin. She warned me, I got a duty to warn you."

Tex glanced at Sarah again. Her lips were pressed in a thin line, but her eyes were considering.

"What'll we do if we ain't planting?" Tex asked finally.

"Pray, I imagine," Sarah said, startling them both. They looked at her. "If Iscah says somethin's coming to kill the crops, and you believe her, then I think probably we oughta pray."

THE STORM

BLACK SUNDAY OCCURRED on April 14th, 1935.

Cold air, blowing down from Canada in the early morning, collided with the still, warm weather that had settled over the Dakotas. A wind kicked up, brutal in its intensity, and rushed south through Nebraska. As it went it grew in strength, gathering long-dead topsoil and five years' worth of drought dust, roiling itself into a storm the size of which had never been seen before.

The temperature ahead of the storm dropped thirty degrees. It ran a thousand miles long, and blew up to a hundred miles an hour. Three hundred thousand tons of dust were displaced across the country, a dramatic climax to the most severe ecological disaster in living memory.

The storm moved south, rolling across the plains, and it darkened the sky for hours and hours.

Livestock died in droves, smothered to death or stampeded into a frenzy. People caught out in the storm were blinded, suffocated. Some died. Many who didn't die in the storm itself died later of the dust pneumonia.

Storms had happened before. The previous five years had already done plenty of damage. It was simply the size of Black Sunday that was shocking. Never had one storm destroyed so much, so thoroughly. Never had the desolation been so vast and complete.

It picked up speed and dust in Nebraska, and the full weight of it struck Kansas around ten that morning. It was in Oklahoma by three that afternoon. Boise City fell to it around five. By then Garden City was already dark with dust. It entered the Texas panhandle not long after.

The scale of the thing had its own merciless cruelty. Too much damage was done for any single town to be pitied or helped by another. Nobody outside of Wheeler County could care for Lea; nobody who wasn't of Lea itself could. It was a farm community, and everywhere the storm touched was a farm community. Carson and Wheeler also stood in the storm's path. Amarillo and Lubbock, too. By the time the leading edge was hungrily devouring Wheeler, Kansas and Oklahoma had been choking for hours.

When Black Sunday arrived at the height of its strength and power, Lea would be on its own.

Twenty

ON SATURDAY, THE family rested. Wild put the tractor up in the barn, then tied down everything and cleared the yard. He made sure the doors and windows on the farmhouse were secure, without knowing why, or what good it would do against an unnamed threat. Bill went over to help Tex and Sarah do the same. Mama and Adie cooked a couple of chickens and brought some preserves up from the cold cellar, just in case. Iscah, unusually quiet, watched the preparations with big dark eyes. Xolotl and Buddy, sensing something was wrong, paced between family members, sometimes whining softly.

Sunday morning, Adie looked drawn and tired, and Wild said they didn't have to go to church, but she insisted. So Lonnie and Iscah, Bill and Moze, Mama, Adie, and Wild all washed and dressed, and Wild drove the little ones and Adie to church, leaving the older ones to walk with Mama. Nothing happened at church, and nothing happened on the trip home, and Wild's tension began to ease.

Then, just as she was standing to see if Mama wanted help with dinner, Adie doubled over with a cry, clutching her belly.

"Adie?" Wild asked, standing.

"Was that Adie?" Mama asked, coming to the kitchen doorway.

"Baby's coming, Granny," Iscah said.

"Very suddenly," Adie added, breathing deep.

"Moze, you keep Iz and Lonny in here," Mama ordered. "Bill, come to the kitchen and pump a few basins of water and put them on to boil, then call Sarah and Tex and let them know, then call Gert Johnson."

They got Adie into the bedroom, Mama undressing her and piling quilts and towels underneath, Wild hovering in the background. When she was settled, he came forward to hold her hand while Mama washed with strong soap.

"Get out of here, now," Mama said, pushing him gently aside. "Make room for the women to work."

"Sarah ain't answering!" Bill yelled from the kitchen. "Mrs. Johnson says she's ready but you'll need to come fetch her."

"Go on, go fetch the midwife," Mama told him. Wild hurried out, passing Bill in the hallway.

"I'm going to get Mrs. Johnson," he said. "Keep an eye on Moze and the kids. If Adie has any troubles, call Mrs. Johnson back and let her know. Tell her I'm on my way."

"She'll be fine," Bill said. "You know how birthing is. It's always easier after the first time."

"Remind me sometime to tell you how your birth went," Wild said, and Bill grinned.

"Don't bust up the truck," he advised, and let Wild go.

He headed up to the main road as fast as he dared, leaving clouds of dirt behind him in his wake. It was a warm, windless day for April, and not many folks were out, it being Sunday; Wild sped as fast as he could through town, grateful as ever for the paving.

Gert Johnson, who had caught Wild and all his brothers and his daughter, and showed no sign of stopping anytime soon, was waiting with her carpet bag when he reached their farm on the far side of town.

"I hope your mama got dinner on before the baby started," she said cheerfully, when Wild pulled up. "Nobody does a nice Sunday dinner like Mary Platter, and if the baby's dropping now it might be late before your new one arrives."

"Well, I hope it's an easier birthing than last time," Wild said.

"Should be. Adie's a strong one. Breech isn't that common, and none of your Mama's sons were," she said. "That Iscah of yours was mischief from the word go, is all."

"Hasn't stopped being mischief yet," Wild agreed.

"How's she takin' her mama's pregnancy?"

"Hard to say," Wild said, but he barely paid attention to what he was saying, because he could see a thick dark line on the horizon, to the north, and he wasn't sure what it was.

"Wild, what is that?" Mrs. Johnson said, following his gaze.

"Don't know. Can't be sunset," he said, the hairs on his arms rising. At this distance, and the height it was – growing larger every second, and with dry white flashes behind –

"Is it a thunderhead?" Mrs. Johnson asked.

"No," Wild said, throwing the truck into high gear and gaining speed, pushing the engine. "It's a dust storm."

"In Lea?"

"Had to come sooner or later," Wild said. "I drove through one a few years back. We'll try to make it there in time but we might have to stop in town."

"Jesus preserve us," Mrs. Johnson said.

Wild roared through Lea as fast as he could, but by the time he reached the Dry Goods, the air was hazy. Mrs. Johnson was clutching his arm tightly.

"Wild," she said, and he gritted his teeth. "You won't be any good to your baby if you run us both off the road."

"But Adie – "

"Mary's helped catch a few babies in her time, and the storm can't last forever."

Lightning flashed ahead of them and despite her calm tone, she flinched. Wild, giving in, pulled over.

"The bank," he said. "Worst comes to worst, we can shelter in the vault."

He grabbed her hand, pulling her out of his door after him so they wouldn't be separated, and forged his way the ten feet to the bank's entrance. They burst inside in a flurry of dust, door slamming shut behind them. Tellers were cowering behind the long counter, patrons huddled below.

"Mayer, is it the apocalypse?" Lentz Platter roared from down the hall.

"Pretty nearly, sir," Wild called back. "It's a dust storm, a bad 'un. I weathered one in Oklahoma a few years back."

"Well, what do we do?"

"Keep everything shut, wait it out," Wild said. "Can I use the telephone, Mr. Platter? My wife's in labor."

"Saints preserve us, boy," Platter said, emerging and pointing him towards the phone. "Delivering in this? She's a brave woman."

"Baby doesn't really give her a choice," Wild said, swallowing. "Hey, you got water in here? Wet down the curtains and hang 'em shut, it'll help keep the dust out. Gum up the windows if you got gummed paper."

"You heard the man, get going," Platter barked. Wild took down the phone receiver and rang home. Lonnie answered.

"Wild, where are you?" he bawled, clearly terrified. "Adie's droppin' the baby and Mama's in with her and so's Bill but it's so black out we can't barely see – "

"I'm stuck in the storm, Lonny," Wild said. "Listen close. It's a dust storm. I'm at the bank. Tell Mama I'm safe and Mrs. Johnson is with me but we can't get through. Soon as you do that, you and Moze soak bed sheets in water and hang 'em over all the windows and doors. Are the dogs in?"

"Yes, Wild," Lonnie said unsteadily.

"Good. Make sure Iscah stays put. You let Bill look after Adie and Mama," he said, and almost lost his nerve when he heard Adie screaming in labor pain down the phone line. "You got me, little man?"

"Yes, Wild."

"What're you gonna do?"

"Tell Mama you're safe then get Moze to help hang up the wet sheets and don't let Iscah go anywhere."

"There you go. You'll be fine. And tell Adie I love her. I'll call back in half an hour if I can, okay? Call the bank if there's trouble."

"Okay, Wild," Lon said, and hung up. Wild hung up too, leaning against the wall. Soft murmurs in the background and the splash of water told him the bank was being weatherized. Outside, he could hear shouting, but not what they were saying. It was already too dark to see whoever it was who was caught out in it. He could barely see the truck.

"It's like the hand of God," Lentz Platter said, and Wild looked up at him. "There's lights in the storm, but no rain."

"That's how it was last time, too," Wild said.

"How long'd it last?"

"An hour or so. But it wasn't..." Wild swallowed. "It was dark, sure, and the wind howled and the lightning, but it wasn't like this. It wasn't black like this."

"They say they've been getting worse. Newspaper says Congress is supposed to do something but what they're meant to do I'm sure I don't know," Platter said.

"There's pamphlets about it, folks doing social services. Bet's helping, in the summers," Wild said. "But the damage is done. You can't nail bad dirt down once it's sucked dry. The topsoil just blows away, and topsoil's all we got."

"But this isn't Lea land that's blowing."

"No, sir, and I pray it ain't never, but it's someone's land," Wild said.

"How's your family?"

"Bill's there with the women, and Mama's been to a few births. Moze is old enough to look after the little ones. Wish I could be there but I wouldn't be any use."

"Gert would, though."

"Yeah. Best just hope this one comes easier than Iscah did."

There was yelling outside again, someone screaming for help, and Wild started for the door until Platter caught him.

"You can't go out in that, son," he said gently.

"There's folks dying out there," Wild said.

"And you will too if you try to help."

He knew it, in his heart – he couldn't be of help to most of those stranded outside, just like he couldn't help the poor families in Oklahoma or in Kansas, or even outside Lea, where the land was slowly starving. There was a sickness on the whole country, and he was one hick farmer who happened to be luckier than most.

"Mr. Platter, you got them driving goggles for your car?" he asked.

Platter shook his head. "Don't do it, Wild."

"But you got 'em?"

"You won't be able to breathe!"

"I can't just do nothin'," Wild said. "I'll wet a handkerchief. You can hear 'em yelling."

"You got a wife and a mama and little ones to look to."

"And I can't help them. Let me do what I can."

Platter sighed, but he went back into his office and took his driving goggles out of his desk drawer, offering them to him like a blindfold to a condemned man. Wild wetted his handkerchief in the bucket they were wetting the curtains in, then tied it over his nose and mouth, buttoning his jacket to the neck against the driving dust.

"There's a rope, Mr. Mayer," one of the tellers said, and Wild turned around. "In the storeroom. We could tie it to the doorknob."

"Well, go and get it," Platter said. The teller scurried away, returning with a thin hank barely thicker than twine. Wild knotted one end around his wrist, the other to the inside knob of the door.

"You're a god damned fool," Platter told him, and Wild nodded. "If you die out there I'll make sure Mary's looked after."

"I'll see you inside half an hour," Wild said, and slipped through the door, hauling it shut with a hard slam after him.

The wind was immediate, screaming in his ears, and the darkness was nearly complete; the goggles kept the dust from his eyes, but it wasn't as though he could see much. The handkerchief, plastered to his face, grew a thick muddy layer immediately, and he had to wipe it off pretty much continually, but the air he breathed was at least mostly clean.

He made his way down the boardwalk in front of the bank, groping blindly, and found someone huddled just outside the last window, coat over their face, trying to shelter from the dust. Wild bent down and grabbed the man's hand, pulling it to the twine.

"Follow it back to the bank!" he screamed into the howling wind. He felt the man's other hand pat his arm in acknowledgement, and then the jerking of the rope as he followed it. There was yelling from somewhere off to his right, in the road, and Wild bruised his shin on the bumper of his own truck as he tried to find them. The rope jerked as whoever it was he'd found opened the door and got inside.

Wild felt his way around the truck and into the road, pulling the rope over the truck as best he could. The screaming was louder out in the road and he reached what he thought was the other side, bumping blindly into the railing of what must be the porch of the Dry Goods. Huddled underneath it, out of the wind, a woman was curled up in a ball, crying for help. The howl of the wind was quieter here, but dust still filled the air.

When she saw him, the woman screamed "JESUS CHRIST DON'T HURT MY BABY," and Wild knew her voice –

"Sarah, it's me," he said, wiping some of the dirt from his goggles. His nephew Platt, Sarah's youngest, was in her arms. "Sarah, it's Wild. I come to get you to safety."

"I can't go out in it, Wild, I can't," she sobbed, holding her little one tighter. Wild reckoned she'd come into town on some errand, and must've been just arriving when it hit – probably didn't even know why he was there.

"It'll be okay. Look, I got a rope, I'll get us back to the bank," he said. "They're safe out of the wind there. Come on, you can't stay here, you'll suffocate."

"It's the end of the world," Sarah managed.

"It's a bad storm, but I been through one before. Look, here," he said, and untied his handkerchief, shaking the dust loose and retying it over little Platt Muller's face. He squinted his eyes shut and pulled the goggles off, feeling for her face and pulling them down over her eyes.

"I'm gonna hold the rope taut from here and you follow it to the bank. I'll come in behind you," he said.

"Wild, I can't – "

"Come on, Sarah, you ain't a coward," he said, pulling her into a momentary hug. "You got little ones depending on you."

She sucked in a breath, and he felt her nod against his shoulder. He pulled the rope taut, found one of her hands, and wrapped it around the rope. He could feel her crawling out and then the rope rose as she stood; he came out behind her, pulling the rope hand over hand, eyes squeezed shut, coughing as dust blew into his nose, between his teeth every time he took a breath.

Sarah could move faster than he could, since he had to hold the rope tight; he could feel when she got the door open, the way the rope jerked loose and then tight again, but he was still somewhere in the road, he thought.

It would be so good to get one clean breath of air, he would never take it for granted ever again –

Then he tripped, sprawling, a breath knocked from his lungs. Someone was lying in the road, half-buried already, and Wild kept his eyes closed and swore at God Himself.

But there was no choice; he was here and could do this one thing, and so he had to.

He felt up the leg he'd tripped over until he reached a belt, and then hauled whoever it was upwards until he could get an arm around his waist. Heaving, he lifted the man over one shoulder and secured him there with one arm, pulling on the rope with the other. He staggered, almost lost his cargo, and swore again.

There was a flash of lightning he could see through his screwed-shut eyes, which were beginning to ache…and then a flash that stayed, and a sudden silence.

Wild could feel dust fall off him as the wind stopped, and when he inhaled tentatively, the air was clean and cool.

He brushed at his face, clearing the dust from his eyelids and brow, and opened his eyes. All around him, dust raced past on the wind, blowing steadily sideways, a scouring hellstorm. Lightning flashed, but it was barely visible, dim in the face of the light shining down on Wild, in this one little pool of peace.

He turned, searching for the source, and saw what he first mistook for a big round moon, incredibly, impossibly close. Then, as his vision cleared a little, he saw it was the rose window of the church. Light was streaming down onto him from it, in a circle that reached almost to the door of the bank.

He took three deep, clear breaths.

"I suppose this means I got a son," he said. The light shone on; Wild touched his forehead respectfully, gave the light a nod, and then turned back to the job at hand.

It was only ten or twelve feet to the door of the bank, and the light followed him until he touched the doorknob. Then the darkness and the wind returned, and Wild got a mouthful of dirt before he managed to get inside.

There was a moment of silence when he hauled the door shut, a strange tableau. Sarah was sitting in a chair with Platt, a damp rag held in one hand; Wild saw now that the man he'd found sheltering near the bank was a Baptist, who now had a wet cloth over his eyes. Everyone else was in a crowd near the teller desks, far away from the windows, staring at him.

Then the silence broke, and people came forward to help – hands took the man off his shoulder and untied the rope from his wrist, and someone brought him a cup of water that made the dirt in his mouth turn to mud. One of the farmers helped dust him down while they laid out the other man on the floor. With the dust settling, Wild could see in the dim light that it was one of Rohlf's people, in the signature orange and blue.

"Might as well have left him," someone said. "One of the crazies from the Church, and probably dead anyway."

"I wouldn't leave a dead coyote out in this," Wild said. His voice was hoarse, and his throat hurt. When he coughed it felt like dust flew out his mouth, though he knew that probably wasn't the case. Even as he spoke, the man in the orange and blue was coming around, sitting up and spitting mud into a handkerchief. Wild crouched down and offered the half-drunk cup of water. The man drank gratefully, then looked up at him and blanched.

"Hell of a time to get caught outside," Wild said carefully. "Safe in here, though."

"What was it?" the man whispered.

"Dust storm. Came west from Carson, most likely," Wild said.

"But – not in Lea," the man stammered, then coughed another wad of mud into the handkerchief. Wild pushed on the cup, forcing him to take another sip.

"Had to happen sooner or later. If we're lucky, won't happen again for a while," he said.

"But after all we've done – we were promised," the man murmured bewilderedly.

Wild tilted his head. "Promised what?"

"That this was the garden. That if we made the – the sacrifices we had to…" the man trailed off, lips pressing down into a thin line as he seemed to realize, again, who he was speaking to. Wild watched him for a moment, suspicions beginning to stir in his mind, but the man seemed distracted by the water, so eventually he stood and went to Sarah, standing in a corner, being comforted by Lentz Platter.

"Jesus, Wild," Sarah said, her voice cracking as he approached. "I like to died twenty feet from you."

"None of that, now," Lentz Platter said calmingly, patting her on the shoulder. "You're safe here."

For now, Wild thought, but didn't say. There would be folks dead in this storm, and if this wasn't the last, there would be hell to pay in the next year or two. But at least this time it wouldn't be his kin.

The phone rang and literally everyone startled. Wild couldn't help it; he laughed, mostly amused, a little nervous.

"That'll be Lonnie," he said, voice high and tense, as one of the tellers answered it. "Tell him to name the boy Gerhardt."

Every head swiveled from Wild to the teller. He said something quietly into the phone, and then hung up.

"Congratulations, Wild, it's a boy," he said. "How'd you know?"

"Little bird told me," Wild said. "Adie's all right?"

"Mother and son doing fine."

"That's great. Hey, Sarah, you'd better call Tex Junior and tell him you're safe or he's like to go out in this looking," Wild said, and Sarah, after a brief look at Lentz Platter for permission, hurried over to the phone. "How do you like that," he said to Platter. "I got a son."

"How did you know, though?" Platter asked quietly.

"The truth'd make you think I'm off my head," Wild replied.

"Maybe I wouldn't," Platter said, ambling off to take charge of the clerks. Sarah, hanging up the telephone, came to sit next to Wild with little Platt still in her arms.

"Tex says thank you," she said. "And congratulations. I didn't know Adie was in labor or I would'a come over to help."

"It came on fast," Wild said. "Hell, Sarah," he added, pulling her against him with one arm and tucking her head under his chin. "What would I have told Tex if you died under the porch of the Dry Goods?"

"Folks die," Sarah murmured. "The influenza got your daddy and my mama. The war got half their people. Maybe the dust'll be what does it for yours and mine."

"No wonder Iscah said we shouldn't bother planting," Wild sighed.

"If she's got any more words of wisdom I'm prepared to hear 'em," Sarah said.

"Well, I'll ask, but I don't think prophesying's a precise science. Anyway, gonna have to buy more seed."

"It'll be a lean summer until the second crop comes in. And a late harvest. And that's if there ain't another storm like this one."

"And Tex is carryin' the mortgage on your place, ain't he?"

"We could lose a crop and be all right. Can't lose two, though."

"Well, don't be proud. If you can't make the mortgage, call me. Tex Junior ain't gotta know. Don't lose the farm over it."

"Some will," she said, her voice hushed.

"We'll do what we can. Lea's been lucky so far," Wild said. "Means we got a duty to share it around to those who ain't."

"Well, I wish whoever's looking out for us wasn't sleepin' on the job when this storm hit," Sarah said.

"I imagine right now they got other concerns," Wild told her, thinking of Adie in labor, and the kind of energy it took to fight off a storm like this one. "We'll get through it right enough. Now, let's find somewhere quiet to let Platt sleep, and I'll call down to the farm and hear more about my new son."

It was true dark by the time the storm blew itself out around ten o'clock. Lanterns bobbed through the fields as farmers inspected the damage, but they couldn't see much, and most of them went to bed in a sort of dazed shock. In town, people staggered out of their various shelters and gathered in the street, speaking softly to one another, staring at the piles of dust three and four feet high in some places, up against the walls or around the wheels of cars.

Wild dug out his own truck with a shovel hastily borrowed from the Dry Goods; he was heading across the street to dig out Sarah's when she stopped him.

"Tex'll come for it tomorrow. Can you take us home?" she asked, and he nodded. It would take less time to take her home than to dig her out, and Mrs. Johnson had already arranged a ride home with one of the Baptists, since her services weren't needed. Wild concentrated on avoiding the dunes of dust on the road, bumping his way clumsily towards home in the dark. Sarah was very quiet.

"Bet writes to me about Oklahoma and Kansas," she said eventually. "She says she ain't been the same since you drove through them to Chicago. She says trying to fix it…it's like holding back the wind with your hands."

"Sounds like Bet," Wild said. Her letters to him were more about her studies and school.

"I didn't know what she meant until now. Imagine a whole state buried under like this," she said. "How do they stand it?"

"Most go west."

"I couldn't leave Lea."

"Me either, but I suppose plenty of folks in Kansas said the same." He pulled down the road to Tex Junior and Sarah's place, the pretty little Sears home they'd put up so they wouldn't have to live in the old Fischer house. Tex Junior was standing outside, a lantern in one hand. Wild had known Tex Junior since they were born, practically, and had never seen him cry, so he pretended he didn't see it now, when Tex Junior swept Sarah and the baby up into his arms and shook like an old man.

He pulled the truck around while they were still hugging, and offered Tex Junior a wave as he left.

Bill was waiting for him outside their own house, sitting on the steps to the porch, with Buddy and Xolotl sprawled nearby. The dogs ran to greet him as he got out of the truck.

"Swear to God, I thought the end had come," Bill said. He looked about a hundred years old, Wild thought. "I thought all the science fiction stories were right and aliens were bombin' us from space. Happy goddamn birthday, Gerhardt Mayer."

Wild grinned. "One little old dust storm and everyone goes to pieces. How's the family?"

"Adie's restin', got the baby with her," Bill said, leading him inside. "Healthy little thing, screamed like anything, nursed himself stupid, passed out. I don't blame him. Moze and the little ones are asleep, or at least in bed. Mama's seeing about something to eat."

"Good thing too, I'm starvin'," Wild said, as warmth and the smell of hot food washed over him. Mama came out of the kitchen and hugged him, eyes wet. There were little piles of dust all over the floor where she'd been sweeping. There were thin films of it on the tables, too, and in the corners of the windows.

"Thank God," she said. "When the storm blew up I hoped you'd have more sense than to come home."

"Did my best," Wild told her. "Lentz Platter sends his regards."

"Look at you, wearing five pounds of dirt," she said, dusting it out of his shirtsleeves. There was only so much he'd been able to do in the bank. "Wash for dinner. There won't be much, the dust got into everything, but – " she stopped at the expression on Wild's face, smiling. "Go look in on Adie first."

"Thanks, Mama," he said, kissing her cheek.

Adie was sleeping, hair askew in little fly-aways, exhaustion and the pain of labor evident in the dark hollows under her eyes. There was a mess of dirty sheets and blankets from the birthing in the corner, and the floor would need to be scrubbed, but all that could wait. Next to her on the bed was a basket stuffed with pillows, with a damp blanket draped over most of it to keep the dust out. When he lifted a corner gently, careful not to stir up any air or let much light in, a swaddled-up, wrinkled, red-faced little infant lay sleeping. Wild gently touched his cheek with the tip of one finger, feeling the same awe and pride he had when he'd seen Iscah for the first time.

"Well, Gerry, you picked a hell of a time to show up," he whispered. The baby didn't stir. Wild heard a soft shuffle behind him, and turned to see Iscah in the doorway. "Hey, Iz. Want to see your brother?"

She nodded. He lifted her up so she could peer in at him, holding her close.

"Were you scared during the storm?" he asked. She shook her head. "You weren't even scared for your mama?"

"Mama got protection," Iscah said.

"Oh? From who?"

"You know, daddy," she told him. He supposed he did, at that. He let the corner of the blanket fall and carried her out into the hallway, back towards the room she was, at the moment, going to have to share with Lonny.

"Daddy," she said. "The storm wasn't no good."

"It sure wasn't."

"The crops're gonna fail."

"Whose? Ours?" he asked, but she was shaking her head.

"Our crops won't. But someone's will."

Wild laid her in her little cot, looking down at her, concerned. Lonny snored obliviously nearby.

"Iscah, you're just a little girl. You shouldn't worry about the crops. That's my job."

"They're gonna be mad when they do."

"You just let me handle the crops," he told her, stroking hair off her forehead. "I'll make sure you never, ever go hungry."

"It's worse'n that," she said softly.

"How?"

"Just is," she told him. "But it'll be okay. You'll see. Remember it'll be okay, daddy."

"Sure will, darlin'. You go to sleep now."

He tried not to think about what she'd said, as he ate dinner that was only a little gritty with the dust. Bill, across the table, was carefully cleaning his disassembled typewriter with small damp rags; Mama had gone to bed.

"What do we do tomorrow?" Bill asked.

"I'll need to spend a little time with Adie," Wild said. "Get out tomorrow morning and see what the damage is, as best you can. We won't worry about planting until we know how much we got to clear. Suppose we'll have to plow the dust under; it'll smother anything we try to plant in it direct, but we can't shovel off acres of dust."

"What'll it do to the crops?"

"No idea, but what else can we do? I'll get Moze to go in to town tomorrow; Sarah left Tex's truck there, so he can drive Tex in to get it, and while he's there he can put in a new order at the seed store. You got a list of what we planted?"

"Sure, I'll send it with him."

"Good. Ask him to keep his ears open about anyone else needing help with re-planting, and..." Wild paused.

"Anyone who died?" Bill asked. He kept his eyes on the little typewriter part he was scrubbing clean, not looking at Wild.

"Might as well." Wild stood, taking his dishes to the washbasin.

"Wild," Bill said, still not looking at him. "Will the farm be okay? I got some insurance to the tune of two hundred dollars."

"Keep it for now," Wild said. "We'll be fine as long as there ain't another storm."

"But there won't be, will there?" Bill asked.

"No," Wild said. "I don't think so."

"Because of Adie?"

"Maybe." Wild shrugged, staring out the window. In the darkness you could almost believe nothing had happened today, that his land wasn't suffocating under some other farmer's misfortune. "You weren't wrong, Bill. About there being some...some powerful science fiction in Lea today."

"Did she cause it?"

"No. She just couldn't stop it. A bad coincidence, maybe."

"Some folks might call that witchcraft," Bill said.

"Do you?" Wild asked.

"I think if there was evil in Lea today, it was the storm, not Adie," Bill said. "I think…the land ain't been used well, Wild. Ain't been cared for like it should. Maybe that's nobody's fault; most folks don't know any better. But any creature ill-used enough'll bite its master. I think the land's tellin' folks to do better."

"I hope they listen. We've been trying in Lea, you know that."

"I do. And if Lea's got a guardian angel it might be a woman who still ain't ever said where exactly she comes from."

"Adie's a woman, Bill, not an angel."

"Sure thing," Bill said. "I'm going to bed, soon as I get this put back together. You bunking with me tonight?"

"No, I'll make up a pallet next to Adie. Wake me for breakfast if I ain't up."

Bill nodded and left Wild alone in the warm, silent kitchen, with the dust in the corners, and the memory of what he'd seen in the storm that afternoon.

TWENTY ONE

LIFE, EVEN AFTER the storm, moved onwards like it always did; they tallied their dead, plowed the dust into the good strong earth, re-planted when they could, and slowly cleaned their homes, clearing the roads.

Some folks had to re-mortgage their land. The churches, Baptist and Lutheran, took up collections for the worst-hit. The Church of the Redeemed Abandoned didn't take up collections, but nobody had the heart to snub them for it; they were the hardest hit by the storm. Two of their buildings had blown completely down in the high winds, and a lot of their equipment was damaged beyond repair by the dust as a result. A lot of their food stores were spoiled, too, and their fields were drifted three feet deep, being a little lower than most of the farms in the area.

Five of the seven people who had died in Lea during the storm came from the church – Wild had brought one of them inside, but the rest had made it another thirty feet before collapsing, and were found huddled together under the eaves of a nearby building. Wild wondered if Rohlf still preached about sacrifice these days.

A month after the storm, Bet came home from Chicago. She brought a crackling-new diploma, her now much-battered suitcase, and an earnest-faced friend named Elaine who'd been rooming with her, to save on money and housekeeping chores. They arrived in Elaine's old four-seater jalopy, which didn't look like it would survive a heavy rain, let alone a trip from Chicago to Texas, but they got there somehow. Mama, by now resigned to Bet traveling where and when she wanted, just hugged them both welcome and helped set up the cot in Bet's room.

Wild took in Bet's cheerful new demeanor and the way this friend of hers, Elaine, looked at her, and drew his own conclusions.

"You fixing to stay in Lea?" Wild asked at dinner that night, already knowing the answer. Bet and Elaine looked at each other.

"Well, I owe Lentz Platter my education, and if he wants me to work for the bank for a year or two I can't tell him no," Bet said. "But I'm wanted back in Chicago – they got a job for me there, helping out in the immigrant houses and surveying the city. Important work, even if it doesn't pay very well."

"Pay well enough to live on?" Mama asked. Bet nodded. "Then it pays enough. I hate to think of you in that big city for good, but I suppose you been there years already."

"Bet fits Chicago like a glove," Elaine said. Wild could see Bet trying to quiet her, but Elaine pressed on. "She was meant for a big city, I think."

"You come from Chicago, Elaine?" Adie asked.

"Just outside it, Oak Park. When Bet said she came all the way from Texas to go to the University I thought she must be the bravest person I ever met," Elaine said. "I was scared just thinking about living in the city itself, and here was this girl from a farm in Texas moving in as easy as you please."

"Is it really as busy and full as they say?" Bill asked. "What's it like living right next door to another person?"

"People!" Elaine said. "Our little apartment's got neighbors on both sides and above and below, too. But I like it – I can't imagine living out here without anyone around. Sorry, that's rude," she added, but Mama just smiled. "What I mean is, I've always lived so close to someone, if you yelled, help'd come running. I don't know what I'd do with myself so far from other people."

"It makes a body self-sufficient," Mama said.

"There's lots of publishers in Chicago," Bill said.

"Bet said you were a writer! She said you were always sending stories off to Chicago," Elaine replied. "You get anything published lately?"

Wild cast a sidelong glance at Bill. The corrected proof of his novel had come back to him just that morning. The check for $200 had come a week before, but he hadn't deposited it yet.

"A few things," Bill said.

"Bet says it's all science fiction, men living on the moon and such.

It's thrilling to think about, isn't it? Do you suppose one day we'll really find out what's up there?"

"Sure. Hopefully in our lifetimes."

"There's all kinds of new rocketry science," Moze put in. "I been reading about it. The Germans're all studying it now."

"Makes me nervous, to be honest," Elaine said. "Nobody builds Mr. Hitler's kind of rockets because they want peace. No offense to....to Germans," she added, sudden nervousness in her tone.

"We're Americans, anyhow," Moze said. "Ain't we, Mama?"

"We sure ain't Mr. Hitler's kind of Germans," Mama agreed.

"Sure ain't," Iscah echoed. Wild glanced down at her, but she was busy pushing the last of her vegetables around her plate. She'd been quiet since Bet arrived, which Wild supposed was understandable; she barely knew her, really, and Elaine was a complete stranger.

"I'd like to take a rocket to the moon," Lonny announced. "Wouldn't you, Bill?"

Bill grinned at him. "That'd be an adventure, I suppose, but I got more Earthly concerns to see to first, Lonny."

That evening, while Mama minded Iscah, the others spilled out onto the back porch – Bet and Elaine, Bill, Adie nursing Gerry, Moze climbing the porch pole to work on his wiring, and Wild, gazing out across the land, watching Lonny bug-hunting in the field. Rain had come not long after they plowed the dust under, and against odds the corn was already starting to show green shoots out of the dirt.

"You have such a big family," Elaine said, leaning against the porch railing. "Bet told me, but experiencing it is something else altogether. In Oak Park, it's just me and my Mom and Dad."

"We're lucky," Wild said, and then, "Bill, you been writing to Bet about moving to Chicago, ain't you?"

Bill shrugged, a little guiltily. "Ain't made up my mind yet."

"But there are publishers in Chicago. You could get a good job. Maybe even write for the newspapers," Wild pressed.

"Bet's shown me some of Bill's work," Elaine said, giving Bet a loyal look. "You know how good he is, Wild, you must."

"Sure, I do," Wild said. "I'm not the one you got to convince, Bill. Mama...."

"It's hard on her," Bet said. "God knows. Having one child in

Chicago's hard."

"Maybe she'll get comfort in it," Adie said. "If Bill's there too. You can look out for each other."

"Still not easy, having your son a thousand miles from home," Wild said softly. He looked to Bill, who nodded. "Going to have to be your choice, Bill."

"I ain't made for farming," Bill said, and it felt like a confession to Wild. "I ain't bad at it, Wild, but I ain't made for it."

"Well, that's all right," Wild said. "Another few years and we'll probably have to apprentice Moze out to some electrical genius or other. If you're gone too, it means I won't have to split up the farm, unless Lonny's got a passion for it. I can just hand it down to Gerry."

Adie smiled over their son's head. "What if Iscah wants it?"

"Iscah ain't want it," Wild replied easily. Elaine looked fascinated by the whole discussion. "Maybe if she's got an uncle and aunties in Chicago, she'll make her way there, too. Now," he said, leaning forward, before anyone could remark on Iscah's aunties, "the question is, how to break it to Mama."

"I can do that," Bill said stoutly. "Just need some peace is all. Hard to get with all of y'all underfoot."

"We ought to get out of your way, then," Wild said. "Now that planting's done again, I could make myself scarce for a day or two, long as you keep an eye on the fields."

"Where?" Bill asked. "Carson? Ain't got business in Carson this time of year."

"What about Palo Duro?" Adie asked.

"What's Palo Duro?" Elaine said, intrigued.

"It's an old canyonland, south of Amarillo," Wild said.

"They just made it into a state park," Adie added. "I been itching to see it, Wild, you know I have."

"You think Gerry's old enough?" Wild asked, considering the idea. "Iscah might like it."

"We could take a couple'a pallets and some tarpaulin," Bet said. "Go see the canyon, sleep out under the stars. I never been to a state park before."

"And Elaine ought to see how pretty Texas can be, lord knows she ain't seeing its best side in Lea," Wild said.

"I like Lea just fine," Elaine said. "But I've never seen a canyon at all. That'd be something to tell the folks in Oak Park!"

"And give Bill some peace to hash it out with Mama," Wild said. "Fine. Moze, you mind going camping out in the canyon a day or two?"

"I ain't mind!" Moze's voice drifted down from above.

"And if Iscah goes, Lonny'll want to go. Well, that's settled," Adie said. "I ought to put Gerry in his crib. Wild?"

"Iscah'll be wanting her bedtime story," Wild said. "Hey! Lonny! Come on in now, it's time to wash up and say prayers. Moze, stop your wiring things and come inside."

"And I got writing to work on," Bill added.

"Bet, why don't you show Elaine the land?" Wild asked. "Nothing like seeing the fields at sunset to give a person an appreciation."

Bet gave him a puzzled look; Elaine, who seemed to understand, looked grateful. She and Bet lingered as the others went inside, and Wild stood, shoving his hands in his trouser pockets. They watched him expectantly.

"My family's old German Lutheran," Wild said to Elaine, considering how to phrase this. "My granddaddy married a Texican and some folks didn't like that. My wife used to go to Baptist services, and plenty of folks didn't like that either – me marrying outside the faith – but there wasn't a one didn't like Adie, or my granny Maggie, once they got to know them. We're old-fashioned in Texas, particularly in Lea, but I got good eyes to see with. And I've seen a little of the world outside of here."

"You strike me as a man who knows a few things," Elaine agreed warily.

"A few," Wild said. "For instance, I know Bet couldn't be happy in Lea."

"Wild," Bet said.

"I ain't know exactly why before now, but now I know," Wild continued. "And I want you to know that I know, Miss Elaine, so you'll understand."

"Understand what, exactly?" Elaine asked.

"Where I stand on it," Wild said. "Maybe my mama ain't know, and maybe if she did she wouldn't understand. Maybe nobody in Lea would understand. But so long as you look after my sister, there's always a place in my home for you and yours."

Elaine pushed away from the railing, standing up straight, even if she still had to tilt her head a little to look him in the eye. "You ought to know, I'd look after her even if there wasn't a place for her or me in your home, Mr. Mayer."

Wild grinned. "I see why Bet likes you so well."

"If you two're done," Bet drawled, and Elaine stepped back, offering her hand for Bet to take. "Wild, you better see to Iscah."

"So I'd better. Enjoy your walk," Wild said, and ducked inside.

TWENTY TWO

THEY PLANNED THE trip out to Palo Duro for the following Friday, intending to leave in the morning and sleep over Friday night, back in time for dinner on Saturday. Mama clearly suspected something was up, but she didn't protest, so on Friday they loaded bedding and tarps and rope into the truck bed with Moze and the dogs, packed food and sundries and Lonnie and Iscah into Elaine's jalopy with Bet, and took off down the pretty, new-paved road to Amarillo. Wild, arm around Adie with Gerry in her lap, was pretty satisfied with life.

Palo Duro was the prettiest land he ever saw, full of deep russet stone cliffs striped with chalky white, the whole thing flocked with green juniper, mesquite and cottonwood. There was plenty of space to make a camp, and when Adie told Moze that she'd read there were dinosaur fossils always being found in the canyon, he took Iscah and Lonny off straightaway to go looking, Xolotl and Buddy following along curiously.

"Is that even true?" Wild asked, laughing, as he assembled stones for a firepit. Elaine and Bet were swearing over one of the tarpaulins, trying to stake it out as a shelter in the hard earth.

"Sure," Adie said. "Knowing Iscah, wouldn't surprise me if they found something."

"What's Iscah going to find?" Elaine asked, dropping down next to them with a huff. "I think we got the shelter up."

"Looks fair," Wild agreed, eyeing it. There were one or two stakes could go a little deeper, but he'd take care of that before nightfall. "Adie told the kids there were fossils in the canyon. If anyone's like to find a big dinosaur buried under our feet I suppose it'd be Iscah."

"She's a quiet little thing," Elaine said. "Lonny mostly chattered at her in the car."

"Still waters," Adie said, as Wild piled dry grass in the fire pit, stacking sticks on top of it. "Hope they weren't too much of a trial."

"No, Bet kept 'em busy. Though I did have a question about something Lonny mentioned, about another family in the area."

"Sure," Wild said. "Lea's a small town – tough to understand what's happening if you come in from outside."

"You get used to it," Adie added.

"Lonny said he and some of his friends went ghost-hunting in an old house near your land – the Fischer place?"

"Ah," Wild said.

"Ah," Elaine echoed.

"It's a sad story, I didn't want to tell the details while they were in the car," Bet said, joining them. "You were there, Wild, you tell it."

"Happened a few years ago, before Iscah was born," Wild said. "Been a couple of sad stories in Lea these past few years."

"If it's not my place to ask – "

"No, it's fine," Wild said. "The Fischers were our neighbors, though not so close as they'd be in Chicago," he added with a dry smile. Elaine nodded. "John and Georgia were older'n me, younger'n our parents, so we didn't know them so well as we might have. They had two little girls and a son. Christmas day, Tex Muller came and fetched me – he was up there to borrow a ladder, said their truck was there but the house was dark, and oughtn't to be. When I went in I found 'em all dead."

"All of them?" Elaine asked, wide-eyed. Wild nodded. "Jesus, Bet, you never said."

"It's not polite conversation," Bet said. "And anyway – "

"It's a bigger story," Wild told her. "The Fischers had been murdered, pretty awfully too. Lonny and the Muller kids go ghost-hunting in the old house 'cause Tex Junior – he's married to our sister Sarah, their boys are our nephews – bought the Fischer farm. I imagine the old farmhouse is starting to fall down, these days," he said to Bet, who nodded. "Ought to have a word with Tex Junior about salvaging the wood and such. Any rate, it was a shock for Lea."

"They don't know who did it," Adie said. "Wild called him the Roggenwolf. It's an old German legend, about a monster that comes out of the corn."

"Ain't the last time, either," Wild said. "There's been a few more families dead, these last few years. Came after us, one night. Whoever it was, we ran him off, but it didn't stop him."

"Like the axe man of New Orleans," Elaine said with a shiver. "And you still let Lonny and the others play in the old house?"

"Well, it ain't no harm in the daytime," Wild said. "Other than they might take a tumble on the stairs, I suppose. And these days most folks keep a guard dog."

"It's just...sort of accepted?" Elaine asked.

"Well, what're we gonna do, sell up and move?" Wild asked. "Sooner or later he'll get shot for his troubles. I winged him last time."

"I don't like it," Adie said, and Wild glanced at her, surprised. "None of us women do. But there's nothing to be done about it, not now anyhow."

"I ain't know it made you so uneasy," Wild said.

Adie shrugged. "Can't be helped. No point complaining."

Wild was opening his mouth to say something, he wasn't sure what, when there was a whoop and excited barking from nearby. Coming up a low hill was a proud procession – Iscah in front carrying a rock, with Lonny behind her carrying another one, and Moze and the dogs bringing up the rear.

"Told you she'd find something," Adie remarked, as Iscah and Lonny brought their discoveries to her to be examined. Wild concentrated on lighting the fire, so that it would be big and well-fed by the time darkness fell.

Adie knew the most about Texas fossils, having taught about them, but Elaine had taken classes in prehistory before entering the math program at the University, and that night under the moon and stars she regaled them with stories about the behemoths and leviathans who had inhabited the wilds before humanity came. The children listened attentively, eyes huge, while Moze used his pocket knife to carve hardened mud away from the fossilized vertebrae Lonny had found. Iscah fell asleep in Wild's arms, curled around a little row of ancient teeth set in stone. Lonny wanted to go off looking for a really big one, "A whopper!" but Wild told him to wait until sunrise at least.

That night, lying in their tarp shelter with the stars wheeling overhead, Gerry sleeping fitfully on his chest, Wild said, "I ain't know how upset the murders made you, Adie."

"I told you," she murmured. "There's nothing to be done."

"We could move. Sell up and shift out."

"Wild, your family's been in Lea for generations."

"When I first came home after Lon died, we thought we might sell and move to Lubbock. And the farm's worth even more now."

"What would you do in Lubbock?"

"Don't know, but there'd be something. I ain't afraid of hard work. With Bill out of the house it's just Moze and Lonny to get launched, and there's schools for them in Lubbock. Iscah'll be going to school in another year. Mama's getting older, be good to be close to a doctor if we need one."

"But you wouldn't be happy," she said.

"Don't matter, if you ain't happy now."

"I am happy, Wild," she said, and he relaxed a little. "I'm not...not haunted, not afraid. I don't like it, and it makes the winters darker, but I wouldn't let that drive us out of Lea. Besides, I...feel like we should stay. For Iscah's sake."

"To be near the church."

She nodded in the darkness.

"Well, I don't imagine Buddy and Xolotl would like a city anyway," Wild said.

Adie patted his shoulder. "Go to sleep, my love."

They came home the following afternoon, sunburned, covered in red dust, with more fossils packed in the now-empty food basket, guarded fiercely by Lonny. Mama looked tired and sad, and Bill had a set to his chin that said he'd had to stick pretty hard to his guns, but they didn't seem *angry* at each other, at least. He could tell Bet saw it too.

"I'm going into town on Monday to see Lentz Platter," Bet said at dinner, after they'd all washed up and Mama had fussed appropriately over the tiny skull Moze brought back for her. "I need to ask him if he'll want me at the bank here in Lea."

"It does seem a shame, him paying your education and you not staying," Mama said. Bill looked like he had a sore tooth. "I understand why," she added with a sigh, glancing at Bill.

"Well, I like to think that he's sending me out into the world to do more good in his name," Bet said. "And you know, especially with more roads being paved all the time, pretty soon I could visit Lea at least once a year."

"Chicago's got some big thinkers," Elaine put in. "There's always new ideas she could bring to Lea."

"It's what I did," Wild added loyally. "When I did my year at the aggie school, I came back full up with ideas for new farming."

"Rotating the crops is what kept the dust out for so long, I imagine," Bill said. He shot a sidelong look at Mama. "Elaine says the University sometimes offers free writing classes."

"I imagine so," Mama said quietly.

"Wonder who'll get the scholarship now Bet's done with it," Wild said. "There's some likely kids coming up, I suppose. Bound to be one of them who wants to see the big old world."

"Is that what you wanted when you got it?" Moze asked.

"Hell, I didn't know. I just thought I might learn something," Wild said.

"I did," Adie said. Everyone looked at her, and she smiled. "I wanted to see as much of the world as I could."

"And after you did, you stayed in Lea?" Elaine asked, sounding a little skeptical.

"Well, I saw enough, after a while," Adie replied. "And sometimes you find people you want to put down roots with. But you can't force it. All you can do is make wherever you settle the best place it can be."

"I ain't fixed to settle forever in Chicago just yet," Bill said suddenly. "Just to see it for a few years. Must be something there to teach me a few things."

Wild saw Mama looking between Bet and Bill. They both had a lot of Lon Platter in them. He had a sense, just for a moment, of great alienation; his siblings all shared a father, and most took after him heavily. Not since Bill was a baby had he felt like such an outsider. Even Bet and Sarah had each other.

But he'd watched them all grow up and even before Lon's death he'd helped to raise them. Anyway, there were more important things to family than blood.

"If you're not wanted at the bank, when will you leave?" Mama asked.

"Probably in a few weeks. Unless…" Bet hesitated.

"Unless you need me for the harvest, Wild," Bill said. "Though Bet and Miss Elaine could always go ahead without me, and I'll go on the train after we've sold the harvest in Carson."

Wild glanced at Mama, but she gave him no hint of what she'd prefer. Bill seemed hopeful that he could go when Elaine and Bet did, and Wild couldn't blame him. It was hard to wait on the life you wanted, when you could see it so close.

"I imagine Moze and I'll get along all right without you this year," he said. Bill let out a soft huff of relief. "Might hire on a few hands to help, but we've managed that before."

"Will you need a suitcase?" Mama asked, clearly trying to be conciliatory.

"Might look in town when Bet goes to see Lentz Platter," Bill said. "I think the Dry Goods has some cartons I could use."

"Mama," Wild said, because the tension was hard, and he didn't care for it. "What do you think Daddy Lon would think of Bill upping sticks to Chicago?"

Bill and Bet both smiled. Mama looked surprised, then seemed to give it thought.

"I imagine after the roaring he'd have done over Bet going there, he'd give Bill a six-gun and tell him to stay away from the saloons," she said, and then she started to laugh. "Lord above, can you imagine Lon trying to give a farmer's advice on the big city."

Bill chuckled too, and then Wild and Bet were laughing as well. Elaine seemed amused, though it turned to worry when Mama wiped her eyes, sniffling suddenly.

"I ain't know why I'm bein' so stormy about it," she said. Adie rubbed her shoulder. "I never wanted anything for any of you but what'd make you happy. You go on to Chicago with my blessing, Billy."

"Yes, Mama," Bill said. The way he said it made Wild wonder if he could let his own children go into the world with as much good humor as Mama was. The thought of it made his heart clench.

"Well, now, Gerry," he said, turning to where the baby was sleeping in a sling over Adie's chest. "You ain't going to Chicago until you're eighteen, I don't care what Uncle Bill and Auntie Bet say."

HARVEST 1935

BILL, BET, AND Elaine left for Chicago in early June. Lentz Platter said he couldn't see what good it would do to stake a fine young woman like Bet down in Lea if she had ideas to change the world. Later, to Wild, he said that he wasn't sure Bet's progressive ideas would do well in Lea, and it was just as well to have her trying out all these newfangled ideas elsewhere. Wild, knowing discretion to be the wisest course, nodded to Platter and did not tell Bet what he'd said.

He spent a full day working with Elaine on her car, making sure the engine was running as smooth as it could be, the tires were in good shape, and every bolt and screw they could find was tightened. Mama loaded them up with as much food as they could fit that wouldn't spoil, and Wild had to dig Lonny out of the pile of luggage in the back seat when he declared he wanted to go with them to see the dinosaur bones Elaine had told him were in the Field Museum in Chicago.

"Quit your fussin'," Wild told him, as Lonny wriggled in his arms. "Behave yourself and help with the harvest and maybe Bet'll let you visit come winter."

"I'll send you a postcard of some of the bones," Elaine promised him, which mollified him a little. Mama, meanwhile, was hugging Bill and Bet together, whispering last-minute advice and benedictions.

Just before he got into the car, Iscah toddled up to Bill and wrapped her arms around his leg.

"Be safe," she ordered him, solemnly.

"Promise I will, Iz," Bill replied. "You look after your Mama and Daddy and Gerry, won't you?"

"Ain't have to, they got a guardian angel, Granny says," Iscah replied serenely. Bill laughed and lifted her up, kissing her cheek.

"Tell me my fortune, little one," he said, bouncing her onto his shoulder. Iscah looked down at him, eyes dark and solemn.

"Tell good stories," she said. "Your fortune'll look after itself."

"Fair enough." Bill set her down, well back from the car, and then climbed in. The family waved them off until the car was out of sight, and then went back inside – Mama sadly, Moze and Lonny a little sullen that they couldn't go, Wild and Adie too busy herding the children to be concerned with what they themselves felt.

"I still think Bill could have stayed through the harvest," Mama said. "For that matter, so could Bet. She drove a good bargain."

"Moze is big enough to fill Bill's shoes," Wild said, and Moze looked pleased by this. "Lonnie'll be more of a help this year too. Adie can come at selling time if you're worried my numbers ain't what they ought to be."

"No, I'm sure you'll be fine," Mama sighed. "It's just…sad, that's all."

It was sad, and it was quiet after they'd gone; Wild hadn't realized how much he'd depended on Bill until he had to train Moze to fill Bill's shoes. Without Bet and Elaine, dinners were a lot less lively. Still, it was the way of the world, Wild knew, and he couldn't be sad that Bill was on his way, however long that journey might be. Someone had to go and someone had to stay behind; that always seemed to be the way of it, and some part of Wild had known that Bill and Bet were always going to be the ones to leave, eventually.

That summer was a hot one, but the rains came regularly enough that the corn thrived. The oats could use a little less moisture, but past seasons had been dry enough, towards the harvest time, that they wouldn't lose the oats. The farmers on Sunday, out back of the fellowship hall, all talked of the dust storm and the seed crop they lost before it was even growing; they worried about another one, and read reports to each other from the Carson newspaper of other storms in Oklahoma and Kansas. They talked in hushed tones about the dust pneumonia and the ruined land. The few who hadn't come round to Wild's way of planting, back when he'd brought crop rotation home from college years ago, now sidled up to him to ask what they ought to be doing.

"I guess your family's a line of prophets," Tex Junior said to him once that summer, without awe or rancor, just as if it were a fact, and maybe even a little bit of a joke.

"Blessed by luck, I suppose," Wild replied.

It was high summer, with the first harvest of the oats already looming large, when the second storm came. Iscah had been fussy that morning, but hadn't predicted anything out of the ordinary; Wild had been so confident that they were safe that he'd let his guard down. Not that anticipating a storm would do much good in any case.

He was out among the corn, the dogs snuffling along behind him, when it happened. The crop was well taller than him by now, and there wasn't much left to be done – just making sure there was no leaf-rot or vermin in the field. But halfway down a row he felt a shudder of recognition, a sense that the air was somehow wrong. Buddy and Xolotl, as if they felt it too, dropped into low growls.

It was ten feet from the row he was in to one of the wide lanes he'd left between fields, and when he turned northwards in the lane, he saw it. Well beyond the farmhouse, beyond his land by miles, there was a dark stripe on the horizon. It might have been a thunderhead, but it was too low, and the edges rolled even at this great distance.

He looked around himself frantically. There was nothing to be done for the crops, which would be damaged if they weren't destroyed. The storm was an hour away, perhaps less, perhaps much less; farmers on the north side of Lea might even have seen it earlier and sounded the alarm, though if they'd called all the farms, nobody had come to warn him.

The corn might suffer, the oats be threshed from their stalks. If he was lucky he'd salvage; if not, his labor would rot in the field. But that was as inevitable as the seasons, and he couldn't fight it.

Then he realized what the oncoming storm might mean, and he took off running for the farmhouse.

He burst in through the kitchen door, panting, yelling "MAMA! ADIE! MOSES!" but nobody replied. His immediate thought was that they might have sheltered in the cellar, but three steps towards the cellar and he saw –

Mama lay in a crumpled heap on the kitchen floor, blood crusted in her hair. Xolotl sniffed the blood in the air and then sent up a howl, Buddy joining him, until Wild gestured for them to be silent.

"Jesus Christ," he swore, bending to scoop an arm under her shoulders, fingers probing the wound. Her eyes flickered, and the pulse at her throat was strong, but —

"ADIE," he called, terrified. "MOSES?"

He heard Gerry send up a wail, then, and followed it into their bedroom, where Adie lay, like Mama had, the same wound across her head. She had Gerry in a sling, askew, on her chest. Wild scooped Gerry up and hushed him, then lay him on the bed while he saw to Adie, moving her gingerly as he dared.

There was a thump in the kitchen, and Wild grabbed his rifle from the hallway rack as he ran back — but it was Moses, pounding on the cellar door. Wild lifted the latch and hauled him up.

"They hurt Mama," Moses said, stunned. Wild helped Lonny up behind him, and peered down, expecting Iscah. "Mama said someone was coming and sent us into the root cellar but Adie was s'posed to come too and — "

"Moze, where's Iscah?" Wild asked, heart seizing in his chest.

Moze looked up at him, eyes huge and terrified.

"Mama told us to be quiet," he whispered. "They came into the house. Mama sent me and Lonny down and said Adie'd come, but she locked the door after us — "

"Iscah was screamin'," Lonny supplied.

"I think they took Iscah, Wild," Moze said.

Wild felt his fingers tighten on the rifle. "Who was it, Moze?"

"They was prayin' as they came," Moze said.

"Was it that sumbitch Rohlf?" Wild asked. Moze nodded.

There was no time to hesitate, he realized. The storm was coming, his mother and wife were hurt and his son and brothers were terrorized, and the Church of the Redeemed Abandoned had his daughter.

"There's a dust storm coming," he told Moze. "Can you carry Mama into our room? Adie's in there."

Moze swallowed, nodding.

"All right. I'm gonna get Iscah back," he said. "You two batten down. I'll leave Buddy in case someone comes back. Moze, get Bill's gun and protect the family. Xolotl and I are going."

"But if there's a storm — " Moze began, already lifting Mama, Lonny trying to help.

"Close and lock the windows and doors. Call Tex Junior and see if Sarah will come see to Mama and Adie, then call into town and see if anyone's seen Rohlf," Wild interrupted. Moze nodded. Wild tucked a box of ammunition in his shirt pocket. "When Adie wakes, tell her I gone after Iscah and I'll kill the man took her."

He stopped only long enough to wet a handful of rags before loading up the truck – Xolotl leapt into the front seat, still growling a low, rumbling bass, and Wild laid the rifle where he'd have easy access as he steered the truck down the dirt to the paved road that would lead him through Lea, up to Rohlf's church. On the horizon, the storm was growing, and the air had a dry, gritty haze to it. He could see less by the minute, and he had to swerve once or twice to avoid cars coming the other direction, evidently headed home to secure farmhouses against the storm.

He meant to try and catch Rohlf before he made it back to his farm, if he could; he'd tear-ass through town and worry about everything else later. But then, as he reached town, he saw it – the amber glow of the old church, and Rohlf's truck parked outside it. Half a dozen other cars were there too.

No one from town was on the street. The porches and front steps were deserted, and the blinds drawn in the bank and the Dry Goods, and every other window as well. But there were people gathered in front of the church, all in orange and blue, heedless of the dust.

Wild slewed the truck to a halt and climbed out, rifle in hand. The congregants of the Church of the Redeemed Abandoned were clustered around the closed gate of the fence, watching something on the other side.

Wild fired into the air. Heads swiveled, alarmed, and people began to back away when they saw him and Xolotl standing too close for comfort.

"Y'all better let me through," Wild snarled, reloading. One of the men started towards him, hands upraised as if to placate, and Wild leveled the rifle at him. "Take me to my daughter or get the hell out of the way."

The man opened his mouth and Wild fired over his head, the bullet pinging off the wrought iron gate of the church. He reloaded again as people screamed and began to scatter.

The way through to the gate was clear, and Wild reached out to touch it as soon as he could. His scars tingled, but it didn't open for him. On the other side, through the dusty haze and the wind that was beginning to bite into bare skin, he could see Rohlf, a bundle under one arm –

No, that was Iscah. Iscah, bound in strips of cloth, blindfolded and gagged.

"ISCAH," he yelled, beating against the metal gate, Xolotl hurling himself fruitlessly against it. She writhed in Rohlf's grip, which at least meant she was still alive. Wild could see a hatchet in a sheath on Rohlf's belt, and his blood ran cold. "Rohlf, you child-stealing *son of a bitch!*"

"It's the only way to stop the storms!" Rohlf cried back, as Wild threw the rifle's strap over his chest and began to climb the gate. "The deaths aren't enough anymore! It wants its own back!"

"You touch her and I'll rip your heart out!" Wild yelled, already halfway up the gate. His boot slipped and he almost lost his grip; the flesh of his palms tore on the rough metal. Xolotl was screaming below, battering himself on the fence.

"I never wanted to be the Roggenwolf!" Rohlf pleaded, his voice desperate. "We had to! The storms would destroy Lea!"

Wild wriggled over the top of the gate and dropped to the ground; he fumbled for the rifle and got to his feet, tucking it under his arm, finger finding the trigger, but he was nearly blinded now by the dust, and he couldn't see well enough to know that he wouldn't hit Iscah if he fired.

"You're a sick monster, Rohlf," he yelled, trying to lure him closer. "The Roggenwolf is a *monster!* Nobody had to die!"

"The land needed blood! The church needed blood!" Rohlf wailed. "I spared your family, I only need – "

"If my daughter bleeds I'll meet you in Hell for it!"

There was a flash of lightning, and the booming roll of thunder; Xolotl began to yelp in fear. Wild steadied the rifle. He'd seen Rohlf at the very door of the church, laying Iscah down while he tried to open it, and if he had one more flash like that he could fire. Just one more flash of light –

Then the doors of the old church opened, and white light and stillness poured out of it, and everything became very clear, and very slow.

Rohlf was turning, his back to the open doors through which light illuminated him, turning and bending to gather up Iscah who lay on the path behind him. Wild wanted to fire, but every moment felt like a lifetime, and even as he tried desperately to pull the trigger, he saw the masonry of the church facade begin to move.

The whole building twisted like a living thing, pale adobe and pretty white stone expanding in some places and contracting in others. It looked like nothing so much as the scales of a snake, as if muscle rippled beneath the stonework. The door expanded, widening hungrily, and Wild watched in a mixture of awe and fear as it loomed upwards, stretching out over Rohlf's head.

As he bent over Iscah, Rohlf saw Wild's face and turned, but it was far too late; he raised his arms and screamed, and the church *fell on him*, fell like a hungry dog on meat, the lintel of the door dropping down over his body. The white, pure light vanished as the building *ate* him, opened its mouth around a living human man and swallowed him down without chewing.

Wild almost pulled the trigger as soon as the light vanished, but the dirty wind of the storm hit him like a slap in the face, and he dropped the rifle, running forward to gather Iscah into his arms. As soon as he did, there was a crack like thunder and the doors of the church opened again. Terrorized, nearly blind, and desperate, he carried her forward, inside, without hesitation. He heard the creak of the gate, and then Xolotl burst inside after him.

The door slammed shut, and the world was mercifully silent.

He didn't even look around himself at first, too occupied with freeing Iscah; he pulled his knife from his boot and cut her bindings, tugging the rag off her eyes and the gag from her mouth. She threw her arms around his neck and buried her face in his dusty chest. He clung for dear life, Xolotl licking them both worriedly, pacing around them and whining.

"It's okay," he whispered, over and over. "Daddy's here, Iscah. Won't nobody hurt you while I breathe. Daddy's here."

"The bad man made the storm," Iscah sobbed, into his neck. "He hit mama and – "

"Shh, it's okay, Moze is looking after mama and granny. The storm'll blow out, and we're safe here," Wild said. Iscah nodded against him.

Over her shoulder, as he held her, he could see the high, white walls of the inside of the church; they were flat and unbroken, even where they vaulted into the roof far above his head. No studs, no beams, just smooth white, like polished plaster. He couldn't tell where the light that bathed the inside was coming from, but it was brighter than anything he'd ever seen, and certainly brighter than the yellow glow he'd seen from the outside, through the rose window.

He stood, Iscah still cradled against his chest, and turned to face where he'd come in. From here he could see where the rose window ought to be, but there was no window on the inside. There were no windows at all, in fact. No pews, no Bibles or hymnals as they'd speculated. And there was no Dan Rohlf. Wherever he was, it wasn't this safe, brightly-lit sanctuary.

"Where are we, Daddy?" Iscah asked softly, raising her head to look around as well.

"Inside the old church," Wild replied. And then, because he knew it had to be true in some sense, "This is where your mama comes from."

Iscah was silent, eyes drinking it in.

"This is your birthright, darlin'," he said. "I ain't pretend I understand it. Maybe you will, someday."

The room echoed with the sound of his boots on the white floor, and when he set Iscah down, it seemed as though the floor glowed under her feet. Xolotl slobbered all over her. After a few seconds of struggling against him, she giggled. Wild dusted the sand of the storm off his shirt, out of his hair. He undid the button on the cuff of his sleeve and rolled it up, oddly unsurprised to see his scars glowing pale against his skin.

He could feel himself being watched, and Iscah and Xolotl too. It didn't feel evil or mean, didn't seem like it'd harm them, just – curious. Perhaps protective. Like a parent that didn't fully understand its new baby yet. Wild could relate.

"Iscah, stay with Xolotl," he said, and she nodded, plopping onto the floor. He walked further into the room, leaving a trail of dust behind him. The only thing in the church, aside from them, was what looked like an altar at the far end. When he drew close, the wall above the altar telescoped apart, forming the shape of the rose window at eye-height. Even though it was in the wrong wall, he could see through it out onto the main street of Lea. The wind seemed to be dying down. He could see his rifle lying in the churchyard, his truck parked in the middle of the street.

He offered his arms to the window, the scars pulsing gold.

"I ain't know what we did to deserve it," he said softly. "I ain't know why you picked me. Done my best to accept my blessings and pass 'em on. Done my best to make Adie happy, keep my children safe. I reckon you ain't really a church and you got not much in the way to do with God."

The window seemed amused, if such a thing were possible.

"Guess this might be the only time you and me ever meet face to face, so to speak," Wild said. "So thank you, I suppose. And so long as I live I'll make sure you stand safe. And my little ones'll do the same after I'm gone. Like the corn," he added with a grin. "We come and go, but we'll do our best to bring in a good harvest."

"Daddy," Iscah called, and Wild turned away from the window. She was standing in front of the door, one arm over Xolotl's shoulders. "We can go now."

Wild nodded, going to her and pulling her up into his arms. "Reckon we can."

Outside, the air was clear, and a light, warm rain was falling. Wild lifted his face into it, letting it wash rivulets of dirt down his skin. The doors to the church were already shut; Wild gathered up his rifle and passed out through the open gate, Xolotl trotting at his side. It closed behind them.

Outside the Dry Goods, people were gathering on the covered porch to stare at the rain, and a crowd had formed at every window in the bank.

"Strangest weather I ever saw," someone said. "You take shelter in that old church, Wild?"

"Closest place to hand," Wild said. "Say, you see any of those Redeemed Abandoned folks go running past when the storm hit?"

Heads turned. Wild followed their gaze. There were half a dozen dust-covered mounds strewn across the street and yards of Lea.

His first instinct was a savage kind of pleasure, and it shocked him; he raised a hand to his mouth, pressing his knuckles under his nose.

"I got to take Iscah home," he said. "Mama and Adie are both poorly. Can someone call up to the doctor and ask him to come to the Platter-Mayer place?"

"Is it the dust?" someone asked, in a hushed tone.

"The Roggenwolf nearly got us," Wild said. There was a ripple of shock. "But he won't bother Lea no more."

"Didja shoot him, Wild?"

Wild shook his head. "I reckon fate took care of him. Send the doctor," he added, settling Iscah in the seat between himself and Xolotl. "Get them bodies laid out for burial, too. I got to get home."

Mama and Adie were both awake by the time he returned, thankfully, and Adie burst into tears when she saw he had Iscah with him. He settled Iz on her lap and left them cuddling under Sarah's watchful eye, Adie with a makeshift bandage tied around her head. Mama, laid out in Bill's old room, was sore and seemed confused, but Moze was giving her water and had Lonny jumpin' around to fix them all some food, so Wild tried not to worry too much.

"Wild," Moze said, gnawing on some cold beef while Lonny heated the rest in a pan, clumsily. "What about the crop?"

"I ain't looked yet," Wild said tiredly. "If it's done for, it'll wait till we've eaten. If it ain't, it'll still be there when we're done."

"What'll we do if the crop's done for?"

"Harvest what we can and live lean for a year or two," Wild said. "Same as we would any year. We can thank God nobody died and that we ain't got more mouths to feed."

"What'd you do with them churchgoers who took Iscah?" Lonny asked.

"I didn't do nothin'. Guess their sins caught up with them, is all," Wild said. "Tell you this, though, Lonny. If I pass on sooner'n I expect, you boys make sure someone's looking after that old church in town. Tex Junior'll help but it's our job, our family. We look after Lea and we look after that old church."

"Why, sure," Moze said easily. "What do you reckon's inside that old thing, anyway?"

Wild thought about the white light, the window in the wrong wall, the sense that the church could speak if it chose – and it simply chose not to. He thought about the sight of it swallowing Rohlf down whole, disappearing him from the world.

"Better not to know, less it wants to tell," he said finally. He saw Iscah in the doorway, Adie in shadow behind her, and got up to help Adie to a seat at the dining table, taking Gerry's sling off her shoulders and settling the baby in his basket on the table. She gave him a wan smile, but her hand settled over his, thumb brushing the edge of the scars on his wrist.

"You went inside," she said softly. He nodded. "You learn anything?"

Wild shrugged. "Never questioned my luck before. Don't seem wise to start now."

"Do you think it was luck?" she asked. Wild blinked at her. "Nothing comes without a price, Wild."

"Rohlf thought the price was our daughter," Wild reminded her.

"Well, he didn't understand how the price is paid," she said.

"I don't imagine I do, either. I know what it ain't, but…" he shrugged.

"We all make sacrifices for each other in Lea," she said. "It's why I stayed here. People mostly do the decent thing. Sometimes it isn't easy. It costs, sometimes. But the cost comes back in the end. So I found myself a town of good people, and I found myself a good man who did right by his, who looked after folks when he ought to. And those sacrifices paid back."

Wild reached down to where Iscah was tugging on his pant leg to be picked up, settling her in his lap and pulling his plate close so she could pick at the food there. He smoothed down her thick hair, thoughtfully.

"Got more back than I gave," he murmured. "Couldn't ever give enough to be worth one of these little ones, let alone both."

"So you say," Adie said, smiling at him, then turned away. "Moze, could you bring me one of those biscuits from yesterday? I don't think I'm up to beef just yet."

"Lonny'll do it, I'm gonna look in on Mama," Moze called, and Lonny ran over with the bowl of biscuits and a crock of butter.

"Doctor should be down when he can," Wild said. "I asked them in town to send him."

"Well, I'll meet him when he gets here," she said. "You should see how the crops are."

Wild nodded, lifting Iscah off his lap so he could stand; he thought about taking Buddy and Xolotl out with him, but Xolotl looked done-in and he suspected he'd want Buddy protecting the family for a while to come.

The corn was still standing, at least, and when he walked down the rows he couldn't see much damage. Silk from the ears strewed the ground, but that wasn't going to harm anyone. There was a thin film of dust on the leaves and ears, and that might hurt the growing, but even as he thought it, even as he ran his fingers through the dust, he felt the wind pick up. Alarmed, he ran through the rows to see if another storm was coming, but the horizon was clear.

Instead, when he turned back, he could see the wind blowing the dust away; it was rising like a thin golden cloud above the corn, spinning away gently, dissipating into the air like smoke.

TWENTY THREE

THE DOCTOR, WHEN he finally came after seeing to folks in town, wanted Mama and Adie both resting, and that meant the menfolk had to take care of the cooking and the washing-up for the next week or two. It took Moze and Lonny a few days to get the house really scrubbed down, while Wild did his best at the stove. It was a week solid before he had the time to sit down and write to Bill and Bet about what had happened, wanting to reassure them that everyone was safe, that nobody had been truly harmed.

It was just as well, since it was a week before he got real news about the Church of the Redeemed Abandoned, too. He was reasonably sure that without Rohlf, the yearly killings would stop, and at any rate he now knew that something, whatever the old church was, would protect the family. But he still wanted to know what they were up to, and Tex Junior finally caught him up, sitting on the fence overlooking the corn fields, fresh from town.

"They say it was the freak dust storm," Tex Junior said. "Killed near half of them all told. Every one of them that was in town. I reckon everyone who came for Iscah," he added, and Wild nodded. "Folks say they didn't have the sense to get in out of the storm. A lot of the survivors went back to their families. Out of towners mostly caught rides back out of town."

"They ain't carrying on up at Rohlf's place?"

Tex Junior spat in the dust. "Storm took care of that, too. Damndest thing – most farms only got half an inch or so. Barely had to sweep out my barn. Crops're fine. But that place took a pounding. Three feet of dust, crops destroyed, and every single building blown down. Someone was mad as hell at that place."

"You don't say," Wild said sourly.

"It'll take a while for Mrs. Rohlf to get on her feet again. She might sell up. Don't know who'd buy it, though," Tex said. "I do feel sorry for her. She weren't happy."

"Might buy it," Wild said, surprising himself. Tex raised an eyebrow. "Well, if the corn sells good this year. And at least I'd know I was giving a fair price for it. I ain't want Mrs. Rohlf swindled."

"It's clear on the other side of Lea. You can barely manage the land you got, now that Bill's gone," Tex pointed out.

"I could tenant it out. Maybe let it to some poor Okie who lost his own. Or we got paved roads now – maybe Lea'll build out a little. Like Wheeler or Carson. Could sell the land for houses eventually."

"Well, don't dig too deep. We might still get more of those storms."

"Maybe. Don't think so, though. Thanks for the news, anyhow."

"Thought you'd want to hear. I best be getting on – give my and Sarah's love to your mama and Adie."

"Sure. Come over for Sunday dinner next week, I just about got the hang of roasting a chicken."

Tex Junior laughed. "How about you come to ours, so it's edible?"

"I won't say no," Wild agreed. "See you at church if I don't before, Tex."

Wild's letter, when it arrived, caused a stir in the little apartment Bill shared with Bet and Elaine in Chicago. They'd developed a tradition of opening letters from Lea over dinner – it helped Bill with the sharp homesickness of his first few months in the city, feeling as though he was sitting down to a meal with the whole family, and it was one of the only times all three of them were sure to be together, anyway.

This letter felt different, though. For one thing, it was extra thick, page on page of writing, which was unusual for Wild; he mostly wrote short letters, covering news of the family and of Lea without much flower or fanfare, to the point where Bill often wrote back to ask him to elaborate on certain things just to get the full story. This time, though, it looked like Wild had a lot to share. And it opened with reassurances that everyone was fine, which of course were never all that reassuring.

Bet started to read it over dinner, and then went silent; she set the paper down, rifling through the pages, then went back to the first one.

"What's wrong?" Bill asked.

"He says Iscah was kidnapped," Bet said, skimming Wild's scrawling handwriting. "He says she's fine, but she had a fright."

"Who did it?" Bill demanded.

"Looks like Dan Rohlf. Some fool notion from his prayer group," Bet said. "He says she's back, at least, so I guess it wasn't that serious. And…there was a dust storm."

"Another one?" Elaine asked, alarmed.

"Did he say how the crops did?" Bill asked.

"He says everyone's fine and so are the crops, but…" Bet set her fork down, using both hands to flip through the pages. "Jesus," she muttered. "He's been in the old church, Bill."

"The *old* church? In town?"

"What's wrong with that?" Elaine asked. "It's not illegal, is it? I thought you said nobody really owned it."

Bill and Bet exchanged a look – discussing the church wasn't even done in Lea, let alone with outsiders, but Elaine wasn't quite an outsider, even if she wasn't quite family yet.

"I'll explain it to you later," Bet said to Elaine, passing the letter to Bill. "Point is, Iscah's safe, and it sounds like the Roggenwolf's been caught."

"Well, praise be for small mercies," Elaine said. Bill ate without paying attention to the food, engrossed in the letter, detailing the inside of the church and Rohlf's half-confession, the wrath visited on those who had taken Iscah and those who had belonged to a church run by a murderer.

His publisher had asked if he had anything written about his life in Lea; interest in rural *roman-a-clefs*, whatever those were, was on the rise. He said he hadn't, too taken up with leaving Lea by means of his own imagination, but that he had more in the vein of space adventures, if they wanted it. The reception to that had been fine, but not overly heated.

After dinner he went to his desk in the corner of the kitchen, where it was boiling hot in the summer but far enough from the sitting room that he wouldn't disturb Bet and Elaine with his typing, and studied the letter again.

I ain't saying whatever good fortune came our way wasn't earned, Wild had said in the letter, *But it don't hurt to show a little gratitude. I'm going to paint the fence after the harvest, sweep out the yard if it'll let me, and I mean to bring Iscah and Gerry with me when they're older. Ain't much you can do from there in Chicago, I know, but I suppose I told you all this on account of I want you to remember it too. Out there in the world, someone ought to keep hold of it.*

Bill set the letter aside, thoughtful. It had been written to all of them, but he could hear in it the extra meaning it held for him, and he understood what Wild was asking. And anyway, he owed Wild for the idea about the sun-farmers. So he rubbed his hands together, cracked his knuckles, and set to work at the typewriter.

It must've been some sort of hypnotism, because the church had always been there when it arrived one day. Everyone agreed that the church had been there as long as living memory, but some of them seemed to know deep down that it also hadn't been there the day before.

January 20, 2019:

Last night I dreamed I was a farmer in the early 20th century, and the strange thing about the local town was that it randomly had a small but extremely ornate gothic-style church that had fallen into ruin and nobody used. It wasn't scary, it was just kind of there and sad.

Then one day, someone was digging postholes to put in a new fence and hit some kind of wire or power button and THE CHURCH WOKE UP and started growing more towers and stuff, and my entire simple farming community was like, "oh, it's probably a Crashed UFO. Best just leave it be."

Which we did until we started having SUSPICIOUSLY GOOD FARMING WEATHER for the crops, and every good crop year the church would get a little taller and fancier until it started putting out other infrastructure like roads and stuff, and when it sent a road down to my farm the whole town was like "welp, looks like it wants a sacrifice, better go get your toddler."

Both I and, it must be said, the UFO were very unimpressed by this and eventually my child was returned to me but not before the church ate the guy who took her, who had been poking annoyingly at it for years anyway. And then the church turned into a skyscraper. I don't know, guys.

And that's the story of the time my imaginary daughter was rescued from an angry mob by a UFO posing as gothic architecture.

Content Warnings:

This listing is to the best of my ability and made in good faith.

- Mention of pandemic, death by pandemic, and aftermath (Chapters 2 and Lineage). Brief, no gore.

- Injury from purported lightning strike (Chapter 5). Brief, no gore.

- Mentions of scarring from electrical injury (throughout book).

- Description of religious revelation (Chapter 7) and discussion of mental illness connected to it, including period-accurate attitudes and terminology (throughout book). Generally brief.

- Brief mention of child death from prior to the start of the book (Chapter 8).

- Descriptions of violent death, including the deaths of children; some gore, but no portrayals of the murders themselves, just the aftermath (Chapter 9, Harvest 1931, Harvest 1933, Chapter 17, Chapter 22). No main characters are killed.

- Sexual content, heterosexual, consensual; brief (Chapter 10, Chapter 16).

- Discussion of unwanted pregnancy, brief mention of miscarriage, and description of abortion (Chapter 11); the abortion scene involves some blood and vomit.

- Descriptions of cultlike behavior, escalating (Harvest 1931 and continuing throughout book); brief, no descriptions of cult abuse but mentions of various controlling behaviors.

- Descriptions of economic crisis associated with the dust bowl, including dust storms and resulting deaths (Harvest 1932, Chapter 20, The Storm, Harvest 1935); descriptions of the storms are somewhat graphic, deaths are not.

- Brief verbal abuse including an anti-sex-work slur (Chapter 17).

- Description of an attempted murder (Chapter 17); very brief.

- Mention of period-specific homophobia (Chapter 21); very brief.

- No dogs are harmed at any point in the story.

Printed in the USA
CPSIA information can be obtained
at www.ICGtesting.com
LVHW090004180124
769274LV00008B/271

9 781716 475887